THE HIGHLANDER &
THE LADY OF MISRULE

The Queen's Highlanders
Book 2

Heather McCollum

ARE YOU SIGNED UP FOR DRAGONBLADE'S BLOG?

You'll get the latest news and information on exclusive giveaways, exclusive excerpts, coming releases, sales, free books, cover reveals and more.

Check out our complete list of authors, too!

No spam, no junk. That's a promise!

Sign Up Here

www.dragonbladepublishing.com

Dearest Reader;

Thank you for your support of a small press. At Dragonblade Publishing, we strive to bring you the highest quality Historical Romance from some of the best authors in the business. Without your support, there is no 'us', so we sincerely hope you adore these stories and find some new favorite authors along the way.

Happy Reading!

CEO, Dragonblade Publishing

Additional Dragonblade books by
Author Heather McCollum

The Queen's Highlanders Series
The Highlander & The Queen's Sacrifice (Book 1)
The Highlander & The Lady of Misrule (Book 2)

Dedication

For Keri, my dragonfly sister.

We met after having our first babies and had two more each in the following years. Growing old with you is going to be a hoot! This book is also for all the pups we've loved. Miss you, Cody, the best reading dog ever (who could turn the book pages with his nose).

Scots-Gaelic Words Used in Book

bòidheach – beautiful

daingead – damnit

Darach – Oak (Name of Greer's horse)

mattucashlass – dagger sharpened on both sides of the blade

mo chreach – my rage

sgian dubh – black handled dagger with only one side of the blade
    sharpened

CHAPTER ONE

"Bear-baiting [sic] was a very pleasant sport to see. To see the bear, with his pink eyes, tearing after his enemies' approach...with biting, with clawing, with roaring, with tossing and tumbling, he would work and wind himself from them. And when he was loose, to shake his ears twice or thrice with the blood and the slather hanging about his physiognomy."
Robert Laneham, court official, 1575

24 December 1573 AD
Bankside Street across the Thames, London
Bear Garden Kennels

LUCY CRANFIELD FLATTENED against the brick wall of the kennel and motioned for the three children who had followed her to do the same.

"We will be caught for sure," twelve-year-old Alyce whispered, keeping her cowl up to cover the scar on one side of her pretty face. "Then they'll make *us* fight instead of the cocks and dogs."

"Then we'd be gladiators like from Lady Lucy's stories," ten-year-old Nick whispered. His voice held a certain hopefulness that made Lucy question the history lessons she'd been teaching the three orphans. And she certainly wasn't presenting an example of propriety with this clandestine plot.

"Can we keep one of the dogs?" Catherine, the youngest, at six years of age, asked.

"They'll likely be too large," Lucy said.

"How about a bear?" Catherine asked.

"Don't be dull, Cat," Nick said, rolling his eyes. "A bear would eat you up."

From the size of some of the mastiffs Lucy had seen battling the bears, a dog might also eat them up. "The three of you should return to Cranfield House," she whispered. "I'll be right along after I save the dogs." *And attempt to not be eaten.*

Whereas the giant bears were prized and so expensive that their masters withdrew them from battle before they could be seriously injured, the poor dogs were considered inexpensive victims for the bears. And if they showed any kind of fighting talent, they were then set upon each other in other arenas. Bear baiting, bull baiting, and dog fights were brutal and horrid. It made Lucy question the state of humanity with so many Londoners enjoying the blood sports.

"Don't forget the cocks," Nick said. "They don't deserve to have to wrestle and peck each other's eyes out to survive."

"They'd be cooked otherwise," Alyce said.

"Rather cooked than hurt week after week, and then cooked," Nick said.

Lucy agreed. No animal should be made to fight one another to survive. Lucy exhaled long, her heart pounding with worry. The scheme to free the dogs was becoming more dangerous by the moment. Whereas she might be sent from court for her crimes, the children could be thrown into the Tower or the stocks as thieves.

"Let's only free the dogs this time, Nick," Lucy said, holding the boy's gaze until he nodded, although mutiny sat in his fierce frown.

"I have a snowball to defend us," Catherine said, holding the white ball in her gloved hands. "It has a rock in it to make it sharp."

"Dirt works best," Nick said. "You freeze it in water and break a shard of it to put in the center. Once it melts, there's only dirt." He shrugged. "No evidence of a weapon at all."

"Clever," Catherine said, obviously impressed with the boy who'd taken on the role of big brother to her.

The sound of a horse clopping on the road beyond made them jump back to flatten against the kennel's cold wall. Alyce held a finger to her lips as the sound faded.

"Stay here," Lucy whispered, and she peeked around the side of the dogs' prison. The door was unguarded. Granted, the animals were fed and given shelter against the cold, but was that sufficient reason for making them fight bears or each other until they died? Of course not.

If they wish to return to their kennels, they can. But she would give them the choice. Clutching a bag with food scraps in it, she crept along to the door, pushing inside. She released her breath when she saw the kennel was empty of humans. Several of the mastiffs and bulldogs stood up, barking. They were large with tawny coats and scars that showed their battle prowess. They looked ferocious.

Lucy swallowed against the narrowing in her throat. *First make friends.* She hurried over, snatching off her glove and pushed pieces of meat and rolls through the icy bars of the cells where at least twenty dogs were now straining to reach her. "Here, my loves," she said.

There were three to four dogs in each run. She should have asked Nick to hold the door open so they could run out. *God's teeth.* There was nothing with which to prop the door.

Saint Francis be with me. Without another thought, she started lifting latches on the cells, letting the doors swing open. She flattened herself up against the bars as large and medium-sized dogs tore out of their prisons, tails swatting one another as growls and barks rose in a battle of canine greeting and excitement. Some of the animals' backs came as high as her waist. *Holy Mother Mary,* she could ride one like a horse.

"Good pups," she called several times but could barely hear her own voice over the snapping and barks. The last kennel held the smaller dogs. She released the latch, and half a dozen tore out to jump between the legs of the larger dogs. Two puppies hid in the corner with a blanket. They looked old enough to be weaned, but not by much.

Lucy turned, waving her arms as she waded through the mass, hoping her heavy skirts would keep any of them from biting her legs. Step after step, she dodged massive heads and thick tails. Would they turn on her, devouring her as she tried to liberate them? Her sister, Cordelia, would say she deserved it for risking herself so outrageously to free the hounds.

Lucy fell against the stone wall after tripping over a bulldog, but she reached the door, swinging it open. The surge of yelping, barking beasts rushed around her like water from a shattered damn. They hit her skirts and legs, pushing her forward with the flow. Her arms flailed as she hurtled toward the ground. Eyes squeezed shut, it took her a moment to realize someone had caught her.

GREER BUCHANAN PULLED the woman toward him, turning them both so that they moved out of the violent rush of hounds. The dogs raced off behind a circular building that looked like an arena.

The woman wore laborers' clothing and smelled of strawberries. The hair that had escaped her linen cap was golden, and her skin lay smooth against high cheekbones.

The dogs could have torn her apart. "What in bloody hell are ye doing, lass?"

She turned blue eyes up to him. "Put me down," she ordered. When he didn't immediately, she began to kick and twist in his arms.

"Let her go!" a boy yelled.

A heartbeat later, a cutting pain broke across Greer's forehead, followed by an explosion of icy snow over his face. He dropped the woman, and she landed with a thud.

"Holy hell," she said.

"Mo chreach!" he yelled, wiping the ice and snow from his face.

"Run!" the woman yelled, and three children ran off across the field, the boy in the lead. The woman pushed back onto her heels and straightened, her gaze going back and forth between him and the kennel she'd liberated. "You're bleeding," she said.

He wiped at the sting. "Bloody snowball had a rock in it," he said, but the lass had already run back into the kennel.

Greer yanked a rag from the belt that held his woolen plaid in place and wiped at the blood on his forehead. Aye, she was mad, and her lad had a most accurate aim.

Going to the door, he pulled it open. The woman nearly ran into him.

"Here," she said, thrusting a smallish dog into his arms while she held onto a second tan-coated pup.

"Ho there! What's going on?" a man dressed in guard's livery called from around the corner of the now empty kennel.

"Holy Mother Mary," the woman whispered.

"Bloody hell," he murmured as he and the lass stood there looking guilty enough to march directly to the gallows. Three other guards followed the one in charge, and all Greer could do was hold the pup against him as it tried to lick his face.

Greer Buchanan had already deduced that the portly man on London Bridge had sent him the wrong way to Whitehall Palace. As a Highlander in dress and speech, many of the English thought nothing of lying to him, even when he used his mother's advice on being polite.

"Thank goodness you've come," the woman said as the guards halted before them, short swords drawn. Tears filled her eyes, and her gloved hand shook as she pointed after the hounds. "I was but walking this way and all your dogs barreled out."

Fok. Her statement made him the obvious culprit.

"Who are you?" a frowning guard asked him as two of the men ran into the kennel.

"Greer Buchanan," he answered, "with a message from Lord Moray on behalf of King James to your queen." The dog squirmed in his arms.

"'Tis empty!" the second guard yelled, running back out. "Look!" He pointed toward the pack breaking off into three groups around the fishponds.

"Did Lord Moray send you to steal the queen's dogs?" the leader said, nodding to the pups in their arms.

"I'm not stealing dogs," Greer said. "I was trying to find my way to Whitehall Palace when the noise drew me here, and I came to the aid of the lady."

Tears slid down the woman's cheeks. "These two poor pups were being trampled. I persuaded this man to help me save them."

"Whitehall 'tis on the other side of the Thames, Scot," the guard said, turning outward at the sound of squawking.

"Holy hell," the woman whispered next to Greer. They all watched as the lad who'd hit him with the rock-laden snowball ran out of another animal kennel behind a flock of roosters that he'd apparently freed. They were squawking and flapping their wings as they scrambled in a haphazard race to escape the lad's flailing arms.

"Did you see the lad release the dogs too?" the guard asked, looking between them with suspicion.

"Oh yes," the woman said. "I saw the boy clearly." She gave a dramatic shiver. "About fifteen years old with red hair."

The guard looked back to where the roosters were running, a few stopping to peck at the ground. The boy had run off, and Greer didn't see the two young lasses.

"I think he had dark hair," the guard said.

Greer shifted the puppy who continued to try to lick his face as if he was coated in honey.

"Oh no," the woman said loudly. "I saw him up close. Red hair when seen in the light. And his eyes…" She shook her head. "Unnatural. One was blue and one was brown." She touched her face to the right of her lip. "And an unusual, dark mark right here on his face."

Greer hadn't seen any of that on the boy and yet she met the guard's gaze without blinking. The woman was a masterful liar.

"Would you like to write my description down?" she asked. "Or I could draw something and return it to you if that would help you find the villain."

Before the guard could answer, the woman's gaze diverted, and she let loose a scream that made both puppies yelp and the guard jump.

"Damnation, woman!" the leader of the guards yelled. "What is it?"

She pointed toward the circular arena. "I saw Blind Bess! The fiend opened the bear cages! They'll eat us alive!" She placed her hand on Greer's arm as if she might swoon.

"Edgar, Gabe, get the poles!" the lead guard yelled, running off. "We can't let the bears get away!" Chickens and dogs were replaceable, but not the champion bears that had been imported from the continent.

A horse whinnied, and Greer looked toward the road that ran along the Thames where he'd left his large black horse, Darach. Two of the large dogs were circling him. They were used to chained bears, not a horse that could deliver a blow to their heads that would knock them dead.

"Be gone," he yelled as he ran toward Darach, while clutching the pup to his chest.

The lass ran after him but stopped short while he chased off the dogs. She began to walk quickly away from the arena. "Lass, the pup," he called to her.

"I'll show you to Whitehall," she called back. "You'll need to go back over London Bridge."

"Lord help me," he mumbled. It had taken him nearly an

hour to traverse the crowded, shop-lined bridge the first time. Dog tucked under one arm, Greer took Darach's reins, turning him in a wide circle. His horse's shiny black coat was covered with dried mud from the week's long trip down from Edinburgh. Actually, they were both coated in dirt.

"Come along," she called over her shoulder and continued at a pace that fell somewhere between a walk and a run, both her arms holding the pup against her bosom.

Barking in the distance wove with the sound of Darach's clopping and their footfalls on the cobblestone. The lass glanced behind them at the empty street and exhaled fully, her smooth cheeks puffing out with it. "Thank the holy Mother Mary," she whispered.

"Ye're Catholic?" Greer asked.

Her eyes snapped up to his face. "No."

"Ye pray to the Virgin Mother."

She kissed the dog in her arms on the top of its tawny head. "'Tis merely something I learned as a child. My mother... She was Catholic." The dog looked up at her, its tongue hanging out as it panted. "Ho there, little one. You're safe now."

Greer looked down at the young mastiff in his own arms. "Ye know they won't stay little? They're mastiff pups." His father had owned several.

"They're just old enough to be weaned from their mother." She frowned. "She wasn't in the run."

"What exactly was your plan back there?" he asked.

"To free the dogs so they would have a choice if they wanted to return and fight." She smiled. "Mission accomplished." She looked over the head of the puppy in her arms and continued to march forward.

"You risk being arrested for stealing from the crown?"

"For the dogs? Yes." She laughed when the dog licked her face. "For your kiss, little one, yes."

They continued to wind through the streets. The guards didn't seem to be giving chase. "Did ye release the bears too?" he asked.

She chuckled. "I am soft in my heart for animals, milord, not soft in my head. I have no desire to loose a bear on the citizens of London. And 'tis the dogs that get maimed and killed in the ring." Her smile faded.

As they approached the congested London Bridge, Greer exhaled long as they were forced to slow. Londoners were busy preparing for the twelve days of Christmas when no work was to be done. The only exceptions were feeding animals and people and providing medical care. All other industry screeched to a halt while people celebrated with feasting and games until Epiphany on the sixth of January.

"If ye could point me toward Whitehall, I can find my way."

She spoke loudly while walking between people. "After London Bridge, we need to go up Thames Street to Saint Andrews Hill to Luggate Hill to Fleet Street to the Strand, and finally to King Street, which runs right past Whitehall." She dodged a cart, her lovely face turning his way. "You'll never find it by nightfall without me. The street signs are not placed."

"Ye go there often?" The woman was dressed as the average young goodwife, although her gloves looked quite rich.

"My home *is* Whitehall." She smiled, giving him a nod. "You may call me Lady Lucy. My sister and I are ladies to the queen."

They waited until a cart of buns moved on. "A lady to the queen who releases dogs and cocks," he said, his mouth close to her ear.

She snapped her eyes to his. "The cocks were not my idea."

"The young man with red hair and one blue eye and one brown eye with a mole?" Anyone who stood out from others were noticed by the common man. 'Twas why Greer's pockmarked mother no longer visited the Scottish court.

"They needed someone to search for," she said, shrugging. "I wasn't going to let it be Nick. He's an orphan who loves animals as much as I." She shifted the puppy in her arms.

"Hopefully the guards won't find some unlucky lad who fits

your description."

"I sincerely hope not," she murmured and then glanced up at him, her smile gone. "If they do, I will confess, of course."

Greer pulled her closer to stop her from running into a ladder. A dark-skinned man balanced on it as he lowered a sign painted with a goose.

"Pardon," she said and walked around. Her cap came loose, the wind plucking it from her golden hair.

Greer caught it with one hand. "Hold still, and I'll fix the pins."

"You know how to fix a lady's cap with pins?" Her blue eyes stared upward, long lashes framing them.

Greer pushed the second pup into her arms, and the lass balanced it on her other hip.

He glanced to the top of her shiny waves of hair. "My mother has the same type of pins, and I help her secure her cap sometimes." The lass's hair was soft, clean, and fragrant.

Wagons rumbled by on the flagstone, horses clopped, and people laughed, stopping any further conversation between them as he finished and took the pup back. Off the bridge, Greer and Lady Lucy made their way up Thames Street until she tugged him to turn with her onto a side street where the steady stream of jostling people diminished. Och, but he missed the wide-open moors of home, flanked by mountains and cut through by crystal-clear streams instead of the brown, stinking Thames.

They turned up another street where laundry hung across. "You're in London because Lord Moray thinks there's an assassin who will strike down our queen over Christmastide?" she asked.

"Aye."

"Are you hunting the assassin?"

"Aye."

"Is it your job to hunt for assassins?" she asked.

"For the crown of Scotland, aye."

She trudged forward and shifted the puppy to the other hip. "Can you spot them easily?"

"Nay," he said. "A clever assassin can be hidden in plain sight with no one the wiser. They gain the trust of advisers and courtiers so that their small actions are overlooked until 'tis too late."

She stroked her pup, looking sideways at him. "Perhaps you are actually the assassin, sent by the Scottish regent." Her brows arched upward in question.

"Lord Moray has no reason to see Queen Elizabeth dead. It would only incite treasonous violence by the Catholics who support young King James's mother, Mary." Queen Elizabeth had been holding Mary Stuart, once queen of the Scots, prisoner in England for the last five years.

Lady Lucy held the dog close under her chin. "There seem to be whispers of assassins all the time at Whitehall. What makes Lord Moray think this plot is serious enough to send an assassin hunter all the way down from Edinburgh?"

They halted to let a wagon creak out into the road, and he met her suspicious gaze. "Because," he said, "an intercepted letter originated from within Queen Elizabeth's circle."

Her eyes opened wider. "Who?" she whispered.

"Perhaps you know a Lady Cranfield?"

CHAPTER TWO

"We went into the royal residence known as White Hall. It is truly majestic, bounded on the one side by a park which adjoins another palace called St James's, and on the other side by the Thames, and it is a place which fills one with wonder, not so much because of its great size as because of the magnificence of its rooms which are furnished with the most gorgeous splendour [sic]."

Moravian aristocrat and gentleman-traveler,
Baron Waldstein, 1598

L UCY TURNED TO stone, right there on the cobblestones of King Street. "Lady Cranfield?" she whispered, feeling her stomach drop too far in her body. Had her sister, Cordelia, sent something to their friend, Maggie, that sounded like she was plotting murder? Surely not, knowing that they were watched very carefully by the queen's spy master, Lord Walsingham.

She cleared her throat. "There are a number of Cranfields in London. Which one are you considering?"

"I have not seen the letter, but Lord Moray said it was signed by a Lady Cranfield."

Lord help her. She must talk to Cordelia.

Lucy nodded her head toward the palace gates. "Welcome to Whitehall, Master Buchanan."

Whitehall Palace was a sprawling estate made up of many structures, privy gardens, and parade fields, all of which butted up against the Thames. Even though Queen Elizabeth traveled on progress throughout the year, visiting the people of her realm, Whitehall was considered her seat or home since she was coronated fifteen years ago.

The pup was becoming heavier and heavier through the long walk. Lucy grunted as she shifted him to the other hip again. Both pups stared out at the people, animals, and basic mayhem of London. The one the Highlander carried rested along the man's thick arm. Lord, was he as muscular everywhere? It was almost as distracting as his strong jawline and intense eyes. Strength was an obvious requirement for hunting assassins, but his rugged handsomeness must factor into his success at persuading ladies to talk.

Lucy huffed. "I need to put this pup down or my arms will never recover."

"Take Darach's reins," he said. The black horse was massive like his owner. The Highlander lifted the dog from her arms, and she groaned, shaking the pain from them.

"We can leave them in the barn with your horse," she said, "and I'll take you to Lord Walsingham."

She strode forward and right up to one of the palace guards at the gate. She presented her sweetest smile. "Henry Marr," Lucy said.

"Lady Lucy." The man grinned. "I barely recognize you in those rags." He turned his gaze on the Highlander, and his smile retreated. "Who's this? Did you bloody him?"

Greer rubbed his fist over his forehead, but the blood had dried.

"A misguided snowball," she said. "Not thrown by me."

"With a rock in it," he grumbled.

A second guard, Giles Garner, walked out of the bailey, holding a matchlock musket while another one stood up high in the tower at the gate. "Good eve," Lucy said, looking between the guards. "This is Master Buchanan, come on official business from Lord Moray in Edinburgh in the name of King James."

"'Tis Christmastide," Giles said. "There's to be no business for twelve days."

"Assassins don't follow strict rules concerning festivities," Greer said.

"You're an assassin?" Giles frowned and raised his musket halfway.

Lucy *tsk*ed. "Giles Garner, raising a musket before a lady of the court?" The firearm tipped back to the ground, and she smiled fondly at the guard. "He's not an assassin."

"How do you know?" Henry Marr asked, studying the Highlander with narrowed eyes.

"Do assassins carry puppies about?" she said.

"They could," Greer Buchanan said.

"Aye, he's right," Giles said. "They could."

Henry stepped up and scratched one of the pups on the head. "Are they Twelfth Night gifts?"

"Yes. For the orphans I've taken into my house in town."

"The Scot needs a letter of introduction to enter," Giles said.

Greer nodded to the horse. "'Tis in my satchel."

Lucy slid her hand along the side of the large horse, so she wouldn't spook him. He swung his head around and eyed her but didn't move away. She dipped her hand in the bag, grabbing the letter at the top.

"Here." She waved it as she walked back.

"It could be a forgery," Henry said, looking at the writing above the wax seal.

"Don't be contrary," Lucy chastised. "He's come all this way to warn our queen. I'll take him directly to Lord Walsingham."

The guard sucked on his teeth and narrowed his eyes at Greer. "See that you do, milady."

Lucy walked under the raised portcullis and into the open-air bailey before the large stone-wrought buildings. "There are stables ahead," Lucy said, leading the massive steed. "You can pay a stable boy to care for him."

Outside the wooden building, Greer lowered both dogs, who

shook and pranced around. One puppy lifted his leg to piss on a pile of snow against the barn.

Greer's fingers momentarily slid against Lucy's hand when he took the reins. The contact was through her glove, but the brush made her heart thump a bit faster. Drat the man for being handsome. She needed to stay well away from him if he was hunting a traitor named Cranfield.

INSIDE WHITEHALL, HOLLY was strung around the lit chandeliers and over doors, giving the entry chamber a cheerful look despite the weapons hung about displaying English military strength. Lucy led the Highlander down the corridor toward the Great Hall. Their boots rapped on the floor as they strode along without speaking.

"Lord Walsingham is probably in the Great Hall."

Lucy peeked around the corner into the large room. A huge log was being hoisted by ten men into one of the hearths, most of it sticking out into the room. "'Tis the Yule log," she said, her voice hushed. It would burn until the sixth of January, slowly being eaten away and shortening to eventually fit entirely into the hearth.

Before the other hearth, which was burning brightly, stood a small circle of men in hose, voluminous breeches, and ruffs about their necks, reminding Lucy how lowly she was dressed. She tugged her cloak closed and retreated out into the corridor. The Highlander hesitated for a moment and followed her.

Lucy's cheeks were flushed. "Sir Francis Walsingham is there," she said, nodding toward the room. "With Sir William Cecil, Baron Burghley, and Robert Leister, Earl of Leicester, and a few other of the queen's advisors. And I'd rather they not see me dressed so."

"Lucy?"

Cordelia Cranfield strode toward her, making Lucy look between her and Greer, the assassin hunter. *Holy hell.* Always dressed immaculately, with her red hair topped with a French hood, Lucy's sister frowned as she stopped before them. "Whatever are you wearing?"

Lucy clutched her cape closed. "Just something to help me blend in with the crowds. I told you I was going out to see the orphans who've been sleeping at our house."

"Simmons hasn't thrown them out yet, I hope," Cordelia said.

John Simmons, the aging man who watched Cranfield House alone since Lucy's mother died, did not like disruption. Allowing the three orphans to sleep in Lucy's bedchamber had ruffled the older man's feathers. The baby mastiffs might push him over the edge to quitting.

"No, and I increased his allowance to buy them food."

Cordelia wiped her hand down the front of Lucy's cape. "You're covered with dog fur." Cordelia lowered her voice, her gaze narrowing. "What did you do?"

"I found two puppies who need a home."

Cordelia grimaced. "You cannot save everyone."

"Percy and Pip will be the last," Lucy answered, knowing full well it was a lie. Her sister knew it, too, and gave her a doubtful look.

"Ye've named them?" Greer asked.

"I very well can't call them pup one and pup two," she said, her eyebrows rising. "The one I carried seems like a Percy. Will Pip fit yours?"

"Yours?" Cordelia said. "You assisted in this—"

"Rescue of puppies," Lucy finished. "And let's not talk about it where others can hear."

Cordelia released a long breath. Turning to Greer she crossed her arms over her chest. "I assume you also have a name?"

Cordelia's gaze slid down the Highlander. Lucy couldn't fault her. Despite the lack of refinement, Greer Buchanan was riveting, with his obvious strength, chiseled features, and the most intense gray eyes.

"Greer Buchanan from Edinburgh, here on royal business," Lucy said quickly. "Master Buchanan, this is my sister, Lady Cordelia." She linked her arm with her sister's, hopefully distracting her from correcting her name. She should be called Lady Cranfield.

Cordelia frowned. "Another Scotsman's come to court." She tipped her head as she studied him. "The last one stole away our closest friend."

Greer frowned. "Stole away?"

"By choice," Lucy said. "Maggie Darby and Kerr Gordon are now wed and living in your northern country, with one daughter already born."

"Ho now, who is this?" Lord Leister's voice stiffened Lucy's back. There would be no sneaking up to her room to change before she was seen. She turned to Lord Leister and Lord Walsingham standing in the doorway. The two men were dressed in regal court clothes with ruffs about their necks. Their slender builds made them seem tall except when they stood near Greer Buchanan, who towered over them.

"Lord Walsingham, Lord Leicester, this is Master Buchanan from Lord Moray at the Edinburgh court," she introduced once again. "We met near London Bridge today, and I guided him here."

"You met in the streets?" Walsingham asked, clearly suspicious.

Sir William Cecil, Lord Burghley, a portly man of the highest rank, walked out, slowing to listen to Walsingham's question.

"Yes," Lucy said. She and Cordelia gave slight curtseys to the older man, who was Queen Elizabeth's chief advisor.

"On London Bridge," Lucy continued.

"On or before London Bridge?" Walsingham asked.

"Before actually," she said.

Walsingham tugged slightly on the curled tip of his mustache.

"Interesting. A runner just brought me news of a criminal releasing all the hounds at the Bear Garden."

"And the cocks," Robert Leister, Lord Leister added. "'Twill ruin my bets placed for Saint Stephan's Day."

Lucy gasped softly. "Were the dogs stolen?" She held her hand to her chest in a look of dismay that was quite accurate. If she were caught lying, it would be another strike against her. Apart from her mother's treason, Lucy had been caught sneaking food and half-used candles out to the poor, as well as being seen attending plays performed at the Boar's Head Inn. Walsingham could use this latest incident as a reason to expel her and Cordelia from court. At the very least, Lucy would likely lose the two pups hiding in the stables.

"Are the destitute so hungry that they would eat a dog?" She looked to Cordelia.

Walsingham pinched the other side of his mustache. "Many were rounded up, and we anticipate the rest will return on their own for the evening feeding. Her Majesty's animals are all fed exceedingly well."

Walsingham was known as Elizabeth's spy master and was talented at reading lies. Therefore, it was best to jump in with both feet instead of trying to hide from him. Lucy stared up into his black eyes. "Do they have a suspect? For they should be punished for endangering those poor creatures. Out on their own, anything could befall them. The poor may resort to eating them."

Leister cleared his throat. "An odd lad with red hair, one blue eye and one brown eye, and a dark mark on his cheek."

"Sounds like witchcraft," Cordelia said, and her glance to Lucy told her that her sister knew full well that Lucy was responsible.

"What interesting clothes you're wearing, milady," Lord Walsingham said.

A blush infused Lucy's cheeks. "I was feeding the poor on the bridge. 'Tis the eve of Christmas after all, and I would not see anyone go hungry. My pockets are safer from being pinched wearing these rags."

Walsingham's gaze swept over to Greer. "The runner said you, Master Buchanan, were there at the Bear Garden with a woman." His gaze swung back to Lucy. "And I know you have a fondness for dogs."

"Any animal actually," Lucy said. "Although I have never had much exposure to reptiles. And rats are vicious, so I stay well away."

Walsingham waited, but the silence continued. "That wasn't an answer."

Lucy's brows pinched. "To what question?"

"Were you stealing dogs at the Bear Garden today?" Leister asked, his words succinct.

It was the perfect, wrong question to ask. Lucy smiled at him. "No, Lord Leicester. I was not stealing *dogs* at the Bear Garden today. I came across Master Buchanan on Bankside Street and led him back along the bridge. He was quite alone when I found him and certainly lost. He said someone told him Whitehall was on the opposite side of the Thames. I say, they were leading him astray because of his costume."

No lies. She'd stolen two young pups, not dogs. And was rescuing really stealing? Also, Greer was indeed alone when she'd met him. She glanced at Greer. "What happened to the woman with whom the guards saw you?"

He didn't even blink. "Hastened away after we saw the lad chasing off the cocks."

Walsingham stared at Greer for a long moment and then released an exaggerated sigh. "Go change into appropriate attire, milady, before the queen sees you."

He walked closer and reached toward her cloak, picking off one of Percy's dog hairs. He flicked it, frowning at her, and turned to Greer. "And you will tell me why Lord Moray feels it necessary to send you south to Whitehall over Christmastide."

Cordelia looped her arm through Lucy's, and the two of

them bobbed quickly and strode off together. When they turned the corner, Cordelia leaned closer. "The Highlander lied for you? Why?"

Lucy let out a gusty sigh. "Well, I was praying quite hard." In truth, she had no idea. Perhaps he loved animals too.

GREER HAD LIED for the lass. The whole incident had happened so fast. She'd thrown her trust at him as if she knew he wouldn't fail her. He'd played along without thought. Had surprise been her strategy, like when someone throws a ball, and you instinctively catch it to avoid being hit?

Greer followed Walsingham, while the Earl of Leister departed to do whatever pompous aristocrats did on the eve of Christmas. The impressive great hall, decorated with portraits and tapestries, had been adorned with holly garlands swooping along the walls between sconces. Expensive cloves studded oranges, hanging on ribbons, gave the room a sweet and spicy smell.

"See that a bedchamber is readied for Master Buchanan as the emissary from Lord Moray, regent of Scotland," Walsingham said to a man in Elizabeth Tudor's scarlet and gold livery. "And see that his horse is tended in the stables."

Walsingham indicated a set of padded chairs, and they sat before the fire that was opposite the one where the yule log awkwardly burned at the other end of the hall.

Walsingham tugged on his beard and fixed his dark eyes on Greer. "So, Moray is confident that an act of treason will be done over these twelve days of Christmas? Done toward her majesty, Elizabeth?"

"Aye. Confident enough that he sent me to warn ye and find the culprit."

"From where does his information stem?"

"Intercepted from a Lady Cranfield of London."

Walsingham's brows rose, and he glanced toward the doors. "Which Lady Cranfield?"

"It did not say. In fact, there were only initials, but the crest pressed into the wax seal with the shield, crown, and fleur-de-lis, was identified as the Cranfield crest."

"And the initials?"

"AC."

Walsingham leaned back in his chair. "Agatha Cranfield was killed as a traitor two years ago. And this was recently intercepted?"

"Aye," Greer said, crossing his arms. "Perhaps her accomplices are still active and using her name and crest to remain in the shadows."

Walsingham sniffed through his long nose. "Or it could be an old letter that resurfaced to cause alarm." He sat straighter in his seat. "Lord Moray worries over the health of Queen Elizabeth?"

"He doesn't want Mary Stuart to be released from her prison here in England. She will rally the Catholic nobles to put her on the throne of England and perhaps try to take Scotland from Moray and her son."

"Moray wants James named as heir to the English throne," Walsingham said.

"I'm not privy to his thoughts, but I believe he'd want to see our king named as such by gaining Elizabeth Tudor's favor."

Walsingham shook his head. "There's an assassination plot hatched every week it seems. Some dissolve to nothing more than disgruntled men drunk in their cups. Others grow into real threats against Her Majesty's life."

Several women and men entered the room, silently laying out a light meal for the last day of the advent fast before the decadence of Christmas began. Did anyone watch them? Surely, Walsingham employed someone to taste the queen's food before she ate.

Walsingham shook his head. "Catholics continue to rise up,

because Her Majesty does not actively suppress their activities when they are vicious in their convictions. The brutality I witnessed in France last year on Saint Bartholomew's Day was nothing short of a massacre of Protestants."

Walsingham grasped the arms of the chair, his watchful gaze sliding over the room. "And the Irish grow more agitated with the queen's support of Protestantism. 'Tis Lord Burghley's main goal to take complete control of that green isle to our west." He shook his head. "Making him as much disliked as Her Majesty."

Walsingham cleared his throat. "And you say, you've never met Lady Lucy before today?"

"I have not," Greer said. Which made the fact that he'd lied for her, both at the Bear Garden and here to Elizabeth Tudor's spy master, that much more surprising. Greer made it a point to stay away from intrigue when he visited the court in Edinburgh. Lies only ended up tangling around the perpetrator until they eventually hanged themselves. Lady Lucy seemed like trouble, and he'd avoid her while he was on this mission.

"You'll want to keep an eye on her," Walsingham said.

"Lady Lucy?" Greer's hands fisted where they sat perched on his knees. "Why is that?"

"Because Lady Lucy Cranfield could be your assassin," Walsingham said.

CHAPTER THREE

*"Lords of Misrule, ever contending without quarrel or offence,
who should make the rarest pastimes to delight the beholders.
They provided fine and subtle disguisings, masques and
mummeries, with playing at cards in every house, more for
pastime than for gain."*
John Stow's 1598 *Survey of London*

"PLEASE WILLIAM," LUCY said as she held one of the pups. "I can't get them both to Cranfield House alone."

"You should have thought of that before you brought them here," William Darby said, frowning at her in the lantern light of the stables.

If she hadn't needed to bring Greer Buchanan to Whitehall, she would have taken them directly to her family home. "Well, they are here now, and I need to save them before Walsingham finds them."

"He already suspects you," William said. "That's why I followed you out here. He's tasked me with keeping a close eye on you and Cordelia."

"He suspects me of everything," Lucy said, rolling her eyes. "Because of my mother."

"No," William said. "Because you can't seem to stay out of trouble."

She frowned at him, her lips pinched tight. "I care, William Darby, about animals and the poor. Does that make me a criminal?" She set the wiggling pup down and glanced around for a rope to leash him.

"It does when you…" he indicated her masculine clothing, "dress outside your station and steal the queen's dogs," he whispered.

"Well, a lady can't be seen sneaking around the London streets at night," she said, pushing her hair once again up under the cap, but it tumbled right down her back. She snatched it off her head and began braiding the mass.

William was tall and some would say handsome. Although Lucy couldn't think of him as much more than the brother of her best friend who'd moved with her new husband to Scotland. "And you are a lady," he said, "so you shouldn't be doing any of this."

"Come now, William. I'm only trying to save some pups from being torn apart in the ring. Surely you can help me."

"Then I will be an accomplice," he said.

"An accomplice to treason?" The deep voice made Lucy gasp and spin around to stare down the dark aisle.

Out from the shadow stepped Greer Buchanan, a short sword held in his hand.

>>><<<

THE TALL, THIN man standing before a strangely dressed Lucy Cranfield seemed sturdy enough but unarmed from what Greer could see.

"God's teeth," Lucy said, her hand to the tie of her tunic. "My heart is pounding, you startled me so." She flapped her hand at them. "William Darby, this is Master Greer Buchanan from Edinburgh."

"Exactly how many costumes do ye own, lass?" Greer asked. Even in the hose, tunic, and short breeches, there was no disguising that Lucy was a woman. She had a softness about her, and her glorious hair lay over one shoulder, half plaited.

Lucy looked down at herself as if to see what she happened to be wearing. "'Tis easier to move around in town dressed as a lad."

"Especially at night when ye are involved in some covert actions," Greer said.

"Yes, I mean no," she said. "I mean to say, I am merely taking Pip and Percy to my house in town, and William was about to help me."

"No, I wasn't," the man said, crossing his arms. "I'm here to talk you out of this crime."

Lucy scooped up one of the pups that trotted over to her. "You call it a crime, but I call it saving innocents."

"'Tis a crime, Lucy," William said.

Greer crossed his arms over his chest. This crime he already knew about, had even helped her accomplish. He frowned even more. "I'm not concerned about this incident," Greer said. "I'm more concerned with why ye didn't tell me your last name is Cranfield."

Lucy turned toward him, pup still clutched to her as if someone might yank it away to toss to a bear waiting outside the stable. "Because I don't like the name."

"Because your mother was a traitor and tried to kill your queen," Greer said.

"Of course," she said, as if it was the most foolish statement she'd ever heard.

"And are you also a traitor?" Greer asked.

"Well, William would call me one."

"No, I wouldn't," William said. "I would say you are rash, take too many risks for others, and don't follow the rules meant to protect you." There was a softness in Darby's rebuke.

"I don't need protection," Lucy said. "I need someone to help me carry a pup to Cranfield House tonight."

"Ye didn't answer my question," Greer said, picking up the second pup, Pip, who'd lifted onto his back legs to paw Greer's knees.

"Which question?" Lucy asked.

"Are you a traitor plotting to kill the queen?"

"Of course not," she answered.

"Of course not," Darby added on the tail end of her answer.

"Although, if I were, I certainly wouldn't say yes," Lucy said. Darby slapped his palm to his forehead.

"Well, 'tis true," she said. "And Master Buchanan is clever enough to know that."

Lucy looked at Greer. "Why would you even bother to ask?"

They stared at each other, both holding dogs, and Greer frowned at the loops she was weaving. Lucy Cranfield was disarming and very clever. It wasn't often he was at a loss for words.

"I will help ye take the dogs to Cranfield House," Greer said. That way he could see the lair of Lady Agatha Cranfield.

Lucy's frown inverted into a sweet smile, that surely won over the hearts of those at court. "Thank you, sir." She walked past him, completely ignoring Darby.

"What shall I tell Walsingham?" Darby called after her.

"Don't mention Pip and Percy or you'll be answering to your sister if I'm thrown into the Tower, William Darby," she called.

Greer strode after the lass masquerading as a lad. Several people, dressed in the winter woolens of servants, were traveling in and out of the arched gates onto King Street. Lucy tucked Percy under her cloak, and Greer did the same with Pip. They didn't say anything until they'd blended into the shadows beyond the gate house.

Occasional laughter and carol singing broke the quietness of night. A gentle snow fell around them. The more Greer held Pip, the more he couldn't imagine the sleepy fellow ever charging at a tethered bear. Although children were raised to be warriors every day. Was Lucy raised to be a traitor?

"Thank you for helping me," Lucy said as she pointed them up another street where a few encased oil lamps were lit. "William wasn't bending tonight."

"Does he help ye often?" he asked.

"William wants to help me," she said, "but he struggles with his loyalties. Working for Lord Walsingham is the way he can keep his father and himself employed as poison seekers in the queen's service."

They walked farther until he heard Lucy's labored breath. "Let me take Percy too," he said, and lifted the sleepy pup from her arms.

"Thank you," she said softly. "I think he may have gained weight over the day." She rubbed her arms.

"Does Walsingham *think* ye are a traitor?" Greer asked his question slightly different from before. Although, he already knew the answer. *Lucy and Cordelia Cranfield's mother was a fanatical Catholic who tried to kill the queen two years ago. Although no connection between the daughters and the conspirators was found, I watch them closely.* Walsingham's warning proved he was looking for evidence against the sisters. And yet Lucy took chances like releasing dogs.

Lucy huffed, her exhale puffing out white in the freezing night air. "My mother was involved with a plot against the queen over two years ago now. Cordelia and I knew nothing about it, but we are still suspect." She glanced at him. "I don't mean to implement you in my need to rescue animals and children, but your assistance 'tis needed tonight." Her gloved hand rose to rub Pip's head. "There's too much injustice in the world, as you probably know. Here in London, poverty is rife, and the poor are arrested if they're found begging. Almshouses can only handle so many, and people like my three children end up sleeping in the streets."

She shook her head as she marched forward, looking like a lad heading with conviction to war. Her boots crunched on the frozen straw that someone had thrown out to prevent people from slipping. She turned her face to his. "That's where I found them, the three of them in rags huddled together beside a shop on London Bridge. I must help in some way, even if that puts me at risk."

Greer studied her face before she turned forward again. Either Lucy Cranfield was the best liar he'd ever met, or she was a woman of strong conviction. Instead of sitting back and complaining behind silk and ostrich plumes, she was acting on those convictions.

Bloody hell. She acted on her convictions very much like an assassin would.

⇶⇷

RAP. RAP. RAP. "Don't let them run off," Lucy said, her knuckles resting on the locked door. She heard Greer crunching along the snowy street after the dogs he'd set down.

Rap. Rap. Thump. Thump. She pounded harder. "Come along, Simmons." Or Nick, Catherine, or Alyce. Something moved behind the door. "Simmons," she called. "'Tis Lady Lucy. Open the door."

Behind her, the dogs started to bark. "Come back here," Greer said, his commanding voice making her turn. Two men and a lady hurried along the side of Cranfield House.

"Be gone," one of the men yelled at the pups and brandished a walking cane.

"Stay back," the lady said, taking the arm of another, taller man wearing a feather in his cap. He wore a coat but looked thin in it. The light from a distant tin lantern lit the man's face, showing heavy brows and a shaved chin.

"Lady Lucy?" Simmons said in the open doorway. "How are you dressed?"

"Were you having a meeting?" she asked, her voice low, watching Greer scoop up both pups so they couldn't chase after the people hurrying down the dark street on foot.

Simmons, his bald head covered by a bit of hair that he brushed over to hide it, peeked out into the night as if he didn't know who she was talking about. "Just some details to make firm." He turned back to her. "What are you doing here at this time of night, dressed like a lad?"

Simmons's eyes widened as Greer strode back, the pups under his arms. "And who is that? And what are *they*?" The last word was said with such dismay, she wondered if he'd quit on the spot.

No matter. It was cold outside, and she pushed past Simmons to enter. Greer followed her and set the pups down inside, where they each shook and began to run about. Pip found a scarf and ran with it, while Percy stuck his nose into every corner, his tail wagging.

"This is a friend from Whitehall who kindly helped me carry Pip and Percy. Where are the children?"

Simmons's mouth hung slightly open as he surveyed Greer. Outside and in the massive rooms of Whitehall, Greer looked tall and broad, but in the confines of the Cranfield House entryway, he looked giant. With his northern wrappings and laced, fur-lined boots, he looked like a Scottish version of the Norse invaders of old. And very out of place in the cloth-draped walls with a crystal chandelier hanging overhead.

"Lady Lucy?" Catherine called from above, and Percy tore up the stairs to her.

"I am glad you're here." Lucy smiled up at her. "Are Nick and Alyce?"

"And two roosters," Simmons said, judgement heavy in his voice.

Catherine smiled down at the elderly man. "We named one of the birds Simmons."

Nick appeared. "I managed to save two of them from the fighting ring."

"Even though I asked you not to," Lucy said, giving him a frown.

His face turned red-hued. "I had to save something, and I didn't know you'd go back for the pups."

"Lady Lucy?" Alyce said as she came between the two others.

Alyce didn't have her hood up, and the circular burn scars showed clearly on her cheek. Burns that she'd confided to Lucy were from her uncle's ring, which he'd heat up as a grotesque form of punishment. It explained why she'd sought the safety of the streets rather than remaining under his roof.

"I've brought Pip and Percy to live with you here," Lucy said, smiling up at them.

Catherine gasped and crouched on the landing in a robe over her sleeping smock that Lucy had bought for her. "So sweet," she crooned and laughed as Percy licked her face. Pip ran up to join in, abandoning the scarf halfway up the stairs. She laughed, glancing back at Nick. "They are much cuddlier than Simmons and Xerxes."

Lucy's brow went up. "You named a rooster Xerxes?"

"Xerxes is that king from the bible you told us about," Alyce said. "Who made Ester marry him."

Nick grinned down at her. "I call him Berserk Xerxes."

"Lady Lucy," Simmons said. "I cannot abide all these…creatures in the house. The animals should be turned out and the children taken to an almshouse." It seemed that he ranked the children with the roosters as far as those who deserved comfort.

"When you have your own home," Lucy said, "you can turn away orphans and homeless pups."

"Your mother would never allow this."

"My mother is no longer here," Lucy said, motioning Greer to follow her up the stairs.

"She is turning in her grave for sure," Simmons called.

Lucy stopped halfway up to stare down at the man that her mother trusted to see to her comfort. "And what grave is that, Simmons? The simple pine box planted near Tyburn?" The reminder of the shame her mother had wrought on the Cranfield name made Simmons look away, and Lucy continued up the stairs with the chatting children and the panting dogs.

Greer followed behind the parade. "Where are Xerxes and

Simmons roosting?"

"I think they were brood mates," Nick said, "because they don't seem to want to fight each other."

"Without hens about, they may get along," Alyce said.

"We have them in one of the small maids' rooms," Nick said. "'Tis too cold to throw them in the yard." He frowned toward the stairs. No doubt Simmons had suggested it.

They strode in a loose jumble down the hall to Lucy's room, and she was happy to see that it was as tidy as when she'd left it. Only the large bed was rumpled where the children had exited upon her arrival. One lone lantern lit the room along with the remains of a small fire in the hearth.

"Lord Walsingham is searching for the culprit," Lucy said. "He'll surely take Pip and Percy away if he finds them."

"They'll be safe here with us," Catherine said, dropping to her knees to hug the bouncing puppies again. "I'll take them out, so they won't foul up the room."

Lucy smiled. "Thank you, Catherine." She looked at Alyce. "Pups can be trouble. Do you mind?"

Alyce smiled, her kind heart showing in the pretty face she hid most of the time. "We are very familiar with the cold and neglect of people, so we would never turn away a creature in need, whether they have two legs or four."

"Like my cocks," Nick said, crossing his arms, and Alyce sighed. "They have two legs."

"Cranfield House is the best of all almshouses," Catherine said.

Lucy looked at Nick. "I want you all to stay away from the Bear Garden. No trying to release any more animals or Walsingham will catch you. I would have your promise. At least for now."

She waited until each one nodded.

"Does that go for ye too?" Greer asked quietly, his deep voice a rumble that sent a small shiver through Lucy. She'd been trying to ignore the foolish fluttering in her stomach when he was near, but that intimate voice stirred something within her. He stood near the hearth where he'd rekindled the flames, bringing more light and warmth to the room.

"Of course," she said. "For now." She smiled.

Catherine ran over in her slippers and threw her arms around Lucy, hugging her. "Stay safe, Lady Lucy."

Lucy ran her hand down Catherine's small head where Alyce had braided her hair. The little girl's warmth tugged easily at Lucy's heart. "I always endeavor to do so," she said, kissing the top of Catherine's head. Had Agatha Cranfield ever kissed Lucy's head? If she had, Lucy couldn't remember it. Even without parents, Lucy would make sure Catherine felt cherished. She hugged her tight.

Greer walked over to peer past the window drape. "Do ye know who the three visitors were? The two men and a woman who left when Lady Lucy knocked at the door?"

Alyce shook her head. "Simmons made certain that we were above stairs when they came in. We were to make no noise at all."

"But we saw them," Catherine said. "They met in the parlor for about an hour before you came."

"They were merely some friends of his," Lucy said.

"Sneaking out of the house?"

"He was afraid I would be angered by the guests."

Greer frowned, studying her. "We should return to Whitehall before ye're missed."

Nick scooped up a wiggly Pip in his arms and closed his eyes and mouth as the dog licked his face.

Lucy hugged Alyce and Catherine, scratched each pup, and closed the door behind Greer and her. Simmons was nowhere to be seen. "He's probably gone to bed," Lucy whispered.

"I would like to ask him some questions." Greer's gaze slid about each wall and corner.

Lucy shrugged. "We can return on the morrow."

Greer tipped his head back under the chandelier in the entry.

"Ye grew up in this house?"

"Yes. With my mother, father, Cordelia, and Simmons. Father died about ten years ago, which is when I think Mother became involved with scheming."

"'Tis a rich home."

"We are comfortable. Luckily the crown did not take it away from Cordy and me."

They left Cranfield House, striding in silence along the snowy lane and turning up the road that would take them to King Street. The shadows didn't seem sinister with Greer walking beside her. He was large and well-muscled. And that sword—

"Do ye think Simmons supported your mother's treasonous cause?" Greer asked.

"What?" she said, the word sounding too loud in the quiet street where only a few drunks walked in haphazard lines.

"Your butler was close to your mother, wasn't he?"

"Yes, but he seemed surprised that she was involved with Ridolfi and Norfolk."

"Surprised or afraid of being caught?"

Lucy wrapped her arms around herself. "No one mentioned Simmons by name."

"Your mother died before she could implement him."

Lucy frowned at Greer. "Simmons confides things to me, and he's never mentioned wanting to harm the queen." she whispered.

Greer continued walking. "He is still on my list of possible assassins."

"Well, that must be a very long list indeed," she said. Was she on it? She opened her mouth to ask but closed it.

Giles stopped them at the gate, his brows rising when he realized it was Lucy in the hose and jerkin. "I was out feeding the poor who couldn't find room at an almshouse," she said.

"With him?"

She leaned in toward the man, ignoring the smell of onions on his breath, and smiled. "Can you think of a fiercer man to chase away the thieves? Apart from you of course."

Giles snorted but grinned, waving them through. "Next time, ask me to accompany you, milady."

She smiled but sighed softly as they walked across the bailey. "He will talk of this," she whispered.

They strode past the posted guards at the doors of the palace and down the shadow-filled corridor.

"How now? Lady Lucy and a northern warrior."

Lucy jerked around. Richard Whitby was born into the gentry, but his family no longer owned land. He'd risen in the court because Elizabeth found him humorous, and she'd chosen him as Lord of Misrule for the upcoming Christmastide. Master Whitby sauntered toward them, his cane wrapped in ribbons for his jester role. The elderly man had always worked at his humor, making it almost painfully forced, but he was pleasant and sincere.

He smiled, his brows raised and his cheeks flushed. "And look how you're dressed. Are you helping with the Christmastide merriment?" He pressed a hand against his heart. "Seeking to replace this merry fool?"

"Not at all, Master Whitby. The role is firmly yours. I was but visiting Simmons at Cranfield House to make sure the orphans residing there had plenty to eat on this cold night."

"Your heart is large, and luckily your pocket is full enough to help."

"But I could get in trouble sneaking out." She held a finger to her lips. "No telling anyone."

He bowed low. "I am at your service and discretion, milady."

Richard walked on, leaning every so often on his cane, and Lucy began hurrying once again toward her room. Greer hadn't said a word to the man and kept his silence until they maneuvered through the hallways to her bedchamber.

She turned her key in the lock, her door swinging inward. The fire she'd banked cast a glow about the comfortable room. Smoothed bed, chairs by the fire, wardrobe, trunk, and a privacy screen. All exactly how she'd left them.

Greer stood in the open doorway. "What do ye know of the jester?" he asked.

She peeked behind the screen like she usually did, but no one hid there. "Richard Whitby has worked for the court for several years. He likes to tell jests, so the queen chose him to play the Lord of Misrule this season. His antics will start tomorrow, but he's been planning the pageants to entertain the court for weeks."

"How does he know your butler at Cranfield House?" Greer asked.

The splashes of warm color from the hearth cut across the Highlander's serious features, making them almost look menacing. Lucy's heart squeezed. He'd noticed Richard's flushed cheeks, evidence of him hurrying through a cold night. "They might be acquaintances, perhaps friends," she said. "Richard Whitby used to help with the entertainment at Cranfield House on occasion. Why?"

Greer met her gaze. "Because Richard Whitby was definitely one of the three who hurried out tonight when we arrived."

CHAPTER FOUR

"Elizabeth needed a long time to get ready each day. She would line her eyes with charcoal and her face, hands and neck were then painted with a mixture of white lead and vinegar. And, of course, like many ladies of the time, she wore a wig every day. What's more, Elizabeth was always determined to be the most eye-catching woman in the room. She would always dress in colorful gowns made from rich materials, while she would insist that her ladies-in-waiting would only wear plain black or white gowns."
History Collection.com

G REER WATCHED LUCY'S face tighten. With confusion or guilt? She met his gaze without blinking, so it was hard to decipher. Could she be playing the innocent while her butler and Whitby were creating a way for them to get close to the queen?

"Are you certain?" she whispered. "It was dark."

"That wrapped walking stick was what he used to keep Percy away from him."

Her mouth dropped open and then closed. "We will ask Simmons in the morning."

"And Lord Walsingham?" Greer asked.

"And reveal that we were out in the night, witnessing a possible meeting of traitors at my own house where I'm harboring two liberated pups? We need more evidence of wrongdoing before I condemn both of them to the Tower and torture." Her words came fast and succinct, once again full of conviction.

He stared at her, trying to ignore how her braid had fallen from her cap to lay across one slender shoulder. Even in lad's clothing, the lass was beautiful. Her cheeks were rosy from their walk in the cold night, and the escaped curls around her face were tousled and free as if a Highland breeze had teased them out of the braid.

"Then we will return to question your butler first thing in the morn," he said and glanced about her spacious chamber, but he saw no one lurking. It was full of luxuries, like her home on St. Martins Lane. Even though she mingled with the poor, she'd never known the feel of hunger or cold.

"'Tis Christmas. I will have to accompany Her Majesty to church services and then be part of any festivities at Whitehall. I'd think you'd like to remain close to her."

He huffed softly. "The next day then."

He stepped backward into the dark corridor, and she walked to the door. Rich white gloves encased her long fingers. They wrapped around the edge of the door, slowly closing it, but her gaze remained connected to his until the crack became too narrow. *Click.* The door shut, and he remained, listening to Lucy Cranfield turn the key in her lock. Was she totally innocent? Of mischief? Nay. Of planned treason? He frowned as he stared at the door. "Possibly," he murmured.

"LUCY? WAKE UP. 'Tis Christmas morning." Cordelia's voice penetrated Lucy's bedchamber door. *Tap. Tap. Tap.* "We must follow the queen to the cathedral. Lucy?"

The incessant rapping on her door pulled Lucy from the lurid dream she'd been having. She'd been standing naked before the fire with a fully dressed Greer Buchanan. Even though he didn't touch her with his hands, she'd felt his gaze like a caress.

Lucy ran a hand under the warm blankets, touching her sensitive nipples that were raised through her smock. She ached below and ran a hand down to press it away.

"I'm coming, Cordy," she called, sliding her legs out of the warm blankets to hurry to the door, unbolting it.

Cordelia pushed inside, fully dressed in white, which made her red hair stand out even more. "Still abed?"

Cordelia's eyes narrowed, and Lucy's eyes tipped up, watching her sister's hand rise to press against her forehead. "You look flushed, Lucy. Are you ill?"

"No, just tired."

"Hmmph." Cordelia strode to the wardrobe where several petticoats hung. "We are to wear white, black, or silver this morning so as not to outshine the queen. Colors are held off until the feast later."

Lucy yawned behind her scarred hand. Cordelia was the one person from whom she didn't bother to hide her burns. "The black then, to offset your lovely white costume. Sisters who are opposite. You are the good one, and I am the wicked one."

Cordelia snorted. "I fear we shall have to switch gowns if we're covering ourselves that way." Cordelia had always been flirtatious, and Lucy was certain her sister had given into her lust on at least one occasion, although she wouldn't talk about it. After the passion-filled dream from which Lucy had woken, she could understand her sister's weakness.

Lucy pulled on a clean smock and secured warm hose to sit above her knees. Cordelia helped her dress with stays, tied-on pockets, inner and outer petticoats, sleeves, and a stomacher. The black silk was embellished with small freshwater pearls down the front and, in swirling patterns on the inner petticoat, showcased in the open V. Lucy slipped on long black gloves that would keep her warm and hide her imperfection, which was not permitted at court.

"Your pale hair stands out so nicely against the black," Cordelia said. She brushed the wide curls, taming them before she placed the French hood in black velvet and pearls on Lucy's head. "There, a vision of rich humbleness."

"Or pretentious mourning," Lucy said, but smiled at her reflection in the polished looking glass that stood tilted on her desk. Would Greer think her beautiful? *Good Lord.* The dream was affecting her head. Certainly, Greer Buchanan had other things to think about. Like whether she was an assassin or not.

Lucy looked to Cordelia. "We must stay close to the queen today, in case the assassin Master Buchanan has come to find decides to strike."

"Maybe that means we should stay well away from Her Majesty," Cordelia whispered, her arched brows even higher. Cordelia had been trapped with blades slashing when their mother had tried to kill the queen. It wasn't something she would ever forget.

"Master Buchanan says Lord Moray has a treasonous letter from Mother," Lucy said, watching Cordelia.

Her sister's face tightened with surprise. "From the grave?" She gave a dark laugh.

"He fears the assassin is using the Cranfield name and crest to further her cause."

Cordelia sighed long. "Will we never wash the taint from us?"

"You don't have any information about it, do you?" Lucy asked.

Cordelia took both her hands, squeezing gently as she stared into Lucy's eyes. "I was drawn into plots when Mother was alive," she whispered even though they were alone. "I know how close I came to the execution block." She shook her head. "I won't even let myself think a negative thought about the queen, and I pray daily for our names to be cleansed. So no, Lucy," she shook her head, "I don't know anything about the letter or the assassin. My heart hurts that you had to ask."

"I only want—"

"I know," Cordelia said. "And I assume you are not a secret assassin either."

Lucy smiled, knowing her sister only asked to make the exchange even. "I am not."

"Good," Cordelia said and linked her arm through her sister's.

Petticoats lifted to prevent their toes from getting stuck on the hems, the sisters hurried out of the room and down the corridor to the front of Whitehall. Several carriages waited to take the queen's ladies to Westminster Church, all of them dressed in white, black, or silver. The ensemble of these colors made a beautiful group, punctuated by Elizabeth coming out in bright green, her fiery hair in striking contrast.

The men were also dressed in black, silver, and white, except for the queen's favorite, Robert Leister, the Earl of Leicester, who wore a green doublet and breeches to match the queen. The queen's councilors grumbled over Leicester's audacity, but the queen laughed and called him her peacock or dear Robin.

The only other man who stood apart was Greer Buchanan in his green and blue plaid over a bright white tunic. Beard and hair trimmed, his stern face accented by blue-gray eyes was causing a stir amongst the ladies of the court.

"Who is he?" Lady Margaret Russell asked.

"Is he married?" her sister Anne added. "Not that that matters," she whispered, making several ladies laugh behind their gloved hands.

"He's Greer Buchanan on mission from Edinburgh," Cordelia said. "He's rough and dangerous; no one with whom to trifle."

Did her sister realize that her warning only made Greer more attractive to the bored group of ladies? They all watched from their spots in the carriages as Greer mounted his large black horse, master and animal matched in strength, stature, and seriousness.

"Does he never smile?" Lettice Knollys asked.

Cordelia turned to Lucy. "Have you seen him smile?" All the ladies followed her gaze.

Lucy thought of the softness that had come to Greer's mouth when she teased him. And the look of sweet indulgence as he let

Pip lick his chin. "No. I have not seen him smile," she answered, which wasn't a lie. "He always looks ornery enough to bite the wings off little sparrows." Which was a lie, but it had the desired effect because several ladies gasped, their eyes growing large. Lucy shook her head. "Think what he'd do to punish an impudent woman." She shivered dramatically and looked away from Greer. "I imagine he'd be a cruel lover."

The carriages shook as they started to rumble across the cobblestone in the cold winter air, making all the ladies grab hold of the sides or seats.

Pretending to glance up the winter streets, Lucy noticed that Greer rode several rows behind Lord Walsingham, and William Darby and his father rode behind Greer. William's frown bounced between the Highlander and her. 'Twas his own fault if he was angry that Greer had escorted her last night.

Westminster Church was close enough that they could have walked, but the queen wanted to arrive in stately style and their satin shoes would be marred by the snow. The horses came to a stop, and the ladies filed out of the open-air coach with the assistance of the royal footman. Cordelia leaned toward Lucy's ear. "You like him, don't you?"

Lucy's gaze turned to her. "Who?"

Cordelia rolled her eyes. "Greer Buchanan. He helped you with the dogs, and you just tried to throw the ladies off his scent."

"None of that means I like the man," Lucy whispered back. "At least not the way you're insinuating."

"See that you don't," Cordelia said, clutching her cloak closed against the cold breeze. "I already lost Maggie to Scotland. I won't stand to lose my sister as well."

Lucy pulled the small purse of coins from her pocket to hand out to the poor as they entered. Each of the ladies had been fashioned with them, but Lucy had added coins of her own. "Cease such ill talk on this fine Christmas morning," Lucy said, pulling her most brilliant smile up from her core of merriment. Her father had once told her that her cheerfulness and smile were her best assets. What would he think of the ruined Cranfield name?

A touch of her elbow made Lucy turn, but her smile wavered when she saw William. Greer stood much farther behind with Anne and Margaret. Apparently, Lucy's warning had only enticed the boldest ladies.

William leaned toward her ear. "I didn't tell Walsingham about the dogs. Only that you headed out to feed the poor last night dressed as a lad."

"Thank you," she said, relief lowering her tight shoulders.

"I'm not heartless," William said.

"I know. You're just…too honorable sometimes." She blushed slightly at what he might construe from her words, but there was no time to correct things. Elizabeth was walking toward the cathedral, and they all must fall in line behind her. Lucy walked slowly, pressing coins into the hands of the people lining the walk. Her smile widened as she saw Catherine, Alyce, and Nick peering at her from around several men.

"Merry Christmastide," she said to them and pressed coins in their little hands.

"Merry Christmastide, milady," Catherine called cheerfully, and Nick and Alyce bowed and bobbed. Lucy would bring them some remains from the feast at Whitehall and had gained permission to bring them up for one of the fetes.

"Merry Christmas," a deep voice said behind Lucy, and her inhale stuttered. She turned to see Greer. Up close he was even more handsome in his crisp Highland costume. His hair was dark and given to curl. It looked slightly damp as if he'd bathed that morning. He too pressed a coin into each child's hand, along with the women and men nearby. His arm brushed Lucy's as he moved, and the touch felt like it drew her to him. As if his brawniness was a magnet.

"And Merry Christmastide to ye, Lady Lucy." The deep voice held merriment in contrast to the serious expression he wore.

"You wish me merry when you seem quite the opposite," she

said, purposely separating her arm from his. "But thank you." Lucy glanced about, noticing several ladies watching their exchange.

"Oh," he said. "Do I look like someone who bites the wings off wee sparrows?"

Lucy felt the creep of warmth in her cheeks but met his gaze. She tipped her head, studying him. "You don't look hungry at the moment, but you do look like you might toy with them before swooping in for the kill."

He grunted slightly, and they walked together up the steps to enter the large church. The smell of candles filled the cold space, which always reminded Lucy of the tombs under the polished stone floors.

"I must keep close watch," Greer said. "Have a safe and merry day." He bowed his head to her and went to turn away.

"Good day to you, too, sir," Lucy said.

Greer paused and turned back, quickly whispering in her ear. "And I'm a very generous lover, Lucy. Never cruel, no matter how hungry I become."

Before she could draw in a shaky breath, Greer pivoted and strode along the back row of pews, his gaze scanning each aisle. Cordelia took Lucy's arm, pulling her along to join the ladies, where Lucy was reminded that secrets didn't remain hidden for very long at court.

"Do men of high rank wear your particular costume in Edinburgh?" Lord Leicester asked Greer where they stood outside the Great Hall. "At court?"

Lord Leicester was dressed like a peacock in bright greens and blues. There were even peacock feathers jutting from his tall cap made of matching silk.

Greer turned his gaze back to the bustling hall. "Yay and

nay," he said. "Lord Moray prefers the English garb, and young King James as well. Those coming from the mountains however wear the broad woven wool kilted up around the waist."

"Is it not…" Leister lowered his voice, "breezy beneath?"

'Twas difficult not to laugh at the man whose head looked like it sat upon a ruffled platter. "Aye, but to a Highlander who is always hot and ready, it suits us well," he said without breaking his frown.

Leister's eyes opened wider, his gaze dipping to Greer's jack. "Always hot and ready, you say?" His open mouth broadened into a smile.

"Aye, but don't tell the ladies, else I'll get no peace here in England. Pardon." Greer walked away and into the Great Hall, his gaze scanning the people who had gathered around the queen. Elizabeth was bedecked in bright peacock colors to match Lord Leicester. Even if she refused to wed, there was no doubt of the man she favored, the man right now probably wondering about the size of Greer's jack.

Greer had no need to speak to the queen directly, but he wanted to stay close. It was dangerous enough that Walsingham hadn't demanded the forfeiture of weapons before entering the hall. His gaze swept the festively decorated room. Holly and mistletoe were hung in long garlands.

Greer's gaze halted as Lucy stepped up to the doorway with her sister, both in bright silk gowns. Cordelia wore green, and Lucy wore a bright red, a shade Greer had never seen before. It caught the attention of many in the room. Before Greer could move, William Darby, who'd been standing with his father, Reginald Darby, walked straight to the sisters, offering his two arms to escort both.

Lucy's smile was brilliant, lighting up her lovely, smooth face. Did she fancy the poison inspector who hadn't given her away to Walsingham? Greer walked to the side table where wine was being served and took a goblet of chilled wine.

"You look splendid." Lucy's voice made Greer turn. She

stood alone. "May I have some wine?"

He handed her a goblet, nodding to her. "And ye look radiant. I am surprised the queen would allow such a color to outshine her."

Lucy glanced down at the bright red. "'Tis a color called cochineal and produced by an insect in the Americas. Quite rare." She glanced at the queen who was laughing with Lord Leicester. "I hope the queen doesn't mind. William said it was from a Spanish envoy years ago when King Phillip thought he might convince Elizabeth to wed him after her sister died. The queen refused to ever wear it, so William passed it to me."

The man was in love with her. He hadn't exposed her to Walsingham, showed up at her side often, and was giving her rich cast-offs.

"Do ye love William Darby?" Greer asked, his brows lowering in annoyance at himself for letting the question roll from his mouth. What did it matter? He was on a mission, and Lucy Cranfield was a suspect.

"Pardon?"

"'Tis none of my concern," he said, and took another swallow of wine. His gaze slid over the crowd. "Ye are drawing the eyes of every man in the room, and I am certain that every woman envies ye."

"I don't love William Darby," she said, the smile fading from her voice. "Why did you ask that?"

"I'm watching him to make certain he's not planning to harm your queen."

"Nonsense," Lucy said. "He checks her gowns for poison. He and his father are trusted more than nearly everyone at court." She looked back out at the crowd. "If he wanted to harm her, he'd have done so by now. You're wasting your time focusing on him."

"Like I said before, I have a long list of potential assassins," he said.

"Am I on it?" she asked and took a sip of wine.

Their gazes connected over her silver cup. In the low light, her pupils were large in her smoothly pale face. "Everyone is on it."

"Ah," she said, nodding knowingly. "But does my name have little stars next to it?"

"Stars?"

"To mark all the times I do assassin-like things, like giving children coins and food, and saving innocent animals from a cruel death."

"I don't make stars."

"May I see the list?" she asked, glancing down his body as if to find a pocket.

"I keep the list in my head."

She snorted softly. "Pity. I'd like to compare it to mine." She tapped the side of her head.

The quartet in the corner increased the tempo of the merry tune they were playing. "Do you dance?" Lucy asked.

Greer looked into her face, only to be captured by it again. Her lashes were long and surrounded her large eyes. Even her nose seemed the perfect size, and her lips were full and rose-colored. "Only in battle," he said.

Lucy laughed. "You dance in battle? La volta or a galliard?"

"The movements of battle are like a dance, a deadly one."

William appeared at her side. "Lady Lucy, would you honor me with a dance?"

Lucy cast her smile on William. "Yes, I would."

Ignoring Greer, William offered her his arm, and she took it. "Perhaps," she said, looking at Greer, "you'd enjoy the game of Snapdragon there in the corner." She nodded toward the game of snatching almonds and raisins out of a pan lit on fire. Squeals of fear and delight came from all around it as the ladies were encouraged to take off a glove and reach through the flames. There amongst them stood the Lord of Misrule, Richard Whitby.

William obviously knew the steps to the English dance where two rows were made, one of men and one of lasses. The red dress twirled around Lucy, and her easy smile made everyone jolly around her.

Several servants had entered the room, dressed in Elizabeth's scarlet and gold livery. Small sweetmeats were placed on trays alongside the wine and then one was placed at each place setting on the long, central table.

Whitby scattered salt into the Snapdragon pan, making the flames crackle. A round of gasps and laughter ensued before the man skipped away. As the Christmas jester, he wore a split velvet cap, also bedecked with little bells, and held his walking stick high, a bell jingling from the top knob. He jostled behind several ladies on the dance floor, playing the bumbling suitor. The perfect Lord of Misrule.

Upon one turn away from the center, Richard pushed William aside and took his place dancing opposite Lucy, much to everyone's delight. Everyone except William of course. But he smiled good naturedly and waited, watching as Richard danced around Lucy in her bright red dress. She was a shining light in the crowd of boring decadence.

As the dance ended, William stepped toward Lucy, but Walsingham strode beside him. With a word, William turned away, following the man over to where his father stood.

Greer left his wine and strode over to her. "Are ye brave enough to snatch the nut or fruit?" he asked.

She hesitated but laid her gloved hand on his arm, and he led her over to the Snapdragon table. Several ladies laughed, daring each other to reach into the flames. The flame was blue, so Greer reached through it slowly and without fear. He plucked several raisins, pulling them out as the ladies around the table clapped.

Greer held one of the raisins up to Lucy, and she took it, popping it into her mouth. "It's a wonder Richard left any," she said. She tipped her head back down the long room to where Whitby was hopping from seat to seat, sampling everyone's sweetmeats. He pretended that he would steal the queen's but then swiped the one at Lord Burghley's place.

"We added more back," Lady Anne said. She smiled across the low flames at Greer, reminding him how she'd whispered to him that morning on the grounds of Westminster. *Some ladies like the sting of a rough lover.* He nodded to her and looked back to the game.

"Try it," Greer said to Lucy. "I promise it doesn't burn."

Lucy's easy smile dropped away. "No thank you. I stay away from flames." She clutched her hands before her.

"You can try it with your glove on," Lady Margaret said.

"She never takes them off," Lady Anne said, but then pressed her hand over her mouth as if she'd let out some great secret.

"A lady keeps her gloves on as much as possible," Cordelia said, coming up behind them, her gaze raking over Anne like a slap. The woman glanced away under the intensity.

"Unless you're the queen," Lettice said, glancing down where Elizabeth had taken to the dance floor with Lord Leicester. "She likes everyone to see her long, slender fingers," she whispered.

"'Tis quite stuffy in the hall," Lucy said.

"I will accompany ye," Greer said, but she shook her head.

"I will return shortly." She nodded to the ladies and turned away, striding across the hall. Richard Whitby walked quickly out before her.

William Darby was in deep conversation with Walsingham in the far corner and didn't see her leave. Bloody hell. With a possible assassin nearby, Lucy shouldn't walk the dark halls of Whitehall alone.

"Pardon me," Greer said. Let the ladies whisper that he followed Lucy out. He'd be gone in a fortnight, and she'd probably be swept up in a romance with Darby. Although she deserved someone stronger, someone who wouldn't let his loyalties to a queen make him turn his back on her. Wouldn't he do the same for the Scottish king? The thought twisted his gut, and for a moment he pitied the tug Darby must feel. Greer had felt the tug between duty to his king and his aging mother before.

In the corridor, Greer caught sight of Lucy's red dress as she passed the large wine cellar, entering the corridor beyond. He followed, his much longer stride taking him to the door quickly. He pushed through in time to hear Lucy's gasp.

"Master Whitby? Holy Mary, are you ill? Richard."

Greer jogged down the dark hallway, and Lucy turned her face up to him from where she knelt next to the Christmas jester, her red petticoat spread out about her. Her eyes were wide in the dim light of the glass enclosed sconce on the wall. "He came out of the hall before me and paused here, his hand on the wall," she said. "And then he fell to the floor. I think his head is bleeding."

Greer crouched before the man. Richard Whitby's velvet cap lay on the floor, his flop of greying hair framing his drawn features. "Is there a physician near?" he asked and felt the side of Whitby's neck, pressing. He held his hand over the man's mouth. *No breath.* Just a slight foaming at the corner of his mouth.

"Yes," Lucy breathed. "I can run for him." She straightened, grasping her petticoats.

Greer sat back on his heels. "No need to rush." He met her wide eyes. "He's already dead."

CHAPTER FIVE

The twelve days of Christmas, which ran from 24 December to Epiphany on 6 January, was a two-week period when tools were set down and work was forbidden. To keep women from their chores, it was customary to decorate all the spinning wheels with flowers so they couldn't be used.

HistoryAnswers.co.uk

L UCY SAT AT the long table in the nearly empty great hall. After she'd returned to tell Lord Walsingham about Richard Whitby, all festivities had turned to whisperings and conjecture. Many attendees had rooms at Whitehall and returned to them. Others departed to their houses in town. It seemed that Greer's mission was not in vain. Someone was trying to kill the queen over Christmastide, and poor Richard Whitby had fallen victim.

"Poison," Elizabeth said, sitting in her throne-like chair at the top of the table. "Poison meant for me."

Lord Leister sat next to her, and squeezed her hand, his face grim. "Master Whitby didn't sample anything set before your seat, Bess. The poison was meant for someone else."

"Are we certain it was poison? Could it have been a failing of his heart from the festivities?" Lucy asked. She had known the man as always kind, and the thought that he'd fallen to an assassin's trickery made her ill.

"That is what Masters William and Reginald Darby will determine," William Cecil, Lord Burghley said from his station next to the queen. However, he didn't look hopeful. The slight foaming at the corners of Richard's mouth pointed to poison.

Lord Leicester walked along the table, inspecting the plates for missing sweets.

The entire kitchen staff was assembled along the edge of the room with Lord Walsingham and Lord Burghley going down the line, questioning each of them. Several young maids cried into tattered handkerchiefs, the men standing as if already condemned, their faces gray.

The queen looked up at Greer who stood beside Lucy. Cordelia had remained in the hall while the ladies of the bedchamber had hurried away to kiss and touch every pillow and linen in the queen's bedchambers to make certain no poison was spread upon them. It was a custom that her father, King Henry VIII, had insisted upon, but Elizabeth had relaxed the practice. William and Reginald Darby would investigate anything they found, bringing in their vials and beakers.

"I saw him eat a sweetmeat off Lord Burghley's plate, which was set right next to mine," Elizabeth said, staring at the golden plate where the rest of her untouched food still sat, waiting to be torn apart and tested. "The villain made a mistake, or my sweets are poisoned as well." She glanced along the line of cooks and maids. "I should make them each bite off my plate."

"The Lord of Misrule was also eating from other plates," Cordelia said softly.

Elizabeth's eyes snapped to her. "As if someone would risk their head to poison you, Lady Cordelia, or one of my ladies. Nay. It was meant for their queen, their God-anointed queen." The last of her words came out like a roar, making several servants cringe. "Who made the sweetmeats?"

Lord Walsingham pointed to three women he'd set to stand together. "Come forward Goodwives Mary O'Brien, Fiona MacKenzie, and Jane Welsh." He looked at the queen. "Who all helped bake and set the sweetmeats out."

Jane had tears in her eyes. She shook her head and bobbed a

curtsey, barely raising her eyes to the queen. "Your Majesty. I ate some myself."

Mary O'Brien nodded vigorously, her eyes round. "I sat them out at random, Your Majesty." She swallowed hard, using her handkerchief to wipe an eye. "Could it have been in the wine or a goblet?"

"Or on your plate?" Fiona MacKenzie said.

"Hush!" Elizabeth roared. "I will not be bombarded by your casting of blame." She snatched away from Leister, who had returned to her side, and held her forehead with overlapping hands. The queen's eyes were wide with a mix of fury and fear. It was the type of look that could lead to hangings.

As if realizing the same, Lord Leister slowly pulled her hands back into his. "Let us retire to your salon, Bess. Let your ministers question and find the culprit. Your most trusted ladies will find you safe food."

She closed her eyes. "I couldn't eat, dearest Robin," she said, the anger leached out, leaving only exhaustion.

He tugged her slowly to stand, making Lucy and Cordelia also stand. "Come now," Leister whispered. "You are safe now."

She looked at Greer. "It seems your Lord Moray's concern is valid. You may work with my Lord Walsingham to ferret out this criminal."

"Aye, Your Majesty," Greer said.

"I will appoint another Lord of Misrule," Lord Burghley said. "We must not let a traitor ruin the rest of Christmastide or word will travel abroad. Our stalwart queen has the courage of a lion in the face of such attempts."

Elizabeth looked more like a bedraggled cat, but Burghley's words made her stand taller. "Of course," she said, her eyes sliding to the few people about the room. "Let it be Lady Lucy, with her easy smile and laughter." She flipped her hand. "You cheer me most often, despite your horrid mother."

"Pardon, Your Majesty?" Lord Burghley asked, looking between Elizabeth and Lucy.

Lucy stood, her breath caught, waiting for explanation. Elizabeth waved her beringed hand in Lucy's direction. "Lady Lucy Cranfield. She can be our *Lady* of Misrule for the rest of the season. Through Twelfth Night." A small smile returned to her thin lips, and she nodded to Greer. "I have faith she can even get the ruthless Highlander to laugh."

The pain in Lucy's chest reminded her to inhale. "Yes, Your Majesty." She dipped into a curtsey.

Elizabeth turned around. "Now whisk me to safety and comfort, my dearest Robin."

⟫⟫⟫⟩⟨⟨⟨⟨

GREER STOOD OUTSIDE Lucy's bedchamber door. *Rap. Rap. Rap.* It was well past dawn. She couldn't still be asleep. Could she be ill? Or harmed after she'd returned to her rooms, escorted by her sister last night. "Lucy?" he called, but there was no answer. "Lady Lucy."

"She's gone to meet with Master Darby."

Greer turned to see Cordelia Cranfield walking toward him. He should question her about her mother's treason. She'd witnessed it firsthand.

"To see about the poisoning of Richard Whitby?" Greer asked.

Cordelia stopped before him. "I'm sure the topic will come up, but I believe she went to him for…personal reasons."

Personal reasons? Greer's stomach tightened, and he crossed his arms over his chest. What could Lucy be doing with Darby that was personal? She'd said she didn't favor him.

"What type of personal reasons?"

"The definition of personal, Master Buchanan, means that it is not knowledge for the common man." Cordelia's insincere smile gave Greer the impression that she really didn't like him.

"Have I wronged ye, Lady Cordelia? Or do ye dislike all

Scotsmen?"

Her eyes widened slightly at his blunt words. "I dislike people who could bring injury to my sister. She's the only family I have left."

"I have no intention of harming—"

"Your honorable intentions don't concern me, Master Buchanan. You could inadvertently tear apart my soft-hearted sister. She's a champion of the outcast, and now she's in a dangerous position at court, one that has recently been vacated through murder." She tugged on one of her long white gloves. "I suggest you keep your interactions with Lucy strictly to protecting her person." Her frown softened. "If you do so without making her fall in love with you, you will be the second Scotsman I've grown to like."

With a rustle of silk, she continued to stride down the long, poorly lit corridor. Greer stood stiffly, watching her. *Champion of the outcast?* Did Lucy see him that way? Compared to her wealth, he was poor indeed, but he certainly didn't need charity.

He grunted softly, turning to stride off. *I bloody hell don't care.* He had a mission to complete, one that had just proven to be deadly. *Without making her fall in love with you.* He would make it clear to Lucy that she should not soften her heart to him. Love only muddied matters and missions. Greer avoided the emotion at all costs.

Therefore, his rapid walk toward the poison chemist's quarters had nothing to do with finding out if Lucy and William were kissing or tupping or anything else that involved the Englishman being allowed to touch her soft golden hair. It took Greer a few turns and one reverse to find the rooms that a maid told him belonged to the father and son tasked with checking everything that touched Elizabeth's skin.

Greer strode up to the Darbys' door. *Rap. Rap. Rap. Rap.*

Footsteps came, and the door swung open. William Darby stood there with his hair mussed like someone had run fingers through it. "Buchanan?"

"I am looking for Lady Lucy." Greer's gaze swept behind Darby to a changing screen with a gown thrown over it. Without thought, Greer pushed past him into the room. "Lucy?"

"Blast it, Buchanan," Darby called after him. "You can't barge in here."

The hell he couldn't. Greer walked around the side of the screen where Lucy stood wrapped in a bathing sheet, her shoulders and arms naked.

"Greer?" she said, her eyes wide, a flush running up her neck into her face. "What are you doing here?" She clasped the edges of the sheet in one hand, the other hidden down by her side.

He looked between her and the young cock who fumed. "I was concerned with your welfare since there's an assassin walking Whitehall. Especially when ye don't seem to understand that *anyone* could be a traitor."

"William's not a traitor," Lucy said. "He is…"

Her words trailed off, allowing Greer to fill some in. "Your lover." Her mouth dropped open, but he continued. "Excuse me for the interruption." Greer pivoted on the heel of his boot.

"Greer," Lucy said, but he continued past the frowning Englishman without breaking his stride. If he did, he might stop long enough to punch Darby in the face. "Master Buchanan!" Lucy called.

Anger made him stalk blindly down the corridor. William Darby hadn't even escorted her into the dark streets of London Christmas Eve when she took the dogs to Cranfield House. And yet she was trusting him with her body. Had the bastard seduced her? He'd heard virgins could be easily tricked, which was why he avoided them.

Greer walked out of the building, striding toward the barn where Darach was stabled. A lad was in the stall, letting his horse lip up a small apple from his palm. "He's well, milord," he said as Greer entered. "Such a grand fella, he is."

Greer clutched the stall door and took a full breath before entering. He ran his hand down Darach's shiny black neck. The horse's ears perked up as he eyed his master. He was sensitive to his master's moods, and Greer's mood right now was made of thunder. He held a coin out to the lad and nodded at him. "Thank ye."

The boy took the coin and backed out of the stall as if Greer had growled at him. Greer moved about the stall, making sure the horse had clean water and plenty of hay and oats. Perhaps he could use the jousting tilt yards or park to train, somewhere he could swing a sword. He grabbed the saddle, settling it on Darach's back. He buckled and secured the tack without a word. The bridle came next.

Light, rapid footsteps neared the stall, but he kept fitting the straps to Darach's large head. "Greer?" Lucy's voice didn't stop him. "Where are you going?"

"Nowhere that concerns ye."

She came into the stall, which suddenly felt cramped as he tried to avoid her and her petticoats. She'd been able to get them back on quickly enough.

"Greer Buchanan." Her sharp voice made him glance her way. "You're jealous?" Her eyes were wide like they'd been when he'd caught her undressed.

"I'm not jealous."

"Then what is all this?" she asked. She stomped her feet with a ridiculous frown and threw her hand up and down as if pointing out all of him. "I thought you might knock William down when you stormed out of his room."

"The bastard deserves worse if he seduced ye."

"He didn't seduce me."

He looked at her, her beautiful innocent face. "Lass, a man can seduce an innocent without her even knowing it."

She planted her hands on her hips. "Have you done that? Seduce a lass without her knowing it?" Her attempt at a Scottish accent was laughable, but he was in no laughing mood.

"Nay," he said, turning back to Darach. "I'm more honorable than your William Darby."

"He's not *my* William Darby," she said. "We weren't... I mean, he didn't... We didn't do anything inappropriate."

"Ye may not know much about me, milady, but I will not stand for lies. They put ye in the same company as traitors."

He heard her exit the stall and then... *Thump.* Something hit his back, breaking apart. He turned to see a demolished snowball on the paddock floor. Lucy frowned at him, her chest rising and falling. Her wet hand was still in the air. She shook the water from it, and he noticed red markings along the skin of her hand, wrist, and arm.

"William and his father are helping me with my...disfigurements." She swallowed hard and dropped her hand, but not before he saw that most of her right forearm bore scalding scars. "I was in his room for a treatment." She wiped her hand on her petticoat and shook out the long glove she always wore. "There are some scars on my back as well, which require me to disrobe. William's father had stepped out to get something from the storeroom next door. We were only alone for a few minutes. Just long enough for you to barrel in and conclude the worst of me."

A sickening wave of foolishness washed over Greer. "'Tis none of my concern," he said, his voice low. But he walked over to her, taking her arm in his hand before she could pull the glove up over the puckered skin. "Do they pain ye?"

"No, but they're ugly, and I would have them gone. If possible."

He had seen burn scars before, and these looked fierce. "From when you were a child?"

"This one, yes. An accident." She continued to pull the glove up over them.

"But not the ones on your back?" he asked.

She exhaled, moving away. "Were you going to leave? Ride away from Whitehall without a farewell?"

"Who scarred your back, Lucy?"

She turned to him, her face full of obstinance. "So you

thought to abandon me… abandon the queen over an unsubstantiated, slanderous thought about one of her ladies."

Lucy obviously didn't want to talk about her scars. "I don't abandon my missions so easily," he said.

Her shoulders relaxed, lowering, but her voice still held ire. "Then where are you going?"

He led the horse toward the open stall gate. "To the jousting field to exercise Darach. Warriors and their horses must maintain their strength and agility."

She followed, quickening her step to come astride. They walked together out of the stables into the muted sunlight. They stayed silent across the frosty bailey, Lucy keeping up with his rapid stride.

"Have you any thoughts about Richard Whitby's murder?" she asked.

She was dressed in the blue gown he'd seen over the screen, but she had grabbed a cloak to run outdoors. She pulled the hood up over her blond hair, her warm breath coming in small white puffs in the cold. She wore boots as if she'd been ready to venture out into the snow. To chase him?

The foolish thought loosened his chest. He certainly didn't need a lass chasing him. He had a mission to accomplish so he could go back to Edinburgh victoriously and Lord Moray would reward him so his mother could continue to live in comfort.

"I have many thoughts about Richard Whitby's death. Did the Darbys conclude that it was poison?"

"Yes," she said. "There were traces of arsenic in his saliva. 'Tis a fast-acting poison easily put into food and drink."

"Most likely for the queen," he murmured, and they continued to walk down the long courtyard toward the gates. Lucy seemed intent on accompanying him. He wanted to ask her more about whatever William Darby and his father were treating her for, but he also didn't want her to walk away.

He cleared his throat. "Since ye have a…friendship with William Darby—"

"And his father," she interjected.

"Both Darbys," he said. "We should work together to discover the assassin."

"Together?"

"Aye. Ye and I, with ye interacting with the Darbys."

A soft smile turned up the corners of her lush mouth. *Kissable.* The word surfaced like foam in churned cream, and he tried to push it away. Not because Cordelia Cranfield would hate him for contemplating her sister's perfect mouth, but because he certainly didn't want to hurt Lucy's heart. Was it as vulnerable as it was generous?

"I was planning to work on my own to find the killer," she said, as if deciding whether to take him up on his offer or not.

He frowned. "'Tis too dangerous."

She flipped her gloved arm out before her. "After all, I will be right in the middle of everything as the Lady of Misrule."

"Ye will eat nothing placed near the queen," he said, his tone fierce.

"Of course not," she said. "I have no desire to follow Richard Whitby to the grave. If that happened, no one would agree to play the Lord of Misrule ever again. It would ruin Christmastide for decades at court."

He looked at her, his brows furrowed. Her glance was full of mischief. "'Tis not a humorous matter," he said.

Her grin faltered. "I mean no disrespect for poor Richard Whitby, but I have found that smiling and humor helps many situations." A brilliant smile bloomed across her lips. "Just the act of curving one's lips can make the heart not feel so sick."

Who had made Lucy's heart feel sick? Someone who had scarred her back? The fact that William Darby probably knew made Greer's head ache.

"Like right now," Lucy said, indicating him with a flip of her hand. "You look like you might bite the heads off innocent little animals. If you but smiled, I grant you'd feel better."

"I feel well, and not in the least hungry." He slowed Darach on the edge of a meadow dotted with oak trees.

"I'll leave you to your training," Lucy said and walked farther down the road.

"Where are ye going?" he asked, his voice rising.

"I promised the children leftovers from the Christmas feast," she said, turning to walk backwards as she spoke to him. "And I need to check on Pip and Percy." She turned to face forward but called over her shoulder. "And I must tell Simmons about Richard Whitby if he hasn't heard already. I'll let you know how he responds."

Greer followed her, Darach in tow. "Ye have no food with ye. Ye shouldn't go alone. And we should question Simmons together."

She kept walking, although slower. "I wouldn't give them possibly poisoned food from last night." She patted her petticoat. "I have coin and will purchase food on the way. And I'm very capable of walking to my own house and talking to my house-keeper." She hopped slightly in a skip as if enjoying the winter air. "But you are welcome to join me. If you get hungry, there will be baked bread and goose. I sent a messenger ahead to have them roasted for me at the bakers and poulters."

They walked along the winter-white road and stopped at the bakery and the poulter shop. Greer tied the warm, fragrant feast to Darach's saddle. He patted his horse's neck. "Apologies," he whispered. "Ye've become a pack horse."

Darach snorted but seemed more interested in the turnip that Lucy held in her open palm. He lipped it right up, making her laugh softly. The ease of her happiness seemed to chase off the cold. What would life be like in the glow of such a joyful countenance?

Several shops were closed. Before the doors stood decorated spinning wheels, showing that no work was being done during the twelve days leading to Epiphany. Lucy stopped to admire each one, remarking on the composition to the pleased patron who hovered nearby. 'Twas a simple kindness she doled out with abundance, expecting nothing in return. Greer stayed silent, listening to the inflections in her gentle words of praise. It was almost like a song, one that warmed the hearts of each person she met. She was either an angel or the best liar he'd ever met. *She does lie exceedingly well.* But what would be the reason? To convince him she was good and above suspicion?

"You are certainly quiet," she said, glancing at him as she walked. "I'd almost thought you'd wandered off."

Her foot slipped, and she gasped. Greer's arm shot out, catching her. He pulled her into him off the icy puddle. Her body hit his as if they embraced, and for a moment, he peered down into her wide blue eyes. "If I had," he said, "ye'd be sprawled across the ice right now." Slowly he released her, making himself look away from her face to regain some distance.

Lucy kept her hand on his arm while she tugged at her petticoat as if it had wrinkled. "Thank you for your quick action," she said, the usual smile in her voice. "The roads are treacherous even in my boots." She held his arm as they walked farther along the Strand.

"There is treachery everywhere," he said.

"I hardly think the puddle sought to kill me."

He leaned toward her, his chest warming at her cheerful banter. "Lo, a murderer may have spread water about in hopes of making everyone slip."

She glanced at the sky where clouds hung heavy. "I do believe you're calling God a murderer."

"If He is," Greer said, a grin tugging at the corner of his mouth, "then we are all doomed."

They turned up another lane, walking like lord and lady. It seemed Lucy could take on any role she desired.

Cranfield House looked cheerful in the sunlight. He was about to comment on its upkeep when a scream tore through the icy air. Lucy gasped, dropped his arm, and ran toward the house.

CHAPTER SIX

*"December 25th was a minor feast for the household when
compared with Twelfth Night itself. Sir William Petre of
Ingatestone Hall in Essex sat down to dinner on January 6,
1552 with over a hundred guests, who consumed between them
sixteen raised meat pies, fifteen joints of beef, four of veal, three
of pork – including a whole suckling pig – three geese, a brace
each of partridge, teal, capons and coneys, a woodcock, and one
dozen larks, with a whole sheep and numerous dishes of salads,
vegetables, and desserts."*

Shakespeare.org.uk

"L ET HIM GO!" Nick's young voice had taken on the high-
pitched wail of panic. As Lucy rounded the corner of
Cranfield House, she saw him standing before Simmons in the
snowy yard, Catherine and Alyce off to the side.

"A rooster is for consuming, young man," Simmons yelled
back. "Not for strutting around, eating, and shitting."

"That's what you do, and we don't behead you," Nick yelled,
his hands in fists at his sides.

"Stop," Lucy called and held out her arms.

Catherine clutched hands before her mouth, tears in her eyes.
Alyce held her in the folds of her cloak, her hood thrown back,
showing her scarred cheek. Simmons held the rooster tucked
against his body, standing near a stone where he'd killed
numerous chickens for her mother before.

"Simmons," Lucy said, keeping her voice stern. "We don't kill creatures who are pets."

He looked at her, his gaze rising behind to Greer. "A chicken is not a pet."

"To me, he is. His name is Xerxes," Nick said.

"And you can't kill Simmons either," Catherine added. "He's named after you."

Lucy walked closer. "Surrender Xerxes, Simmons." She held out her arms for the rooster whose head was bobbing left to right as if he might know the dangerous topic being discussed. Simmons had such a tight hold of him that the bird couldn't move much else. "Once they're named, we cannot eat them," she said.

"I didn't name it," Simmons said, but he loosened his hold.

Nick ran up. "I did, and I'm keeping him." He snatched the rooster from the old man's arms, both men, young and old, glaring at one another.

"I will not live in a house with chickens," Simmons yelled.

"Very understandable," Lucy said and looked at Nick who cuddled Xerxes. The rooster was content to stay in his arms. He seemed much more like a hen than a fighting cock. "Then Nick must refurbish the coop out here." She pointed to a wooden structure.

Nick looked at it. "But will it keep them warm?"

"If there's still compost on the bottom from the old chickens, leave it. 'Twill keep them warm enough. But make sure there's a place for Xerxes and Simmons, the feathered Simmons that is, to roost up off the ground. And feed them before nightfall."

Greer walked over to the block and picked up the lethal axe. "Tie a cabbage with string and hang it inside," he pointed to the coop, "from the ceiling. They can peck and bat at it to keep them from getting into mischief or dying from boredom." He tucked the axe under his arm.

Lucy tilted her head at him. "You know about chickens?"

"My mother keeps a flock." The smallest smile tipped his lips.

"And she names each one."

The children ran off to the coop, Xerxes under Nick's arm. Simmons huffed and trudged toward the house, hopefully not to find and strangle his namesake who was still inside.

"She names them?" Lucy smiled.

"Each one, although she gives most of the roosters away, so she doesn't have to kill them."

"She doesn't eat the hens either?"

He shook his head. "She buys unnamed, already-killed chickens to eat, and refuses to ever think they might be one of hers that she sold away."

"Your mother and I would get along beautifully," Lucy said.

His gaze never left hers. "I believe you would."

Lucy chuckled. "Shall we take our unnamed goose inside? Simmons will fuss less with a full stomach." She turned to the coop and held her hands cupped around her mouth. "I brought bread and roast goose."

Catherine hooted in happiness from inside. "We will come at once," Alyce called and all three filed out, Xerxes still under Nick's arm.

"No roosters at the table," Lucy said.

"Just goose," Catherine said, smiling.

"Or unnamed creatures," Alyce said.

Greer tied Darach to a hitching post and pulled a blanket out of a satchel, shaking it and laying it across the horse.

The inside of the house was cold with only the kitchen hearth lit. Simmons's frown flattened to approval when Greer placed the goose on the wooden table in the center. They would have their own Christmas feast, free from poison or having to judge every comment and action as a possible treasonous clue.

WOULD THEY BE missed at Whitehall? Because Greer found he

didn't want to leave Cranfield House. He took the last swallow of the mellow ale that Simmons brewed with pride. The man had roasted some turnips and seasoned some peas to go with the goose and bread. The children proclaimed it the best feast they'd ever had, and Simmons's glare had mellowed. It was an uneasy truce.

"Where does your mother live?" Lucy asked as they carried bowls and the picked goose carcass to the workbench in the kitchen.

"Outside Edinburgh. She has a small farm there." Greer set the simple tableware into a bucket that they would fill with hot water to wash. "'Tis in a valley. My father built it when they were newly married. 'Tis bigger than she needs since she's alone now, but she refuses to leave. 'Tis simple but cozy and smells of the herbs she dries."

"And you live in Edinburgh without her?"

"Most of the time. When I work for the crown." With the proof of the Cranfield riches everywhere he looked, he didn't go into his circumstances any further. "But I visit her often."

"I'm sorry you are away for Christmastide," Lucy said.

Greer covered the remains of combined vegetables with a cloth. "She was happy for me to go."

"Oh?" Lucy asked.

"She wants me to become indispensable to Lord Moray and eventually the king. A mother's aspirations for her son." And his work for Lord Moray earned him enough to care for her.

"Then she can go to court with you. My mother used to...before she withdrew and went mad." Her voice trailed off, but she kept her smile.

"My mother will stay away," he said. "She had smallpox and despises the scars."

Lucy's smile flattened. "I'm sorry."

"I am, too, for she is a wonderful woman who hides away from the world now. The pox took my two sisters and my father, but Mother survived. She doesn't see the scars as proof of her strength, even though they are. To her, they remind her of those she lost."

Lucy leaned back against the wooden table, pain in the pinch of her forehead. "'Tis understandable. I'm sorry you lost so many, well any of them at all." She turned back to the work. "And I'm glad you survived."

"I wasn't at home and was spared the trial." He'd been on another mission, one of his first for Lord Moray. When he'd returned, his mother wouldn't let him inside the house, shooing him away until all but she lay dead. The memory of her stubborn tears as she refused him to get near, pressed, as usual, on his chest.

He glanced at Lucy's ungloved hand. She'd exposed it when she had to wash the table, giving Simmons his Christmas break from service. "What trials did ye face, Lucy?"

She walked over to the hearth, crouching, not looking at him. His gaze followed the loose curls tumbling down her back, half of her hasty updo having fallen.

After a long moment, she spoke. "I was born with…certain marks on my body. Red and raised, although blessedly small. From birth." She stirred the poker under a burned log. "My mother was certain that people would think they were witch's marks, so she was determined to get them off of me." She glanced at him, her smile gone. "Unless the devil pricked me before I was born, and I have no memory of it, they're nothing but defects on my skin."

Greer stood holding the dish towel, frozen with the images of a young Lucy stripped bare while her mother inspected and questioned her. "What did your mother do about them?" he asked, his voice quiet.

Lucy set a new square of dry peat into the hearth, staring at the flames as they licked up around it. "She burned them with hot fat and flame. The scars cover the marks now." She touched her right arm, running her fingers up the puckered skin. "This was an accident. When I tried to hit the bowl of hot fat away, it fell on my arm, coating it."

Bloody hell. Did she feel the searing pain in her memories? Any one of the burns could have become tainted, killing her swiftly with fever. Yet she'd survived, making the world a better place with her natural joy and compassion.

"Lucy…"

She straightened and turned to look at him, giving him a smile that did not lift the sadness from her eyes. "I asked William and his father to help me," she said. "Either to get rid of the scars and any remaining mark or to teach me to cover them." She shook her head, crossing her arms. "William thinks there's not much hope for fixing them. So, we'll try hiding them."

Did the foolish man tell her she should hide them? Anger tightened Greer's jawline. He stepped closer. "Ye don't need to hide your scars, Lucy. They show how strong you are to have survived such torture."

She met his gaze in earnest. "Scars are not permitted at court."

"I don't under—"

"The queen won't allow it. Not even on herself," Lucy said. "She contracted smallpox over ten years ago now. She survived it and hides her scars with thick white makeup. Her loyal nurse-maid through the ordeal, Lady Mary Sydney, caught it, too, and was so disformed that she lives apart from everyone now, even her husband." Lucy shook her head. "Scars from war are permitted if they are not gruesome in the queen's eyes, but other disfigured people are dismissed."

Greer couldn't help himself. He caught her shoulders with his hands, stepping closer to stare into her eyes. "Ye battled against those who did ye harm. 'Twas a war ye won, Lucy, an unjust war. Ye should not need to hide." He threw an arm out toward the other room where the children still laughed. "Do ye think Alyce should hide her face away because of what was done to her?"

"No," Lucy said. "But if she were to work up at Whitehall,

she'd have to hide it."

He ran a hand down his face. "Aristocrats are judgmental cowards."

"You might want to keep that opinion to yourself at court," she said.

"We're going back out to work on the coop," Nick said. Catherine stood beside him, holding Rooster Simmons whose head pivoted sporadically to follow Percy and Pip, who'd apparently been liberated from the bedroom above.

"That's a wonderful idea," Lucy said over the noise. Off they ran, the dogs stopping to jump around Greer and Lucy before following them out. No wonder the human Simmons hid away. Was the man somewhere in the back having a nip of whisky?

Lucy turned back to the dishes that had nearly been licked clean by the children. She lifted a bucket of warm water from off the iron spider sitting over the fire, and Greer took it from her to pour over the dirty plates. They each took up a rag and plate to wash.

"You know how to wash dishes?" Lucy asked, her delicately arched brows raised.

"Not everyone is raised in a home with servants."

"You helped your mother and sisters then?"

"Aye. And I take care of myself when I'm away from her." Under a thatched roof without tapestries and paintings hung on the walls.

Only the clink of the metal plates and the random drip from the water broke the silence.

"There will be sweets back at Whitehall, I'm sure," Lucy said, glancing at him from the side. "I'm not certain I will eat any though."

"I have no need for sweets or Whitehall for that matter," he murmured, irritation in his tone.

"Except that you have a mission there to save the queen," Lucy reminded him.

"A queen who condemns everyday warriors who survive

with scars. 'Tis not very noble."

Lucy set her plate down. Her unmarred hand reached for him, curling around his upper arm. She looked up into his face, hers a mixture of appreciation and chastisement. "Greer, I do not hold the queen's fear against her. I'm certain her distaste stems from worry that she could be struck again."

"And ye forgive her for this cowardice?"

"Yes. She may be a queen with her father's heart, but she's human and mortal. King Henry acted the same way. Only perfectly formed people were allowed around him."

Lucy blinked against a curl that had found its way into the corner of her eye, and Greer reached up to brush it away. His finger lingered, gently sliding along her skin to her golden hair. He couldn't help but remember the sight of her bare shoulders and arms behind the changing screen.

They stared at one another. "I think ye are perfectly formed, Lucy Cranfield."

Her lips had opened, and the whisper of shallow breath was the slightest sound in the quiet house. Greer slowly lowered his hand but didn't back up. Neither did Lucy. It was as if a lodestone nestled in each of their middles, pulling them together, opposites that nature would fit perfectly in place. His hands raised to rest lightly on her shoulders. She stepped the smallest amount closer.

Golden curls half tumbled down around her shoulders with her courtly hood gone, and her soft lips turned up slightly as if smiling was her normal state of being. She looked like an angel. If one considered what she did for animals and children, she didn't merely masquerade as an angel, she was one.

He leaned the slightest bit closer to her face, feeling her shift toward him.

A gasp came from the doorway of the kitchen. "Release her, you scoundrel!"

LUCY SPUN AWAY from Greer to the pinched face of her sister. "Cordy? What are you doing here?"

"The better question is, what are you, and you, doing here?" she answered, glaring at Greer.

Lucy felt her cheeks heat into a full, fiery blush. "I brought the children a Christmas dinner. Greer accompanied me so I wouldn't be walking the London streets alone." Lucy frowned. "Are you alone?"

William Darby walked in the back door. "The children and a menagerie are in the back—" For a long moment they all stared at one another in the kitchen.

Lucy cleared her throat. "Greer helped me bring some Christmas dinner to Simmons and the three children, whom I'm allowing to stay in my room. We were just cleaning up from it," she said, yanking her gloves back on. "Simmons has the day off after Christmas of course."

Greer looked between Cordelia and William. "Why are the two of ye here?"

Cordelia's mouth opened, shut, and then opened as her glare returned. "I live here." Her hands plopped on her hips. "And why are the two of you embracing?"

"Embracing?" William asked, stepping forward.

Holy Mother Mary. Lucy jumped before Greer. "We weren't embracing. He was helping me clean up from the feast." She looked at Cordelia. "For God's sake, be kind and gentle. 'Tis Christmas."

But Cordelia ignored her, her piercing gaze on Greer. "I thought we had an understanding."

Lucy's brow pinched. "Understanding?" She turned to Greer.

Greer didn't take his gaze off William as if he was the bigger threat of the two. "Your sister worries ye will fall in love with a Highlander, one who will whisk ye away from your riches in London."

Lucy's face snapped back to Cordelia. "You told him that?" Her blush was surely burning away the skin of her face. She'd

have nothing more than a bare skull by the time her embarrassment ebbed.

Cordelia didn't say anything, and Lucy looked back to Greer.
"Do you think I'm in such jeopardy?"

Greer's face was serious but gave nothing of his thoughts
away. "I believe you thrive on peril, Lady Lucy, but I have done
nothing to lure ye away from your life at Whitehall."

"I thrive on peril?" she repeated, her frown tossing between
Greer and Cordelia. "Well, I have no time nor intention to fall in
love. So, sister, your worry is unfounded." She strode around
William and out the door into the back yard.

Lucy sucked in a large breath of icy air, the coolness a balm
for her cheeks. When had Greer and Cordy even been talking?
About her? Without her being present?

The roosters strutted about, squawking and pecking at the
pups when they got too close. The sound of hammer striking
wood came from the coop where the children worked inside.

The back door opened behind her, but she didn't turn. From
the heaviness of the footfalls, it was a man. But she didn't hear the
slight jingle of cabinet keys that William carried. So t'was Greer.
She rubbed her arms against the cold.

The heaviness of a cloak settled on her shoulders. "I felt it
prudent for me to leave the house," Greer said. "Without ye in
there, I was much more likely to punch Darby."

Lucy snorted softly. "He's a good friend."

"Who I am certain wants to be more than a friend with ye."

Lucy turned to Greer. "When were you talking about me to
Cordy?"

"When I stopped by your room this morn, but ye were with
Darby." Greer stared out at the coop. He exhaled. "When he was
inspecting your battle wounds, telling ye to hide them."

He crossed his arms. "Even so, he quite clearly loves ye. He
will profess his love, asking ye to wed. Because ye are insecure
about your scars, ye will probably say yes to his proposal. Your
sister will be happy that ye are marrying an Englishman. Ye will

live your days in comfort and luxury at the court, while sneaking out to feed the hungry and rescue animals."

She didn't make a sound as anger licked up inside her. Her relaxed face pinched, her eyes narrowing when Greer looked back at her. "You think you can deduce the complexity of my life into simple predictions." She poked him hard in the chest. "I am not so easily seen; no one is. And your coolness about it makes you arrogant." She poked him a second time. "Of all people, I would think that you'd know nothing about me is predictable."

"You haven't told Simmons about Richard?" Cordelia's voice cut in before Greer had time to reply to her scorn.

"Richard is dead?" Simmons had followed Cordelia and William outside into the snowy yard. "I cannot believe it."

With one last scathing look, Lucy turned away from Greer, hurrying back to the butler, who was more like a family friend. "I didn't want to ruin your meal, sir," she said, taking the old man's hands in her gloved ones.

Simmons's gaze slid over the snow and dead plant fronds.

Greer walked up to them. "What was Richard Whitby doing here the night we brought the dogs?"

"Master Buchanan," Lucy said, "he has just had a startle of the most grievous kind."

"And ye know, Lady Lucy, that I am investigating this murder to find the assassin before the queen is injured."

Simmons lifted his gaze to him but then looked away as if nervous. "I had some friends come by for a nip of brandy." He looked at Lucy. "Your mother would have allowed it at Christmastide."

"Of course," Lucy said, whether her stern mother would have allowed it or not.

"So the other man and woman are also friends of yours?" Greer asked, digging into the distraught man.

"Yes," Simmons said, again not looking at Greer as he answered.

"Richard Whitby, visiting with your butler for a nip of brandy?" William asked, obviously not believing him. "He lived at court."

Simmons shuffled his feet. "We were friendly before his position there."

Simmons looked at Lucy. "What happened to him?"

"Poison," William said, making Lucy frown at the abruptness of the word.

Lucy squeezed the elderly man's hand. "We think it was poison meant for the queen. Richard was elected the Lord of Misrule and was sampling everyone's wine and sweets at the Christmas feast."

Simmons let out a sad huff. "That man couldn't turn away from a treat."

"I'm fairly certain it was arsenic powder," William said with confidence.

"Really, William," Cordelia said. "The details are not helping poor Simmons."

"Pardon," he murmured.

"And now," Cordelia continued, walking closer, "our very own Lucy is the Lady of Misrule." She glanced at the sky. "Who should be heading back to Whitehall to change into the brightly festive gown to play the jester."

"Is there one?" Lucy asked.

Cordelia smiled. "I have found you something that could do, and Margaret and Anne have altered the jester hat into a type of hood."

"I can make you a scepter," William said.

Lucy threw her arms around the old man. Simmons was stiff but didn't pull away. "I am sorry," she said and leaned near his ear. "I will still help you and Lady Wakefield with your plans." Their scheme was a delicate one, but she wouldn't let him give up his dream.

He nodded. "Don't you eat or drink anything there," he said as she pulled away. "You can come back here to eat."

"I'll be careful," she said.

"I won't let anything happen to her," William assured him.

Greer made some noise, but when Lucy looked his way, he was staring off toward the coop.

"I'm leaving," Lucy called out to the children, and all three barreled out, making the roosters scatter and the pups bark.

"Lord help me," Simmons said and turned, trudging into the house. He ran fingers through his sparse hair, standing it up as if he didn't care anymore about his proper presentation.

Lucy gathered the children around her. "Be gentle on Simmons. He's lost a friend."

"I will," Catherine said, nodding solemnly.

"As long as he doesn't try to kill my roosters," Nick said, crossing his arms.

"We will take care," Alyce said. "And thank you again, milady, for allowing us to stay in your grand home." She smiled. Even though it pulled at the scar on her cheek, the happiness was beautiful. She was beautiful. If only she could believe it.

Lucy tugged on her own glove, forcing a smile. "I'm off to court to make merry." Whether she felt like it or not.

William put out his arm immediately for her to take. She took it as Cordelia took William's other arm.

Lucy looked over her shoulder at Greer, who walked to unhitch his horse, but she still didn't feel like talking to him.

With evident strength, Greer rose in the stirrup and threw his leg over his horse. With a press of his booted heels, the horse took off in a fast walk past them.

William murmured something, but Lucy watched Greer ride away. Infuriating man. To think she was predictable, marrying William just because he asked. *If* he asked.

Greer didn't know anything about her if he thought she was predictable. *Damn Highlander. I'll seduce him.* She chuckled.

"Did you say something?" William asked.

"No, I'm just randomly merry," she said, keeping her smile. Wouldn't Greer be surprised. Seducing him would certainly prove that she wasn't a simple sum of bland actions.

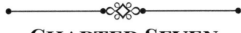

CHAPTER SEVEN

*"The Queen had a notoriously sweet tooth and was especially
fond of candied violets. She ate so much sweet stuff that,
inevitably, her teeth started rotting from a relatively young age.
But since only the rich could afford snacks made with sugar
imported from the New World, black teeth were widely-
regarded as a status symbol and an indicator of not just great
wealth but also cosmopolitan tastes."*

History Collection.com

"**S**TAND IN LINE!" Lucy called over the rabble of brightly
dressed people in the long Stone Gallery of Whitehall.
There were invited commoners and nobles jumbled in the
corridor without any frowns or lifted noses. It was a wonderful
aspect of Christmastide, even at court, where commoner and
aristocrat could make merry together in the celebration of the
season. If only she could get them to line up.

"In a line. Now." The thunderous voice made Lucy jump, her
face snapping to Greer. He stood with his muscular arms crossed,
booted legs braced, and scowl in place. He was far from merry,
but he was quite effective. The parade participants slid along the
wall to form a long line.

Richard Whitby hadn't a chance to lead the Christmas parade
about Whitehall before he was killed. So the responsibility lay
heavily on Lucy's shoulders. Decked in a golden gown with
panels of jewel-tone colors sewn into it, Lucy was ready to take

on the challenge of making people merry. Even the damn Highlander who looked like he could eat baby birds.

She held a scepter made of mistletoe, ivy, and holly. The red holly berries punctuated the greenery, and red and gold ribbons hung from it.

Lucy waved the scepter in the air. "Let us start." She nodded to the minstrels who stood directly behind her at the front of the line and began to walk forward. The minstrels started playing *The Boar's Head* carol, known by all.

"The boar's head in hand bring I,
Bedeck'd with bays and rosemary.
I pray you, my masters, be merry
Quot estis in convivio
Caput apri defero
Reddens laudes Domino"

She strode forward, the long line of finely dressed and masked courtiers mixed with gaily dressed servants and commoners allowed at the castle. Walsingham had inspected each one, but Greer still stood watch. Alyce, Catherine, and Nick had come at her request, full of excitement.

The procession moved boisterously along the Stone Gallery toward the Great Hall, but first they would parade out in the bailey and around the stables and through the gardens, all the way to the Thames.

Once the *Boar's Head Carol* finished, the minstrels strummed and whistled their way into *I Saw A Maiden*. With prejudices put aside, courtier, yeomen, and goodwives sang together and clapped with the thumping of the drums, many swinging each other around on their arms. Lucy wished their differences could be set aside every day of the year.

Even the stone in her slipper, biting her foot every third step, didn't bother her. Lucy laughed, turning in a circle to swish her petticoats about. Greer followed beside the procession, his gaze catching hers. He didn't smile, but his mouth had softened.

Despite the assassination attempt and Richard Whitby's murder, Christmastide was continuing. Playing the part of Lady of Misrule would help prove to everyone that she was no hidden traitor like her mother. Lucy only needed to make it through Twelfth Night alive.

As she made the turn, doubling back on the procession, the three children bowed and curtsied to Lucy as they went by. She stopped to curtsey back, which made everyone in line bow or curtsey to each other, laughing at the absurdity of it.

Make We Joy was the next carol, and they sang enthusiastically as they traveled down the lane to the front of Whitehall Palace, entering in through doors held wide by smiling guards. Lucy stepped to the side, waving the minstrels to continue into the great hall.

Her gaze roamed over the merry people. Could one of them be plotting regicide. Could they hide completely behind their smile and laughter? *I do.* The thought struck her soundly, making her bright smile dim. She'd always used humor to lighten the darkness of Cranfield when her mother ruled it. Even when she was being treated for her marks, she tried to make herself smile. Somehow it alleviated part of the pain.

But could a villain who didn't care if others died in the process smile and sing with merriment?

The ladies of Elizabeth's chamber had been given permission to wear bright colors for the season instead of their usual white, black, or silver. They smiled and complimented each other, some twirling slowly to show off embroidery. Margaret and Lettice strode inside on the arms of Johnathan Whitt, another young courtier. With white ruffs stiff and high about their necks, their heads did look like they were set upon platters. Lucy glanced down at her open ruff, glad she chose it so that her neckline was open.

As the participants came by, they made sweeping bows and deep curtseys to Lucy as if she were the queen herself. It was a struggle not to curtsey back, but she inclined her head with stately seriousness. William escorted Cordelia on his arm, Reginald Darby walking behind them. The older man seemed to watch everyone with suspicion, and William mimicked it whether he knew it or not. The comical similarity made Lucy chuckle. She balanced on one foot, raising her petticoat to grab her slipper.

"Such mayhem is the perfect place for an assassin to hide." Greer's voice in her ear caught her off-guard, and Lucy lost her balance.

"God's teeth," she said as he caught her against him. She clutched his arms to steady herself, her foot still bare under her petticoats. Why did his arms have to feel so incredibly muscular, like a figure out of the Greek story books about gods?

"What happens when I'm not here?" Greer asked. "Do ye fall all the time?"

"You startled me while I was balancing, trying to release a pebble from my slipper."

Without a further word, he knelt at her feet, his hands pushing past the petticoats to find her foot. Lucy looked out at the line of people singing as they circled around, everyone noticing Greer digging at her skirts. "Holy Mother Mary," she whispered. "I will forever be the talk of the court."

She felt Greer's hands grab her stockinged foot. They were warm, and his thumbs pressed up the arch, nearly pushing a groan out of her. But then he slid her slipper back in place and stood. "Pebble released."

The entire line of merry people made their entrance back inside, and Lucy turned to hurry to catch them. They sang *Good King Wenceslaus* as they entered the Great Hall. Halfway through, the boisterous crowd changed "king" to "queen," and Elizbeth clapped in delight from her dais.

She stood in a resplendent golden dress, and the minstrels stopped. The singing softened until the room grew silent. Elizabeth slowly opened her arms to encompass the room. "I welcome you all to my hall to enjoy my graciousness to celebrate the birth of our Christ. May we all know his mercy and the joy of the season."

The room erupted in cheers, but Elizabeth waved them to hush. She looked out over the crowd to Lucy. "I welcome the Lady of Misrule to reside over this court, to make us merry for these twelve days."

Lord Burghley, standing next to Elizabeth, whispered in her ear.

"Yes, yes," she said frowning. "Eleven days." She cut him a glare. "Thank you not for reminding me of the asp in our midst."

Burghley looked back out at the crowd as if he too was scanning the room for killers. But Elizabeth bent her bright red lips into a smile. "Come forward, Lady of Misrule, Queen of Mischief and Merriment."

Lucy walked forward to stand before her queen. They both wore gold, but the colorful additions on Lucy's ensemble marked her as the merry jester. Elizabeth had turned forty years old and was determined not to show any signs of age or blemish from her bout of smallpox. She favored the pale paint made with egg and lead in order to achieve the pristine surface that reminded Lucy of a cold marble statue. William would probably suggest Lucy apply the same type of covering to her scars.

Lucy curtseyed before the queen. "Rise, good lady," Elizabeth intoned. She motioned to one of her ladies who brought a circlet of pearls intertwined with gold ribbon. Elizabeth took it, holding it over Lucy's head. An unseen pair of hands removed her hood, and the queen lowered the crown on her pinned curls. "I hereby crown you Queen of this Christmas Court," Elizabeth said. "For eleven days." Lucy rose to applause. The position had been coveted at times, but surely not this year after poor Richard had died.

She turned to the brightly clad crowd, and they all bowed and curtseyed. Greer, looking splendidly rugged in his Scottish wrap and crisp white tunic, even bowed his head. Lord Leicester claimed Elizabeth's arm as if she were one of the court ladies and not the sovereign, and led her to dance.

Greer walked up next to Lucy. "Where are ye to go now?" he asked, again near her ear. The closeness made Lucy's heart beat even faster, and she leaned away, holding onto her indignance.

Ignoring him, she walked to Elizabeth's throne to perch on it. The cushions were soft, and if she sat back, her feet barely touched the floor. She looked out on the festivities, keeping her gaze away from the damnably handsome and vexing man as he approached.

"I apologize," Greer said, standing beside her chair and inhaled fully. "Ye are far from predictable, Lucy Cranfield."

"Good for you to have noticed," she said, her voice cold.

He lowered into Lord Leicester's seat next to her. "I was taught to make quick judgments about people, right or wrong, in order to assess for danger."

"And after my dangerous release of dogs, inviting orphans into my home, walking about at night in lad's clothing, and taking on the role of Lady of Misrule, you came to the quick conclusion that I would marry the first swain who showed an interest and lead a bland life." She turned her face to him. "I believe your education on assessing individuals was poor indeed."

"Are you the chosen favorite?" Lord Burghley asked Greer as he walked up, bowing his head to Lucy.

"Hardly," Lucy said.

"Not at present," Greer said at the same time. He glanced at Walsingham as he walked over.

Lord Walsingham nodded to her. "I have thoroughly investigated the kitchen staff, utensils, and dishes for the queen. The staff has taken bites of everything the queen shall taste."

"And Lady Lucy?" Greer asked.

"Certainly," Walsingham said. "Anyone close to the queen is protected since she is quite fond of her attendants."

Lucy was still grateful she'd eaten fully at Cranfield House earlier. From what Cordelia said, there were a number of

Whitehall residents and visitors buying food outside the gates in London and ordering their own maids to prepare them food down in the Whitehall kitchens.

"The kitchen staff has constant supervision?" Greer asked Walsingham.

"I have guards watching every station in the kitchen with orders to periodically make the preparers taste what they're putting out for the queen or those closest to her."

Things must not be merry for the kitchen staff. Lucy sighed. There was nothing much she could do for them right now. They were permitted to join in the fun after food was served if they wished, although many would depart early to enjoy their families during this time.

As one of the dances ended, a herald cupped his hands around his mouth. "The sugar works approach." Happy gasps filled the room as Lucy turned to see several sculptures, chiseled out of sugar, brought in. Each one represented a part of London: the White Tower, London Bridge, Westminster Church, and the gates of Whitehall. There were also molds of bears and bulls with renditions of the baiting gardens. Luckily there were no slashed dogs lying at the feet of the creatures in sugar-sweet death.

The crystalline wonders were set up on a cleared table covered with a red cloth so that the white carvings stood out against it. Lord Leicester led Elizabeth to view them, and she smiled, gesturing grandly.

"The sweetest parts of London," she called. "A triumph to the sculptors." She indicated two men and a woman who had followed the structures into the room as if they were nervous mothers following people carrying their babes. "Goodwife Mary O'Brien, recently from Ireland and Goodmen White and Butterbee from the southern part of England." The three nodded to the crowd, who applauded the trio.

"Has anyone checked the sugar works for poison?" Greer asked Walsingham.

"Sugar works are not eaten," he answered as if the thought

was ludicrous. "They are but decoration for the holiday."

"Surely when Christmastide is over, they will be ground back to crumbs to be consumed," Greer said. Lucy saw the side of his jaw twitch like he was clenching his teeth.

Walsingham's frown grew. "I will have the Darbys check it before then." He stepped off the dais, making his way through the crowd toward the sculptures.

Lucy glanced at Greer, who seemed to stand sentry. "You may go dance," she said, pointing with her scepter at the floor.

"I will remain by your side as your security minister," he said.

"I assure you that no one wants me dead, Master Buchanan. Richard's death was a mistake, one I will not repeat."

"Poison could be delivered in other ways, not just food," Greer said.

"Very well." He could stay beside her despite her being irritated. Lucy had received many insults in her life, from traitor to witch, but she'd never been reduced to bland, someone to live out a predictable life. Even though he'd apologized, the wound was still raw. Imagine his surprise if she suddenly kissed him. The thought made her stomach flip.

Lucy watched Catherine stand opposite Nick in the line of dancers. They were both dressed in secondhand clothes that Lucy had found in trunks at Cranfield House, but the garments were much richer than any the children had owned before. As the queen and Leister pass before them, their eyes grew so wide that Lucy chuckled. "From the gutters to dancing with the queen," she said and noticed that Alyce stood apart, her festive mask on to cover the scars on her cheek. Lucy absently rubbed her right hand that remained hidden away in her glove. The wounds had taught her to hide things, even big things that others would notice. And one could hide a million hurts behind a smile.

"You say 'tis the blue flame that doesn't burn?" Lucy asked Greer as they watched one of the young courtiers snatch several almonds out of the Snapdragon basin.

"Aye," Greer said, keeping his voice low. "The brandy burns easily at lower temperatures. As long as the flame is blue, it won't burn you."

"Could I hold my hand in it?" she asked, her brows raised as she looked at him. It was the most she'd looked at him that evening, even though he'd apologized.

With the crown of pearls nestled in her piled curls, Lucy looked royal indeed. Royal, absolutely beautiful, and no one with whom he should trifle. He looked back to the shallow game bowl filled with nuts, raisins, and dancing blue flames. "If ye left your hand there, it would burn, but ye won't feel pain if ye move swiftly. 'Tis less heat than a candle flame."

"Make way for the Lady of Misrule to play," one of the ladies in the small crowd called. People jostled back so Lucy could step up to the table. Several of the court ladies whispered, their heads bending together as they looked at Lucy's gloved hands. Her scars were not a total secret. Perhaps the queen didn't care as long as they were covered. *Mo chreach.*

Lucy took a deep breath and stepped closer. Did the flames remind her of the pain she'd endured under her mother's attempts to burn away her marks? Or the terrible accident with hot fat?

He leaned near her ear. "I can make a game out of carrying ye away," he whispered.

She gave a little shake of her head as she stared at the flames.

"You must take off your glove to reach or it doesn't count," said Lady Anne. She smiled sweetly, but there was a pinch to her eyes that made her look devilish.

Lucy plucked off the glove of her left, unblemished hand. Balling it up, she tossed it across the circle. It hit Anne in the face. "Thank you for holding it for me," Lucy said with such lightness that it sounded sincere. Everyone laughed at the surprised look on Anne face.

Stealing herself, Lucy pointed. "I will have that almond in the middle." She glanced back at Greer. He nodded. Lucy turned back and quickly plunged her hand through the flame, snatching the almond out. She laughed as she held it in the air, and everyone around them clapped. "'Tis not even hot, merely warm," she said and popped the almond in her mouth. "Delicious."

Several ladies removed their gloves, raising them in the air to be the next brave lady to play. Greer stepped before Lady Anne. "I will return her glove."

Anne, having recovered from her embarrassment, smiled coyly up at Greer. "Certainly, Lord Highlander." She held it out for him to take, but when he pulled it, she wouldn't let go. "For a price," she said. "A kiss."

Without hesitation, Lucy held her scepter over Anne's head. "The kissing ball proclaims this lady demands a kiss." Before Greer could even turn to Lucy to find out what she was doing, three men in the crowd pushed forward. A blond-haired fellow kissed Anne's right cheek. A bald man with a cap kissed her left, and a dark-skinned lord held Anne's arm. He boldly slid her glove down and turned her arm so the soft underside was exposed. He kissed her arm, his gaze catching hers with obvious invitation.

The surprise that loosened Anne's hold on the glove turned to a radiant smile over the attention, and Greer easily pulled the glove away. He turned to Lucy. "I think ye better lower that kissing ball."

"Before we are given a carnal display," William said, walking up to them. He sounded like a grumpy miser.

Lucy lowered the scepter. "Who knew such power could be gained with a ball of holly, mistletoe, and bells." Those around her laughed. "We could send kissing scepters to war!"

William nodded to the Snapdragon game. "Have the almonds and raisins been inspected for poison?"

Around the table, the ladies who had raised their bare hands for the next try lowered them. "Ye certainly have a way of dampening the festivities, Darby," Greer said and gestured for Lucy to move away.

"I supplied the nuts and raisins for the two gaming tables," Lord Walsingham said as they passed them.

Greer looked over his shoulder. "And I'm sure Master Darby will explain how if they were tainted, a different color would probably infuse the flames."

"What color would the flames be?" one lady asked, stopping William from following.

"Wouldn't poison be burned off them anyway?"

"How about the brandy, Lord Walsingham? Was that tested?"

Greer left the questions behind for William and Walsingham as he escorted Lucy toward the floor where Elizabeth and Leister were dancing the scandalous La Volta dance with several other couples. It was considered scandalous because the man held the lady around the waist, lifting her with the help of a knee under her arse. The man would turn the lady, setting her down. The dance had come from the continent and had moved up to Edinburgh court too. Greer and the other men of Lord Moray's court had learned the intricate footwork.

"Do you dance La Volta?" Lucy asked Greer when they stopped on the outskirts of the cleared floor where Elizabeth and Leister held all the attention.

"I know the steps, but I don't dance," Greer said, using his sternest voice.

"As Lady of Misrule, I could order you to."

He met her teasing gaze with narrowed eyes. "And take the attention away from the queen and Leister?"

"'Tis allowed at Christmastide," she said and indicated the floor. "Or have I found something that frightens the fierce Highlander?"

Mo chreach! Lucy was going to make him dance before this room of judgmental arses.

"Ye are still punishing me, aren't ye?"

"Yes," she said, giving him a sweet smile.

He crossed his arms over his chest, watching her set her scepter against a bench. Others, especially the courtly men, watched her carefully.

Greer gritted his teeth. He didn't want to dance, but he also didn't want to throw Lucy into a bloody jackanape's arms. He held out his arm, and she took it. With any luck, the minstrels would end the dance soon and take a much-needed break.

Stepping onto the dance floor, he took Lucy's hand, holding it before them as they joined. The room was dim, splashed in light from a hundred candles, some high in the chandeliers, some behind glass globes in sconces on the walls. The fire was fed at one end by the massive yule log. It gave the room a golden glow cut with shadows and the quick tempo of lutes and flute.

Greer was certainly used to the quick pattern of steps, although he'd feel more balanced if he were holding his sword while working through them. Lucy and he came closer as the dance required, and he felt the pull between them that remained. His hands encircled her waist, and he lifted her, setting her down in a turn. He didn't even need to help lift with his knee, despite it being part of the dance. They moved apart, and Lucy's smile held surprise.

"We are not so uncultured up in Edinburgh," he said as they neared and he took her close once again, lifting and turning.

"Scottish warriors learn La Volta?" she asked.

"'Tis practice for war."

Her smile broadened. "You are most accomplished then at warring and dancing." She glanced past him. "You make all the men frown with jealousy and all the ladies fan their heaving bosoms."

He snorted softly, and they moved apart again.

"Was that a laugh?" Lucy asked. "Did I win a laugh from the serious Highlander?"

They turned in their own circles and came together again, his hands now familiar with the span of her waist. "A laugh of derision is not a true laugh."

He held her close as they turned, and she kept her beautiful eyes focused on his. "Allowing yourself to feel merry will not jeopardize your mission, Greer."

"I'm not known for ever making merry," he said, "and I don't make a habit of smiling."

Her brow furrowed the slightest amount despite her smile. "A smile is my weapon to beat back the demons of the past and disarm the would-be villains in my path."

She was close, her petticoats pressed against his legs. "Unfortunately, the villains I know would not be undone by a smile, even from a beautiful lass."

"Beautiful?" she whispered, her gaze unwavering.

"May I claim the Lady of Misrule for her second dance?" William Darby appeared beside them, and Greer realized the tempo of the song had changed to a jaunty dance that brought partners across from one another in long lines.

Greer released Lucy and gave her a brief nod before turning away.

"Thank you," Lucy said, her voice loud.

He glanced back. She looked at him, her smile gentle. "For the dance."

"Are you a leper?" The high voice caught Greer's attention, and he turned toward the sugar works. Catherine, Nick, and Alyce stood there with a lady and lord of the court.

Alyce was desperately trying to fix her mask that had come undone, dropping away from the scars on her face. Several gasps rose nearby from the question. The poor girl seemed paralyzed in fright.

Chapter Eight

"If you're going to splash out at Christmas, you might as well do it in style. After all, 'both meat and cost, Ill dressed is lost'."

Thomas Tusser, *Five Hundred Points of Good Husbandry*, 1573

LUCY WATCHED GREER stride toward the sugar works where Catherine, Nick, and Alyce stood. Something was wrong. If Greer hadn't been but a few steps away, his stride could have been called a charge, as if into battle.

"Pardon me, William," she said, squeezing his arm before striding toward the table. She passed Cordelia on the way. "Dance with William."

"Now?" Cordelia asked.

"By order of the Lady of Misrule," Lucy said as she hurried on.

"She is not a leper," Greer said to Blanche Perry and Johna-than Whitt, who stood with aghast faces, staring at Alyce.

"She most certainly isn't a leper," Lucy repeated, coming up to the table.

Blanche pointed a long, gloved finger at Alyce, who lifted the caul about her neck high enough to cover her chin. "But she's disfigured on her face."

By now, several others close to them had turned to stare. Anne came up beside Blanche, her hands against her cheeks. "We could all be disfigured and scarred."

Lucy's heart ached for Alyce. It had taken Lucy an hour to convince her to come with Catherine and Nick, who had been so excited at the idea. The fact it was a masque was the only thing that gave Alyce the courage. And now she was being called a leper.

"'Tis a scar from an accident," Greer said, walking around to the side of the table where the children stood.

Anne glanced at Lucy. "The Lady of Misrule knows quite well that scars and disfigurements are not permitted at court and should order this abomination away."

"A ridiculous rule," Greer said. "I have scars that show my experience in battle. They're permitted."

Johnathan Whitt scoffed. "They show you're weak enough in battle to have been hit."

Holy Mother Mary, Greer would lop off the fool's head right here in the Great Hall.

"How many battles have ye fought in, sir?" Greer asked Johnathan.

Lucy knew that Johnathan was still young enough not to have gone to war, although he trained with the army. "Several," he lied, expecting that no one would give him away before a foreigner.

"There's no proof of that," Greer said. He stood tall, his broad shoulders back. The expanse of his chest seemed built of muscle beneath his white tunic. He raised a finger to the scar on his face. "This shows that I battled. Ask me what happened to the man who gave me this scar."

"What happened to him?" Mary Hill asked, her eyes wide. She stood next to Blanche, and several others had moved closer to listen.

"I slashed his—"

"The Lady of Misrule rules this not a merry speech," Lucy said, overriding Greer's bloody description. "But you can be assured that this child, who is my personal guest, does not have leprosy or anything that could spread to anyone except kindness and acceptance, if your hearts are open to it."

Lucy had meant to shut down the conversation, bringing them back to merriment so that Alyce could escape the attention that had been cast upon her. Greer apparently had other ideas.

"Scars," Greer pronounced as he stood firm beside Alyce, "whether from an illness or some attack against your person, show that you were strong enough to endure the battle and survived to live and fight another day." His glance slid across the onlookers, ending at Lucy where their gazes connected, holding fast. "They are badges of honor not to be despised."

Lucy couldn't swallow. It was as if Greer spoke directly to her heart.

"So you would have me flaunt the scars that haunt my face?" Elizabeth said as she drew near, her smooth, white face giving her pinched, red lips a ghostly background. "Scars that remind me of nearly dying from pox?"

Greer met the queen's fierce stare. "The very scars that prove ye are stronger than the disease that takes so many away from this world? That ye fought and beat the devil? Aye."

"There is ugliness in them," she said.

"There is strength in them," Greer countered.

They stared at one another, and Lucy, along with the whole room, waited. *Look away.* Royal opinions and fragile haughtiness could send him to the Tower.

He broke the stare and bowed his head to the queen. "I owe that 'tis different when one must represent a kingdom, Your Majesty. That ye must display the perfection of England. But the fact that ye were tested by sickness and won shows that ye have the favor of God and the heart of a king."

Lucy exhaled with relief.

"I have the heart of a king, Highlander," she said, and he looked up, "but I must have the face of a queen."

"Hear, hear!" Lord Leister called beside her, and the room echoed it.

"But," Elizabeth said, obviously happy with the outcry of

support, "for those who do not carry the burden of the crown, marks that show a battle won against death could demonstrate strength in a person."

The queen looked to Alyce, who had backed against the wall where she probably wished to melt away. "Guest of my Lady of Misrule, you are welcome here, as an example of the strength of the common Englishwoman." Elizabeth flipped her hand. "You may cover your scars or not, child."

As if becoming bored with the conversation, she turned with a flourish of her long fingers. "Find me something safe to drink, Robin," she said to Leister. "I am parched from our dance."

The gathered courtiers and listening commoners slowly followed the queen's dismissal, floating away with tentative smiles at Alyce. The minstrels began to play another lively tune.

Catherine raised up on her toes, her hands clasped as she smiled at Alyce. "The queen says you're strong, Alyce! And you don't have to hide your face."

The girl kept her mask in place, but her frightened grimace had softened. She looked at Greer. "Thank you, Master Buchanan," she said softly. A type of adoration seemed to fill her eyes.

"Yes," Lucy said, squeezing Alyce's shoulders. "Thank you for your defense. The common people rarely receive any."

"All people," he said, meeting Lucy's gaze, "need defense, especially at court where nobles play at slander and intrigue in order to elevate themselves."

Lucy glanced away. "That they do." She took a full breath, nodding toward some servants walking in with trays. Each servant had a guard next to them whom Lord Walsingham asked a question. As the guard nodded, Walsingham made the guard eat one of the sweetmeats that he randomly chose. Once the guard ate the sample, Walsingham allowed the tray to enter.

"Are they safe?" Nick asked.

"Lord Walsingham has required each cook be guarded," Lucy said. "So yes, very safe."

Catherine clapped her hands, and Alyce took one to lead her

around the edge of the room toward the long table where the platters were being arranged. Nick, however, cut right through the middle of the floor to arrive there first.

Lucy glanced at Greer. "Your defense of Alyce was so generous." She shook her head. "I didn't even hear the comment."

"I wasn't defending only Alyce," he said. He came closer to her. "There's no shame in your scars, Lucy."

Lucy tucked her hand behind her back. "They're ugly, and I abhor pity," she said with a smile. "I'm fortunate they are easily hidden with clothing, unlike Alyce."

"Will ye let no one see them?" he asked. "Besides a chemist who wants to hide them and a mother who told ye they were ugly?"

"I hide them because they *are* ugly. And if the red and dark marks weren't hideous enough at birth, trying to burn them away made them so." She looked away.

"Did Darby say they're hideous?" he asked, his voice harsh.

She swallowed, remembering the first time she'd shown William. "He said nothing."

"Silence can be as cutting as words."

She looked at him. "And some words can leave scars inside that will never heal." She tried to turn away, but he caught her arm.

"Lucy—"

"I must choose the most festive spinning wheel," she said, nodding toward the length of wall where the household spinning wheels had been set. The ladies of the court had decorated each of the twelve wheels with dried flowers, holly, and ribbons so the wheels couldn't be used for work during the twelve days of Christmas.

"Perhaps one day, ye will show me your scars," he whispered close to her ear. "I will not judge them the way ye fear others do."

Lucy's breath caught at his nearness, and the warmth of his words. *Show me your scars?* He'd practically suggested she undress for him.

"Lady of Misrule, you are needed across the hall," Cordelia said, stopping behind them.

Cordelia found Lucy's right arm in the folds of her gown and tugged her to follow. As she walked away, Lucy could feel Greer's gaze on her back. He really had suggested that she let him see her without clothing. The thought sent a ribbon of heat twisting down through Lucy's middle.

THE REST OF the evening floated by like a play that Lucy acted in while her mind worked over Greer's words. She could still feel the pressure of his strong hands as he lifted her in the La Volta, turning her and setting her down without taxing himself at all. And how he'd leapt to Alyce's defense, even against the queen, deftly turning her opinion while saving Elizabeth's pride. Greer Buchanan was a warrior, but one who had trained at the Scottish court to also be a diplomat. Clever and courageous, he'd shown he could fight battles at court as well as on the cold, rocky moors.

And he wants to see my scars. Her scars were under her clothing, across her back, legs, and stomach. Scattered here and there like ink blots on smooth parchment. Some had been red, some darker. Now the skin around them was mottled with burn marks, turning the marks darker in most places. A failure that her mother had blamed on Lucy, of course.

He wants to see them. What did that mean? Did he only want to see the spots, or the rest of her too? She felt her cheeks warm and snorted softly, wishing she were more worldly like her sister. But there'd been no opportunity to consider a man. Lucy was loath to look at herself, let alone allow another to see her undressed. It had been under great distress that she'd showed William and his father a few of them.

But Greer Buchanan was different. Her heart sped at the thought. Might this be the only time in her life that she could allow a man to see her? All of her? Not just glimpses from under a physician's sheet?

Her mother had said no man would marry Lucy for fear the spots would mar his children. Even when Cordelia whispered to Lucy that she would find a man, Lucy hadn't believed her. After one miserable summer of her mother's torture and mourning the loss of a future she'd never have, Lucy had decided to focus on things that made her and others smile. So, she'd focused on her natural sense of humor. It had become her best trait. Even her mother had said so.

And here I am, Mother, the queen's Lady of Misrule. With a brawny, handsome man who may have suggested that he'd like to see her naked, even knowing about her marks.

Lucy walked along the line of spinning wheels, making people around her laugh with her critical eye, despite her comments always being overly positive. The contrast between words and facial expressions made people laugh. If Lucy saw any lady beginning to suffer from her satire, she'd hold the kissing ball at the end of her scepter over the lady's head, and a gallant swain would come kiss her hand or cheek. The lightheartedness and exuberant attention smoothed the few ruffled feathers her judging caused.

At the end of the row, Lucy turned to survey her domain for the rest of the twelve Christmas days. At least, that's what she attempted to portray. Instead, her gaze sought Greer. He stood with Alyce and Catherine near the table where Nick still grazed, the boy filling his belly with a feast that he'd been denied his whole short life.

Greer motioned to the dancers performing the simple dance in two lines. For a man who did not talk much, he seemed to be doing all the talking with Alyce and Catherine. Both girls had taken on an adoring look. *Holy Mother Mary!* If Lucy allowed herself to look at Greer that way, she would be brutally laughed at when he left.

She turned toward the Snapdragon game. *Well, I'm not giving my heart away. I might give away my maidenhead, but not my heart.*

Lucy raised her fingertips to her lips as if stopping herself from saying the words aloud. She'd already considered seducing him to prove she wasn't predictable.

"William Darby is a kindhearted man with a solid position," Cordelia said beside Lucy. For a split-second Lucy couldn't, for the life of her, remember who William Darby was. "And he's brother to our dearest friend," Cordelia continued. "He has an honorable position at court, is highly intelligent, and had a good upbringing."

"You're right, Cordy," Lucy said.

"Of course, I am."

Lucy opened her eyes wide as she looked at her sister. "I think you should marry him."

Cordelia smile dropped. "Not me."

Lucy rolled her eyes and sighed. "William Darby sees me as a medical curiosity." Despite all the truth in Cordelia's description and the feeling that William might be attracted to her, the thought of marrying the chemist made Lucy's stomach curdle.

"But he's seen your marks and doesn't think badly of you," Cordelia said.

"Greer doesn't think badly of me for having them either," Lucy said.

Cordelia's eyes grew round as she turned on her. "Has he *seen* them?"

"Just my hand," Lucy said.

"Thank the good Lord," Cordelia murmured, and plastered on a smile as William walked up.

"But I've told him," Lucy said. "He has marks too."

"He has scars from battle," Cordelia said, fluffing her dress. 'Tis different from what... from what you were born with." Her sister's words shot like little arrows through Lucy's heart. "Although he suffered, too, from the pain inflicted, like Mother unfairly did to you." Cordelia squeezed Lucy's hand.

Lucy inhaled and placed her practiced smile across her mouth as William stopped before them. She was the jester after all, pierced heart or not. She rubbed the hollow feel in her chest. If one looked inside, would they see her heart bleeding from the jabs or rotting like a diseased limb?

"'Tis very festive, considering the underlying worry," William said, indicating the room, but Lucy barely noticed. Cordelia gave some agreeable reply.

How would Lucy be able to draw another breath if Greer did look upon her scars and turned away? Her heart thudded hard with the thought, and a cold sweat broke along her forehead. How foolish she was to even consider showing him or anyone. If the abbeys hadn't been dissolved, she'd have become a nun.

Maybe she could volunteer at a leper house. Cordelia had been very against that particular idea. *God has a plan for you*, Cordelia had insisted. *And it doesn't involve condemning yourself to a leper colony*. But maybe it did. She might as well help those who understood the pain of being ostracized, of never being touched except through fabric.

Lucy closed her eyes. The laughter seemed sharp and jagged like broken glass against her frayed heart, the music mocking.

"Are you well?" William asked, his hand gripping her arm.

Lucy pulled it away. "I need some fresh air," she said. "Alone, please." She traipsed away, donning the smile she wore like a mask. The press of so many swishing petticoats against her felt like fingers trying to stop her from escape. One step in front of the other, she pushed through the crowd to the arched doorway.

The air was cool in the corridor, and she took full breaths as she continued across to the chapel. Quiet and empty, it was the perfect place to repair her composure. Her slippers pattered against the marble floor as she ran down the aisle flanked by boxed off sets of pews. The ornate alter reminded her of her mother's Catholic masses even though Elizabeth was clearly Protestant.

Lucy nearly fell to the kneeling pad before the table with a central gold cross, her head bowed as she slowed her breath.

When she looked up, the polished cross seemed to glow down at her, reflecting the light cast from the sconces on the wall. "What do I do, dearest God?" she whispered.

Would it be lepers for her? Or William like Cordelia encouraged? The fact that Lucy wasn't sure if she'd rather live with lepers or marry William was answer enough for her that she wasn't attracted to William. At all. She snorted softly. *Then what, God? What do I do?*

Greer's face slid easily into her mind. She shook her head. He would find her ugly despite his kindness to Alyce. *He asked to see them*, she thought as she rubbed her gloved right hand. *I told him they were hideous.* Surely, he wouldn't spurn her after seeing her. Would he?

I am courageous. And she would never allow herself to live a bland, predictable life. Would Greer Buchanan love her tenderly if she asked? He would leave once Twelfth Night was concluded, so there would be no repercussions as long as no one found out.

I'm a very generous lover. That's what he'd said in front of the church Christmas morn. Was it true? The thought tightened the ache that was already forming within Lucy. There was only one way to find out.

CHAPTER NINE

"Some leper hospitals, which housed those believed to have leprosy, also took in those suffering from general infirmity, and by the later Middles Ages many of these leper hospitals no longer housed any lepers at all, instead taking in the old and infirm. Additionally, most hospitals accommodated no more than 20 brothers and sisters, 12 being the most common along with a priest. St Leonard's Hospital in York was truly exceptional, having around 225 beds."

History Extra

G REER GLANCED UP and down the long corridor outside the Great Hall. He breathed in the cooler air. Between the Yule log burning, the press of people, and the dancing, the air was vastly better in the corridor.

"Where did ye go, lass?" he said. She'd probably left to collect herself. What the bloody hell had William said to her? Greer had seen him talking to her with Cordelia, and then Lucy had left.

Greer opened the door to the chapel. The distant smell of incense and candles added to the holy feel to the place. Vast and richly appointed, the Whitehall chapel seemed foolishly redundant with Westminster down the road.

He looked toward the alter. "Lucy?" His voice broke through the layers of holy silence that filled the space like a swollen sea. She knelt there, alone, her petticoats circling out around her over the two steps leading to the altar.

Without bothering to mute his steps in reverence, he strode to her. Startled, she stood, turning to him. Were those tears in her eyes? What did William say to her? "I won't kill him," Greer said, standing before her. "But he will feel pain. What did he do, so that I know how much pain?"

She blinked, taking a full breath. "Who?"

"Darby."

"William did nothing to me."

Greer glanced back up the aisle and then at the altar. "Is that why ye are in here? Because he did... nothing?" Did she want the boy to do something to her? The thought twisted tightly in Greer's middle. His breath swam around in his gut, not leaving his body as he waited for her to answer.

"Pardon?" she said, the lovely arches of her brows pinching.

"Do ye want William Darby? Is that why ye are sad?" He couldn't imagine the stupidity of the boy. Greer was sure the chemist desired Lucy.

"No," she said, shaking her head. "I'd rather live with lepers than be with William."

"Lepers?"

Her hand waved off the comment, and she stepped closer. Standing there in a house of God, Greer tried to ignore the way Lucy's curls lay against her exposed neckline. In the dimness of the few candles placed in glass globes against the walls, her hair looked spun of gold. Her face was pale and perfect with her wide-set eyes and slender nose.

"Greer Buchanan," she said, her voice soft.

"Aye?"

"I want *you*."

His mouth opened and then closed. "Lass..." *Bloody hell.* His hands fisted at his sides to keep from reaching for her. Was this some type of devilish test God was placing upon him here in his house?

"Lass," he started again. "I have no plans to wed."

Her lips were parted, and he could imagine their sweetness.

"I'm not asking you to wed me," Lucy said, her voice slightly above the sound of her shallow breaths. "I am asking you to… take me."

Take me? That's what she said. Take me.

He fisted his hands next to his legs. "Take ye where?" he asked, not giving into the hope that he knew exactly where she wanted him to take her. A place that would leave her panting and moaning in pleasure.

Her eyes met his. "To bed. That is if you want me too." She shook her head. "No need to wed."

With a deep breath that pushed the swell of her breasts higher over the lace edge of her bodice, she reached up to touch his face. Her cool fingers slid along his cheek where he knew his scar sat. He meant to ask her if she were sure, but his arms rose instead, pulling her into him. She came willingly into the circle.

His lips met hers, and the sweetness of the touch tore through him. Lucy was warm and soft, perfect in his arms. She tilted her face, deepening the kiss, and heat tore up through Greer. Her fingers ran through his hair to the back of his neck, and her mouth moved against his. She moaned softly as he cupped her arse through the layers. Did she know what she was doing to him? Promising things with her touch and her body?

He lifted her to slide against him in the most intimate way, damning the silk and cotton between them. Although, he knew she was bare beneath the petticoats. The thought of her heat there rendered him harder still. He groaned against her mouth when she tentatively touched her tongue to his. She might be an innocent, but she knew how to kiss.

Daingead. He was practically tupping an innocent in a chapel. They'd be struck with lightning right through Whitehall's vaulted roof. He shouldn't even be kissing her there.

Without a word, he lifted under Lucy's legs. She clung tighter to him as he carried her back up the aisle like a lusty bridegroom taking his new wife away. His echoing footsteps stopped, and he broke the kiss to push through the door. Thank the devil or the lord or whomever had kept the corridor empty and dark, the sound of music and laughter coming from the Great Hall.

Striding quickly, Greer led her out of the chapel and through the door of the massive wine cellar down the corridor. The smell of wooden casks and dust enveloped them with the deep darkness. No sconces were left burning in the room where servants came to turn the bottles once each day.

He set Lucy down, clasping her face gently in his hands. They couldn't see one another, only feel. He slid his thumb over her smooth cheek. "Ye cannot mean it," he murmured.

"I do want you, Greer," she said, her words breathless.

"Ye are a maid still."

"Yes, but I have no need to continue that way. I will never marry, but I want... I need to know about this heat, this ache inside me."

His breathing was loud in his ears. Lucy's hands found his chest, and he could tell she'd removed her gloves. He caught her hands between them, lifting them to his mouth to kiss. "Ye honor me, lass." His rational mind warred with his want. There was no doubt he wanted Lucy. He would bring her to such pleasure along with him. But why did she think she'd never marry? Because of her scars, her marks? He wanted to argue, but then she pulled his face back down to hers.

Her lips slid against his, banishing all lingering thoughts of talk and treason. He held her to him as if she could disappear into the darkness if he didn't. The soft mews she made tightened his muscles, and he lifted her against him again, molding her intimately to his form. His hands held her arse under her bum roll. "So many layers," he murmured.

"Too many," she said and pulled his tunic up from his wrapped plaid. Breaking free of the edge, her cool fingers slid up underneath to feather across the hot skin of his stomach and chest. It had the same effect as if she'd stroked his hard jack, rolling fire of lust through him.

Greer left her mouth, kissing a trail down the side of her jaw to her neck where her blood rushed under her skin. They backed up until Lucy was pressed against what was probably the door because bottles and casks lined every spare inch of wall and filled shelves up to the low ceiling. Her breathing came fast and shallow, like his. She ran her fingers through the light hair of his chest. She found his hand against her face and led it down to her shoulder and then lower. "Touch me," she whispered on an exhale, her hand pressing his to her breast.

She tugged on her bodice and stays, and he felt them shift downward until her flesh swelled over the laced edge. He could easily imagine her breasts perched on the top of the neckline, two plump mounds of softness.

Hand against her back, Greer lowered his mouth to her skin, breathing in the scent of her in the warm valley between them. Strawberries and cloves. He kissed along the swell over to one taut nipple, sucking it into his mouth.

"Oh God, yes," Lucy said, her words stuttering as with a gasp.

Greer focused his lips, teeth, and tongue on the pleasure point while his hand strummed her other nipple, palming the flesh before moving his mouth over. Her fingers ran through his hair, holding his head to her, and he was her willing captive. She shifted below, pressing against him, and he raised his lips back to hers.

"You are mighty," she murmured against his mouth. "I want to…" She moaned softly against his mouth as Greer pressed against her mound through her petticoats. She pushed her pelvis back, and he could imagine the wet heat there. "Yes," she said. "Please, Greer."

Everything about Lucy pulled him in. Her obvious desire, her words, the strain in her voice, her openness to his touch. *Take me.* Before he could think, his fingers were rucking up the layers of her gown, determined to feel her desire for him. The petticoats came up easily, and he realized she'd reached down to help lift.

Silk, sewn with little pits that he remembered were pearls, puffed up around them. They both shoved the fabric behind

Lucy, like a cushion for her against the door. Her kisses clung to him, and she opened her mouth. When her tongue slid out, touching his, Greer groaned. He slid his hand up her silky thigh, squeezing the roundness of her bare arse.

Lucy breathed heavily against him. She lifted her one leg, giving him access, and Greer found her easily. Wet and warm, she was as soft inside as she was out. She moaned softly.

"Ye are a nymph, lass," he said and kissed a path along her jaw to her ear where his ragged words whispered. "Like sweet honey, heated in the hot sun."

"'Tis so good," she said, thrusting in his hand as he played her tight body.

The rush of blood through his ears blocked the noise at first, but his warrior instincts woke him to the push against the door.

"Is it locked?" a voice came from outside the door at Lucy's back.

Greer's palm flattened against the thick wood as he dropped Lucy's petticoats, the rustle of them breaking the thick silence in the wine room.

"I have the key." It was a woman, the first voice belonging to a man. Were they looking for a secluded place? Or were they servants finding wine to replenish the goblets in the Great Hall?

Either way, he needed to save Lucy from ridicule.

"What do we do?" she said in a whisper barely heard over the iron clink of the key in the lock. Being discovered in a dark room alone together would cause a scandal, something he was certain Lucy didn't want. She'd already lived through so much as a Cranfield.

Greer grabbed Lucy's hand, tugging her behind him as he moved deeper into the room, his hand out to stop him from knocking over shelves of glass bottles. He'd only briefly seen the layout when he'd opened the door to carry Lucy inside. Were there three or four rows of bottles?

Hand before him, he pulled Lucy quickly forward down a back aisle as the door opened. Candlelight seemed bright after the ink-black darkness, and Greer tugged Lucy to stand against the back wall, blocking her body.

The door closed. *Daingead*. Would they have to withstand listening to two lovers? He was still hard as Scottish stone.

"I can't believe Richard is dead," the woman said. "'Tis a sad shock. How could our plan have gone so wry, Simmons?"

Simmons? Plan? Greer could feel Lucy shift against him, trying to see, but they were up near the door.

"The court is a dangerous place." Now Greer could easily recognize Lucy's housekeeper's voice.

"I would rather you return to Cranfield House for our further plans," the woman said. "Jasper says he won't be seen talking with us at Whitehall. That the three of us being together could be noted."

"Cranfield House has children now, and I don't want to involve Lady Lucy further," Simmons said.

Greer's breath stuck in his chest, the heat in his body turning cold. *Involve Lady Lucy further?*

"We need to move forward. That hasn't changed since Richard died," the woman said.

Greer heard bottles being dragged out of their tipped-over positions. "I will keep watch from the kitchens. We want nothing to happen to the queen until we've devised the best strategy."

"Before Twelfth Night," Simmons said. "Jasper says she's at her most vulnerable while making merry."

The two opened the door and walked back out quietly. Darkness fell over them once more.

Greer kept his hand shackled around Lucy's wrist, turning to her in the tight aisle. "What did he mean, *involve Lady Lucy any further?*" His voice was rough, the heat turning to suspicion.

"I...I do not know," she said, and she sounded truly perplexed. But she was an excellent liar.

He leaned toward her until he could tell her face hovered right before his, her back against the wall. "Lucy Cranfield, are ye working with Simmons and that woman to assassinate the queen of England?"

⫸⫷

LUCY'S ENTIRE BODY stood tense, her eyes wide even though it didn't help her see. She blinked as if making sure they were open.

"No," she said, feeling the closeness of Greer's face. He held her against a wall, in a nearly sound-proof room where no one knew she was, but she wasn't afraid. Not of Greer. "I am not plotting to kill the queen or anyone."

Her palms lay against his chest, and she could feel his warmth through the tunic, and the rising and falling with his breaths.

"What were they talking about?" he asked.

She sighed. "If I tell you, you cannot tell anyone. Not yet."

"Tell me," he said.

"They are planning to petition the queen to allow them to own land together." Her words came out in a rush. "Richard Whitby, Mistress Catolina Wakefield, Simmons, and I guess this other man with whom I have not yet been acquainted." Her hand slid down his arm where it hung by his side, and she yanked at it, but couldn't move it much. The man was a mountain of iron. "They asked me for advice, and I suggested they work through Richard since he was closest to the court."

"Work through him to petition the queen?" Greer asked, and she could hear the doubt in his voice.

She frowned, jabbing him in the chest. "Don't sound like that. Yes, to petition the queen. You know, not every plot about Her Majesty ends in her death." She threw her arms out, knocking her bare knuckles against the wooden shelf. She gasped softly and pulled it back in to rub. "Why would they want her dead if they want her to grant them the ability to purchase some of the crown's land?"

"They want land?" he asked, fumbling in the dark until he found her hand, rubbing his thumb across her bruised knuckles.

"Yes. Mistress Wakefield owns her late husband's shop on Gracechurch Street. Master Whitby own's his late wife's small townhouse. Simmons owns nothing but has been saving his pay for years." The more she spoke, the angrier she became.

She growled softly. "You suspected me, and still... We..." She poked him in the chest again. "You think I'd kiss you, and... well, more... That I would seduce you while also helping the assassins you're looking for?"

She heard him exhale through his nose. "Assassins are known to be excellent liars."

"Holy Mother Mary!" She shoved Greer's chest, and he backed up, allowing her to charge off into the dark. She bumped a shelf, making the bottles rattle. "God's teeth, where is the dratted door?"

"Don't charge out there." Greer's voice came from behind somewhere, so she strode forward, her hands sweeping the dark.

She found the door and yanked it open. Blinking against the relatively bright light, she stepped right out into... William Darby.

CHAPTER TEN

"Foolery, sir, does walk about the orb like the sun, it shines everywhere."
William Shakespeare, *Twelfth Night*, 1600

"**L**ADY LUCY?" WILLIAM said, grabbing hold of her shoulders to steady her.

"Pardon me," she said, her hand flattening on her chest. *Please let my nipples be covered.* Thank God she felt fabric beneath her palms.

"What were you doing in the...wine cellar?" Cordelia asked as she hurried up to the two of them.

"Just...finding some solitude after being so smashed inside the Great Hall."

William yanked open the door, letting in a splash of light. Lucy froze, but he didn't say anything like *Good eve, Master Buchanan* or *Was Lucy seducing you in here, Master Buchanan?* So apparently, Greer was hiding somewhere behind the stacks of wine. "'Tis completely dark in there," William said, letting the door shut.

"Which is why I stepped back out after a moment."

Both Cordelia and William stared at her. "Did you two need something?" Lucy asked.

"To make certain you were well," Cordelia said, frowning at Lucy's neckline. "Where is your strand of pearls that the queen gifted you?"

Lucy's hand laid against her bare chest that her sister was studying. Could Greer have left evidence of his kisses? The brush of his short beard? The memory set her heart beating harder.

"And where are your gloves?" Cordelia asked.

Her gloves? She'd taken them off to touch Greer, to feel the warmth of his body under her hands. That was before she poked him. Twice.

"I… I went to the privy."

"Are they in your pocket?" William asked.

"Yes," Lucy said, remembering. She shoved her scarred hand into the pocket that was tied between the two layers of her petticoats. She shook the wrinkles from them and pulled them on up to her elbows.

"Is your necklace in there too?" Cordelia asked, her lips twisted with wryness.

"No. The clasp must have broken," Lucy said, glancing down at her decalage. Her bodice was shifted slightly to the right. When she looked up, Cordelia was studying her from head to hem. Did she look as ravished as she felt, her body still tingling from Greer's touch?

Lucy turned away, her hands going to her bodice, fixing it, and feeling for the pearls. "The strand dropped inside my stays," she said. She slowly pulled them up like a knobby snake. The feel of it against her skin was tantalizing. How would it feel to have Greer run it over her body?

No. He thought she was a killer. Although, she had hidden the plans about Simmons's quest for owning land. And Greer had seen how well she could lie. Lucy sighed.

Cordelia leaned into her, touching Lucy's forehead like she seemed to often do these days. "You look flushed," she said.

"I… I am tired. Perhaps I should take to my bed," Lucy said. Would Greer find her? Come to question her some more? Come to love her some more?

Cordelia took the pearls from her, inspecting the clasp. "The clasp is gone. Maybe 'tis down your bodice too." Her brow rose in question.

Lucy slipped the broken necklace in her pocket. "I'll check when I disrobe." She opened her mouth, knowing a yawn would come, and it did. "I should retire now," Lucy said.

"You're the Lady of Misrule," Cordelia said. "You cannot depart early. The queen expects you to make merry with her courtiers tonight and every night until Twelfth Night." She unclasped her own set of pearls and went behind Lucy to set it around her neck. "Unless you are swooning or purging, you need to march back into the Great Hall and make people smile and laugh." She waved her arm at the doorway as if shooing her as if Lucy were an errant child.

Lord help her. Cordelia was right. "Very well," Lucy said, touching her sister's pearls sitting across her collarbone. "Take me in, sister."

Cordelia led her away, and William followed.

"There you are, jester," the queen called as she entered the room. "We are in need of your scepter as my dear Robin, Lord Leicester, has not kissed me this night."

"A travesty," Lucy said, putting on her bright smile. She inhaled to clear away her heated thoughts, both passionate and furious, and fetched her scepter that was propped against the throne where she'd left it barely an hour ago.

Lucy turned, brandishing the scepter in the air. "Kisses for everyone!" she called out as if casting a spell on the room. Every man turned to the nearest woman, taking her hand or leaning in to kiss her cheek. Robert Dudley, Lord Leister, however, kissed the queen's painted red lips.

Cordelia stood beside Lucy, watching William pick up two goblets of wine. Her sister leaned into Lucy. "Were you with Greer Buchanan?"

"'Tis my affair, not yours, Cordy."

Cordelia's sharp look dissolved as a shine came to her eyes. Tears? "I forbid you to fall in love with him," Cordelia whispered. "He will either break your heart when he leaves, or you will break my heart when you leave with him. Either way, meddling with him will leave us torn asunder."

Her sister was afraid for her? Lucy squeezed Cordelia's hand. "What if lust, not love, is what I feel?"

Cordelia's eyes opened wide. "Have you slept with him?"

"In the wine cellar just now?" She frowned. "No, sister. If I'm going to learn the ways of love, I need a light to see."

"Lucy, you looked…undone when you ran out. Did he take liberties?"

"No," she said. She'd been the one who started it all. In the chapel of all places. She felt her flush increase.

"But you were running out," Cordelia said, her gaze outward toward the merry room.

"I was angry about something else."

"What?"

Lucy huffed. "He thought I might be the assassin."

Cordelia stepped in front of her, staring in her eyes. "Why ever would he think that?"

"Well…he's seen me lie," Lucy said. "Well enough to escape Walsingham. And I'm a Cranfield." She threw her arm out. "I swear I will start going by another name altogether."

"Oh, that won't look suspicious at all," Cordelia quipped.

Lucy sighed. "And he heard Simmons talking about a plan he has to get close to the queen and mentioned that I know about it."

"What plan?"

Lucy stared at her sister. "It involves purchasing land not killing anyone, especially not the queen."

Cordelia's hand had gone to her cheek. "People assume the worst about us."

"To be fair, Greer assumes the worst about everyone." But that hadn't stopped him from kissing her when she threw herself at him.

Cordelia tipped her head. "But you were in the wine cellar with him, in the dark, alone, and he wasn't taking liberties?"

Lucy glanced toward the arched doorway. "I may have been the one taking liberties," she whispered.

"Lucy!"

"Don't chide me for adventures you have already had."

Cordelia looked out at the room, her gaze stopping on William. "You would give yourself to a man before you wed? It will ruin your chances of a good match."

"You have," Lucy said.

Cordelia's face snapped around to her. "And I regret it. I was young and foolish and now I cannot bring my maidenhood to a marriage. Don't follow my folly."

Lucy touched Cordelia's cheek. "I have never thought you foolish, sister. Passionate, beautiful, and adventurous, but never foolish."

Cordelia blinked her tears back inside. "Well I do think I've been foolish, and I won't see you throw away a chance at a good marriage."

"I don't plan to marry anyway," Lucy said. "Mother said no man would risk having children with my disfigurement."

Cordelia nodded toward the room. "William Darby would."

Lucy followed her sister's gaze to where William spoke with Nick. "I've already decided I'd rather minister to lepers than marry William."

"Lepers?"

"Mmhm."

"That *is* rather telling," Cordelia said, both of them looking out toward the room.

Lucy's inhale stuttered as Greer walked back into the Great Hall. Her heart picked up a faster beat, and her stomach flipped. He was so dratted handsome in his bright plaid and crisp white tunic, which he'd fixed after she'd dismantled him in the wine room. His hair lay flat even though she'd run her fingers through it, and his mouth looked hard again even though she knew how soft and teasing it could be on her mouth and skin. Just thinking about the slight brush of his short beard on her breast made her nipples pearl with a shiver. Thankfully her stays hid them.

"Either you didn't ravage him very much, or he's fixed himself," Cordelia said.

Lucy held her hand over her mouth as she laughed, and she saw the corners of her sister's mouth raise.

Greer's gaze moved about the room. When he met Lucy's, he paused. She kept her polite smile in place, still irritated over his suspicion of her, no matter how guilty she looked. The tether between their gazes was a tight cord that plucked sensation through her body. How could he affect her so easily from that distance? It made her knees feel soft.

Whack. Cordelia hit Lucy's arm. "At least hide your affection or you'll be the subject of every jest here at court when he leaves."

Lucy tore her gaze from Greer's intense eyes and stepped out into the room. She held her scepter over several ladies who looked like they needed to be kissed. *I should hold it over myself.* Would Greer kiss her again, or had she ended anything between them by not revealing Simmons's plan?

"Lady Cranfield?"

Lucy turned to look at Mistress Catolina Wakefield, the woman from the wine cellar. The prosperous businesswoman was dressed in what was probably her best gown of gray silk.

"Good eve, Mistress Wakefield."

The woman lowered into a curtsey as if Lucy were the queen herself. Lucy squeezed the lady's arm. She'd met with her several times at Cranfield House as they made plans for pulling their moneys to buy a ruined monastery owned by the crown to the west of London. The lady, along with Richard Whitby and Simmons dreamed of owning land and becoming gentry. "I am so sorry about Richard Whitby," Lucy said. Mistress Wakefield and Richard Whitby seemed close, making Lucy wonder if they were courting.

Mistress Wakefield sniffed softly and pulled a handkerchief to touch her nose. "'Twas quite a shock."

"Will you and Simmons have enough moneys to apply to the queen on your own?"

She nodded. "With Jasper Lintel's share, we should have enough to petition for it."

Lucy frowned. "I do not know him. He's not come to our meetings."

"He came into the plan last month. A gentleman in Ireland but not in England. He has had to make ends meet by serving at the Bear's Inn. To use the title, which he did before, he must own land here."

Lucy thought of the man she'd seen briefly leaving Cranfield House when they'd arrived with Pip and Percy. Tall, slender, shaved chin, and heavy brows. "Well, perhaps he will come for Twelfth Night. The queen will want to meet all those involved in the request."

Mistress Wakefield nodded, but her eyes grew wide as she looked over Lucy's shoulder.

Lucy turned and stopped short. Greer was standing right behind her.

GREER DRAGGED HIS gaze from Lucy's luscious lips. *Bloody hell.* He had a mission and yet he'd rather look at Lucy, even when she frowned at him. And he deserved to be frowned at. Kissing her and then asking her if she were the assassin. But those damn lips were irresistible, and Simmons had said some damning things.

Greer looked past her at the woman he'd seen hurrying with Richard Whitby and another man from Cranfield House that first night. "Ladies," he said, bowing his head like he was one of Elizabeth's proper courtiers. They nodded in return.

"Mistress Wakefield," Lucy said, indicating the woman, "this is Master Buchanan from Edinburgh. He's hunting assassins."

The woman blinked several times and didn't quite look like

she could breathe. "I didn't assassinate poor Richard Whitby. He was a good friend."

"I overheard you in the wine cellar talking about a plan." Greer held her gaze like he was gripping her throat. She seemed to have a hard time swallowing against it.

"Did that plan include poison?" he asked.

The bluntness of her question made Mistress Wakefield blanch.

"Of course not," Lucy answered for her. "I told you that their plan was about obtaining property, which is currently in the hands of the crown."

"I would hear it from Mistress Wakefield," Greer said, keeping his gaze away from Lucy and on the flushed woman.

"'Tis true what Lady Cranfield says," the woman answered. "John Simmons, Jasper Lintel, Richard Whitby, and I were, that is to say—*are* pooling our moneys to petition the queen to buy one of the closed abbeys west of here." She glanced back and forth between Greer and Lucy. "When Master Whitby was killed, Simmons decided that he didn't want to involve milady anymore in case that was why he was murdered."

Lucy squeezed the woman's hand. "I am certain Richard wasn't the intended victim, and I am only giving you advice."

The fear in the woman's face was real enough. "If I have more questions for ye," Greer said, "will Lady Lucy know where to find ye?"

The woman nodded quickly like a bird pecking at seed.

"Thank you, Mistress," Lucy said with an encouraging smile. "Now go enjoy yourself."

"I am not sure that is possible," Mistress Wakefield said. "This Christmastide is like no other." She walked off toward the wine table that was being guarded by three men.

Greer stood close to Lucy, both of them looking out over the busy room. Her arm brushed his as she backed against the wall, but she pulled it closer to her body as if she abhorred his touch.

The thought made his chest feel tight. "Your sister is sending scowls my way," he said, also backing against the wall.

Lucy's hand rose to her neckline. "She suspects I was being ravished. My necklace had come undone and was down my bodice, which was slightly shifted to the side." The sound of the minstrels and conversation blocked her words, but she still lowered her voice.

"She's quite clever," he said. "Ye were, and I am sorry for it."

Lucy's face snapped to his. "Sorry? Because you think you kissed an assassin or because you fouled it up by suggesting it?"

He ran a hand up the back of his neck to squeeze it. "Because I lost focus of my mission, and because I made ye angry in the process."

She turned completely to him, leaning in, apparently having forgotten that she was on display for everyone in the room. "Do you really think that I could be trying to kill anyone?"

Greer took in all the smooth features of Lucy's face. He exhaled. "If you are, you are by far the deadliest assassin I've ever met."

She snorted. "Why is that?"

"Because I've never been so thoroughly distracted before."

"Distracted? Is that a good thing or a bad thing?" she asked, the fierceness mellowing in her glare.

He leaned close to her ear and inhaled the scent of strawberries and cloves. "Everything about ye, lass," he said, "pulls the rational and logical thoughts from my mind and replaces them with fiery, carnal want."

Lucy leaned completely against the wall as if she needed it to hold her up. "Oh," she said, the bluster completely out of her voice.

He turned back to stand beside her against the wall. "Ye may decide if that is a good or a bad thing."

THE PARTY DRAGGED on until midnight, and Lucy was required to stay through it all, at least until the queen retired. "Don't wake me in the morning," Lucy said to Cordelia as she hid a yawn behind her glove. "I will sleep until Twelfth Night."

"The curse of being witty, merry, and known for jesting," Cordelia said, following Lucy with her own yawn.

"Go on to bed," Lucy said. "The queen will quit the room soon." She nodded toward Elizabeth, who whispered with her favorite as he fed her sticky pieces of flat gingerbread that had been plated in an exchequer design with dark and light squares.

"What?" Cordelia said. "And leave you here to find your own way back? All alone?" The insinuation in her voice spoke her suspicion even though Greer had left the hall an hour before with three very sleepy children. He said he'd deliver them to Cranfield House safely. The memory of Catherine tucking her hand in his warmed Lucy's heart. But it was the words Greer had whispered in her ear earlier that slid molten rock through the rest of her.

Everything about ye, lass, pulls the rational and logical thoughts from my mind and replaces them with fiery, carnal want.

But he didn't see that as a good thing. She was a distraction, one of which he probably wished to be rid. Lucy let out an exaggerated sigh. "Greer isn't waiting in the hall to whisk me into a dark corner."

"Or a dark room?"

"He thinks I could be an assassin, Cordy."

"Which is utterly ridiculous."

"Agreed."

Cordelia set her wine goblet down. "You wouldn't harm anyone unless they were trying to hurt an animal or child."

Lucy smiled at her. "Exactly."

Cordy arched her brow and lowered her voice. "And the queen owns all those animals you've been trying to rescue."

Lucy frowned at her. "You sound like Greer now." She shook her head. "I would never try to kill someone. Steal their dogs? Yes. Maim them, perhaps, if they harmed a child? Absolutely."

Cordelia chuckled, shaking her head. "You'll end up in the Tower. And Maggie isn't here to break you out, *and* Walsingham has retrained the guards to not be so easily fooled."

"I don't know how you sleep at night, Cordy. Worrying about me so. Will I end up in the Tower or broken hearted and the ridicule of the court?"

"Maybe all of that," Cordelia warned. They stared out as another group leaving the room together. Johnathan Whitt stared rakishly into Anne Bixby's eyes as he escorted her into the corridor. "I could stop by the Darbys' door and have William come escort you back to your room."

Lucy huffed. "And lead the poor boy on?"

"You do every time you smile at him."

"I smile at everyone."

"You need to tell him that you will have nothing to do with him."

"I suppose if he were a leper, I would," Lucy said lightly.

Cordelia turned a frown on her. "Don't say to him that you'd choose living with lepers over living with him."

"Of course not," Lucy said, frowning back. "I wish he could just be my friend."

"'Tis hard when one cares more or in a different way."

Lucy looked at her private sister. She knew Cordelia had given away her maidenhead, and to a man who ended up being a traitor. She certainly had regrets but would never talk about them. Lucy squeezed her hand.

"Fare thee well, Lady of Misrule and Lady Cranfield," Elizabeth called as Leister helped her rise and took her arm. Cordelia and Lucy curtsied low as the queen swept by them.

"To bed now," Cordelia said, tugging Lucy along. They walked arm in arm down the Stone Gallery toward the suite of rooms kept for them.

"I'm yearning for sleep," Lucy said and let another yawn open her mouth like the swelling of a wave. Would Greer have returned from Cranfield House? Was he somewhere in the shadows or already tucked into his own bed? Would she distract him from sleep like she had from his mission?

"Peace-filled dreams," Cordelia said and watched Lucy unlock her door and go into her room.

A maid had kindled the fire in the hearth, shedding enough light to show that no Highland warrior with chiseled muscles lay on her bed or stood in the corners. She took a step and looked down at the gentle crunch under foot.

Lucy scooped up a small square of parchment, dropped her scepter on the smooth bed, and hurried to the fire for better light.

The children are safely home.
I did not harass Simmons.
And I made certain that you are locked in your room.
Good eve. G

A surge of energy rushed through Lucy, and she spun toward the doorway. He must have been watching for her return from the shadows if he knew she was locked in her room.

She cracked her door, peeking out, but the hall was empty and dark, the sconces having been gutted. Stepping out, she closed the door behind her and walked toward the guest quarters, listening to the sleeping palace. The darkness felt thick like the stonewalls flanking her.

Greer must be ahead, somewhere in the shadows. She flew around the corner and gasped as she ran smack into a solid chest.

CHAPTER ELEVEN

"At Christmas of Christ many Carols we sing, and give many gifts in the joy of that King."
Thomas Tusser – 16th century English poet

GREER'S HAND SLID up her arms, steadying her. "Is all well?" he asked.

"No," she said, catching her breath. She raised searching eyes to his. "I cannot sleep."

"Ye've only now returned to your room."

She stayed close to him, her words soft. "And you know that because you've been waiting out here for me."

He inhaled, the struggle to not pull her against him making it difficult to draw a full breath. "I would not be able to sleep if I didn't know for certain ye were safe."

The darkness hid them, and he felt her tremble slightly in his arms. "It seems I distract you when I am near and when I am far," she said.

He nodded slowly, his gaze on her lush lips as she wet them with the very tip of her tongue. Lucy's eyes were dark orbs staring up at him. "Ye don't know what ye do to me, lass, how ye tangle around my every thought." It was surely curiosity that drew him to her. "Ye are like no other woman." His hand rose to her cheek, and he slid his thumb across the softness there. "Willing to risk all to save those who have little hope. Clever and courageous."

She stepped closer so that her breasts and petticoats pressed against him. Could she feel his jack growing rock-hard through all those layers? "You haven't mentioned beautiful," she said, a slight teasing in her whisper.

His face bent toward hers, his fingers lightly grasping her chin. "Och but lass, ye are as freshly beautiful as the moon shining on a smooth loch."

Her lips opened as if she needed more air, and the invitation made his grip on restraint slip. His face dipped down, capturing her lips in a kiss that turned instantly carnal. Slanting against one another, he felt her hands sliding along his chest and dipping lower. He kissed a path across her jaw to her ear. "Your maidenhood and your heart are in jeopardy out here," Greer whispered.

"They are mine to give, and tonight I give you both," Lucy said.

He pulled back to look into her face. They breathed hard as they held onto one another in desperate fashion. "Lucy, I—"

She slammed her finger across his lips. "My virginity is too much trouble to keep, so you may have it as a gift. And my heart is made of steel, so you needn't worry over it." She reached on tiptoes, her body pressing against him.

His breath caught as she kissed his neck and pulled him down so that he felt her warm, wet mouth capture his earlobe. "Take me right here if you must, but take me this night, Greer."

Bloody hell. "Come," he whispered, tugging her hand to follow him, and they hurried on the lightest footfalls down the way he'd come. He'd been given a room on the floor above that belonged to some absent courtier.

Lucy held tightly to his arm as they climbed the stairs, the darkness broken up by periodically lit sconces. She hadn't had time to disrobe and wore the finery of the party, including her gloves. Would she trust him with her scars tonight? Even when he hadn't trusted her? She was either incredibly forgiving or as hot and aching as he.

They made the landing, and he swooped under legs, carrying

her to his door. He unlocked it with one arm still holding her against him as if to shield her if anyone came upon them. They pushed into the room, and he closed the door. Lucy pushed him back against it, her mouth on his, her fingers pulling up his tunic to reach his bare skin beneath.

"I can't stop thinking about this," she said. "How you touched me in the wine room."

He kissed a path to her small earlobe, breathing in the wild strawberry scent. "I want to explore your sweet spots, lass."

"I love the words that come from your lips," she said. His continued kisses, his hands stroking down her back to lift her.

"Unpin me," she whispered.

"Before the fire." He led her over to the blaze he'd set before he'd gone to her room. There was a thick fur rug between two chairs. They stood before the dancing flames, so the gold splashes of light warmed the paleness of her face, enhancing the sparkle in her eyes and the pink of her lips. The tip of her tongue came out to wet them, and he felt another surge of want wash through him.

"Ye render me as hard as a bull with that tip of tongue," he said.

She touched the tip with the back of her smooth left hand. "Who knew such a small bit of me could be so powerful."

"I can teach ye how powerful a tongue can be," he said, and her lips parted as if she needed more air. "That is," he said, "if ye wish it. There is no penalty for asking me to return ye to your room right now. I would see ye safely there, modest and maidenly."

Lucy raised her hands, resting her forearms against his chest. She cupped his cheeks in her hands, one gloved and one bare. "Modest and maidenly sounds dull indeed. I prefer ravished and wanton tonight, Highlander."

"Lucy—"

"I cannot stop thinking about your touch, Greer." She shook her head slightly. "I do not intend to wed and doubt I will trust many to see me… undressed. I would have this one night." She slid her finger across his jaw and down his neck to his chest. "Just one wonderous night to keep me company once you leave."

She smiled then, a mischievous light coming to her eyes. "So, unless you worry about *me* ravaging *you*," she said, "stop warning me away."

He took her finger, unfurling the rest of the digits of her hand. He kissed the tender center. "Ye have every permission to ravage me."

Her smile broadened, her eyes narrowing slightly. "I was hoping you'd say that." She slid her bare hand down his tunic to his wrapped plaid. Her hand cupped along his raging hard jack beneath the wool.

She squeezed and stroked, pulling out a low groan from Greer. It turned more intense, almost like a growl as his arms wrapped her up against him. The *V* of her legs slid right along his jack.

"Your pins, lass," he said, his fingers exploring the front where her stomacher rested over her stays, stays he remembered she'd slid down to prop up her breasts. He'd felt their softness in the heavy darkness of the wine room. Now he wanted to see them.

They both pulled pins from the silk. Her hair was golden in the glow of the flames. She stepped back and unpinned it, letting it fall around her shoulders to her waist, her fingers raking through the curls.

Lucy pulled the ties at her shoulders, letting the sleeves down and off. Och, but she was a delicious mix of innocence and enticement. He yanked the tie at his throat and pulled his tunic up and over his head, tossing it away.

Lucy watched, her fingers pausing at her petticoat ties. "Holy Mary, you are beautifully made." She shook her head the smallest amount as if to wake her from a dream. "Ruggedly, masterfully made. Like a warrior chiseled from marble."

His hand slid under his kilt to his erection. "I am as hard as marble." He stroked himself, and her eyes dropped to his exposed jack.

She murmured something, her mouth slack, her soft lips in an *O* that gave him wicked thoughts of what he could teach her.

Lucy yanked on her petticoat ties and the heavy skirts fell in a whoosh to the floor. She stood in her smock and stays, the white lace teasing the flesh at the low neckline. Her gaze remained on him as he slowly moved his hand, and her fingers went behind her back to the ties of her stays. He would help, but she seemed to like watching him. And having her eyes on him was superbly carnal.

The stays loosened but still hugged around her middle, and she lowered them so her breasts were freed. He inhaled swiftly through his nose as she lifted them up to sit upon the edge. *Perfect.* Round, the nipples hard and jutting.

He walked closer. There was a scar on one of her sides, but all he saw was the perfection of her soft skin. He took up her gloved hand, and slowly pulled each finger out of its encasement. "No hiding tonight," he said, but watched her.

She kept his gaze, her face serious, and nodded slightly. "No hiding."

His chest filled as if he'd won the greatest honor from the battlefield. He kissed her, his hands sliding her untied smock from her shoulders, the fabric trapping her arms before her. She couldn't reach his shoulders, but he felt her cool fingers wrap around his jack. He groaned as he kissed her, and she slanted her mouth against his, opening it.

His fingers rucked up the back of her smock and sought between her legs from behind. She arched her back, giving him access to her heat and moaned as he found it. Liquid heat. Their mouths giving and taking from one another, his fingers stroking her until she panted.

"Oh God, Greer," she said.

His other hand plucked the laces of her stays, loosening them even more until her smock had room to lower, and she slipped her arms free. He cupped her breast with one hand and stroked her below with the other. Their kisses abandoned all restraint, both of them tasting and breathing against one another, completely surrendering to the sensations washing like wildfire through them.

She tugged his belt, and the buckle released, his heavy wrap thudding to the rug beneath their feet. He was completely naked, and the feel of her smock against him was driving him mad.

He lowered his face to her breasts, breathing in the strawberry essence that made him want to show her the wild strawberry fields near his home, where they could roll together in the soft grasses, where he could love her under the blue sky.

Her nipple was taut as he sucked on it, pulling a thready moan from her as if she couldn't catch her breath. His fingers moved to the front of Lucy, rubbing against her sensitive spot. With each gasp and moan she made, he became bolder, pushing her ever closer to her release. Her body was open and ready, but he wanted her to come apart in his arms before he lost his mind inside her.

He felt her weaken where she stood as her breath moved faster, and he lowered her down to the soft rug. He moved over her, rucking up her smock, her long legs still wrapped in soft white stockings. "Bòidheach," he murmured. For she was the most beautiful thing he'd ever seen. Hair wild like spun, golden silk across the dark fur, her long, tapered legs spread for him, her breasts mounded on top, and the look of wanton lust on her lovely features.

Lucy's fingers had slid down to the dark heat between her legs, her knees bending upright, and she touched herself, rubbing the spot he had just left. The sight caught him in a vice grip of want. "Aye, lass," he said, his voice husky, and he moved over top of her to kiss her lips. His fingers met her own as he played her body, the two of them helping her reach her peak. She gasped against his mouth, her body tight, and moaned with a higher pitch to her voice.

He felt her body clench around his fingers, and he withdrew them as the waves broke over her. He stared down into her face, her eyes closed to ecstasy.

"Lucy," he breathed, his jack finding the edge of her heat. She opened her eyes, her lips open for breath, and he surged into her, thrusting deep into her still-clenching body.

"Oh, my God," she cried and thrust back against him until he couldn't climb higher within her. He groaned, withdrawing, but her legs came up to clasp around his hips, urging him back into her, and he thrust again. Both of them cried out with deep need, and Greer started a rhythm.

"*Yes*, keep going," Lucy said near his ear as she clung to him.

She tilted more and propping herself up to him as he thrust into her over and over. He clasped her hip bone, amazed at how fragile yet how strong she was. Sliding slightly up her body, Greer continued to strum inside and out, the coil in him tightening with power.

"Oh Greer," she cried, and he felt her whole body tense around him, her fingers digging into his biceps as she held on.

He answered her with the deep groan of release, his mouth coming down on hers in a fiery kiss. Their mouths clung together as their bodies slowed, wringing out all the pleasure they could.

After long moments of slowing, Greer rolled to Lucy's side, bringing her with him into the circle of his arms. Her body still trembled slightly, pressing against him in a slow rhythm below. He ran his fingers through her hair, kissing her cheeks and each of her closed eyes.

A smile blossomed, and she blinked open to stare into his own eyes. "I definitely prefer ravished and wanton," she whispered.

His mouth curved into a large smile, making her eyes open wide. "I won a true smile from the broody Highlander," she said. "'Tis a Christmas miracle."

LUCY LAY BEFORE the fire amongst the blankets that Greer had pulled off his bed. Light and heat radiated from the charred remains in the hearth, warming her face. The wood snapped every so often, and she watched the cinders glow red when the wind blew down the chimney.

Greer was like a warm blanket against her back as he curved around her. He was completely naked while she had worn her smock through their vigorous, fabulous romp. The thin white fabric had been tugged down and rucked up, but stayed on, hiding the worst of her scars, the ones of her stomach and back.

Greer had brought her again to shattering before they'd both fallen to sleep in front of the raging fire. From the looks of the embers, she guessed it was the hour before dawn.

"Are you asleep?" she whispered.

"Aye."

His lie made her grin. She rolled onto her back. Dawn lightened the sky beyond the window behind him. "I better get back to my room before Cordy finds me gone and sends for William to search for me."

He pushed up on one elbow, and she looked up into his face. Greer Buchanan was the most ruggedly handsome man she'd ever met. His dark, longish hair lay tousled and free about his head. Dark eyes, that she knew were blue-gray in the sunlight, were framed with dark lashes. She reached up to touch his short-clipped beard. "You've lost your smile."

The corner of his mouth rose. "I would rather the sun not rise until ye moan my name again."

"Rogue," she said, smiling broadly. She sat up, her smock hiding her, but he took her ugly arm. He kissed the back of her hand as if the skin was smooth. Instinctively she pulled it, but he didn't let go. It became a mild tug of war, and he kissed it again.

"Greer," she said, and he finally released it.

"Ye are beautiful, Lucy, every bit of ye. I don't like ye feeling ye aren't."

Her smile faded. "Let's not start the day with lies."

He stared in her eyes. "I don't lie."

Lucy huffed and stuck out her leg where her stocking had been slowly rolled off her last night. Bending and turning it so he could see her calf, she pointed at one dark mark that was mangled by a burn that had only made it look worse. "That part of me is not beautiful."

Greer lay his full palm over it. "What was done to ye was ugly and wrong," he said.

She looked away but he bent his head around to capture her gaze. "What I see is that ye survived it and have continued without bitterness making ye cruel and ugly toward people. Even with what the queen dictates, ye work bravely here at court, helping others."

Lucy pulled her leg out from under his hand and stood, her smock covering her to her ankles. "Fortunately, 'tis in my nature to be happy." She smiled. "Or else I would be a poor creature indeed. But I know how horrid my marks are and how they would be viewed by the court and my friends. 'Tis good I can keep them hidden."

Greer stood to his full height, and Lucy's breath caught at the sight of his muscular form. So unashamed by his growing jack, he looked at her. "Would ye tell that to Alyce? That she should stay hidden because people would see her as horrid?"

"Of course not," Lucy said, trying to act as if he were fully clothed and not the god-like creature who had brought her such ecstasy. "But you saw how people view her, how they thought she was a leper. She will be treated thus her whole life."

"By ignorant people who base a whole person solely on their cover instead of what lies beneath in their heart."

Her brows rose. "'Tis the way of the world."

"'Tis a bloody brutal world."

She turned away to pick up her stockings and various parts of her costume. "I thought you already knew that," she said.

She heard his footfalls coming behind her. He turned her with gentle pressure on her shoulders. Greer looked into her face, sliding his thumb over her cheek. "Well, I know ye to be beautiful, Lucy Cranfield, inside and outside. But that doesn't matter at all until ye believe that to be true."

She gave him a smile but knew it was sad. "Thank you for the compliment." She looked over her shoulder at her clothes across the bed. "Now help me put myself together so I don't get caught in the hall undressed or in the same gown I wore last night."

Greer let her go. She watched him walk with the grace of a predator, his taut backside a thing of beauty. It was a shame to cover it.

He stopped before a wooden chest where he'd apparently stored his clothes. He threw on a new tunic and grabbed up his long length of plaid, deftly folding it to cinch around his waist, the sash over one shoulder.

"Such a simple design," she said. "Do the ladies in the north wear such a costume?"

He walked over barefooted to pull her stay laces tighter. "Nay. They wear petticoats and stays like ye. Silk and velvet at the Edinburgh court, but coarser fabric on the populace."

Dressed, Lucy leaned in to kiss her lover before leaving the room. *Lover*. She had a lover. And not just any lover, but this amazing creature who thought she was beautiful. Her stomach fluttered.

"I will walk ye back," he said, going to the door.

"No." She pressed into him and inhaled their combined scent. "Getting caught in my gown from last night would be bad enough, but if you were with me, then would both be slandered."

"I care not."

She hugged him and stepped back. "I do." He frowned at her fiercely, but she smiled. "I know now that you don't eat the wings off little sparrows, so you can stop frowning and gnashing your teeth."

"I'm not gnashing my teeth," he grumbled and rubbed his jaw line.

"I'll go wash and change, and we can meet for the morning meal as if we haven't seen each other since the celebration last night."

He kissed her soundly but let her pull away. "I'll be in the kitchens or the Great Hall," he said, finally opening the door for her to slip into the corridor.

Lucy strode on her bare feet through the darkness. Movement behind some doors made her hurry as if pursued by the devil. Yet she couldn't help the joy that filled her. She was deliciously sore from being loved so thoroughly.

She rounded the corner onto her hall and caught herself. William stood before her door. *God's teeth.* Before she could turn around, he saw her. "Lucy, you are already..." His words trailed off as he took in her gown. A grimace of pain pinched his features. "You've been out all night."

Lucy hurried forward. "Come inside," she whispered. There was no need to bring Cordelia into this if it could be helped. She unlocked the door and pushed inside. William continued to stand in the corridor.

"You were with *him* all night?" he asked.

She turned to him. "William," she said, coming closer. "We can never..." She tipped her head slightly, wishing she knew how to soften the blow. "I think of you as a brother."

"And you let yourself fall prey to a seducing Highlander," he said, accusation in his voice. "He will leave you here, Lucy. Sullied and alone."

She knew he was hurt, but his tone bordered on cruel, and his words picked away at her confidence. "Don't try to hurt me because you hurt, William. 'Twas unintentional."

He took a deep breath, his fingers lifting up through his red hair until it nearly stood on end. His eyes drifted to the floor. "You have a letter," he said, nodding to the ground, and pivoted on his heel.

"William," she said, but he continued to stride down the corridor.

Lucy exhaled long and shut her door, her gaze turning to the folded letter that had been pushed underneath. It was folded in an intricate locking design that required her to tear it to open.

Dearest Lucy,

As beautiful as you are, it will never work between us. I must return to Scotland, and you must remain here in the service of your queen. I do not wish to harm you any further, so I will not speak of this, but you must know that whatever was to be between us cannot be. It would be best if we do not engage in any further correspondence or discussion. I will know you understand when you completely ignore me.

Never Yours,
Greer Buchanan

Lucy looked at the door. William knew that she'd been with Greer all night. Would he have left the letter with that realization? No. Lucy looked at the wall between her room and her sister's. Her eyes narrowed.

"Cordelia Cranfield!"

CHAPTER TWELVE

"Queen Elizabeth I also suffered from a crippling fear of the dark. It's possible that this started in childhood and was almost certainly made worse by the time she spent locked up in the Tower of London. Elizabeth was so scared of the dark that she refused to sleep alone. Each night, one of her trusted ladies-in-waiting would be ordered to sleep in the Queen's bedchamber."

History Collection.com

GREER WALKED ALONG the raised, wooden tables where half a dozen cooks were busy kneading bread for more festive banquets. Others were pulling buns out of the stone ovens that would accompany fresh milk, eggs, and pheasant pie for breakfast. He recognized them all now, and several nodded to him as he passed. Guards also walked along, watching them work and making them sample things at random. Walsingham was clever to order it. Each of the cooks was vigilant about no one touching their creation because they would be the one to taste it.

"Would ye like an egg and bun?" the young Irish woman, Mary, asked. "They be safe. I made them myself." She tore a piece off a bun and popped it in her mouth. "And one can't poison an egg." She smiled. "Unless ye be the chicken, I suppose."

Greer nodded. "Thank ye." He took the offering, cracking the eggshell off to bite into it. Mary nodded, smiling. "A big man like ye needs to be fed regularly." She seemed to inspect his form. "Here," she said, plucking a second off the tray. "Take another."

Someone bumped his elbow. "I churned this butter myself," Jane Welsh said, handing him a rosemary herb bun with a small slab on it. Greer remembered her as one of the other cooks that had been questioned about Whitby's death. To show it was safe, she pinched off a bit of bun and a bit of butter and stuck them in her mouth.

"Thank ye," Greer said and took them, biting into the warm bun. He looked around as he chewed. Several men brought in loads of coal and wood to keep the ovens and cook fires going. Keeping Whitehall fed was a major undertaking.

He nodded to the guards as he walked past them toward the Great Hall, his spare roll in hand to give to Lucy once he found her. His gaze raked over several intricate tapestries hung on the walls as he walked along the corridor. Such riches were rare even at the palace of Holyrood in Edinburgh. And this luxury was the only life Lucy knew. He sighed and turned the corner.

"It was found near the wines sent from the Loire Valley in France."

Walsingham, the queen, several guards, and William Darby stood in the corridor before the wine cellar. The rapid clip of slippers on the polished wooden floor heralded Lucy, walking briskly toward them, her sister trailing behind.

Lucy looked flustered, angry, her lips clenched.

"We must have all the wines tasted before serving," Elizabeth said. "Would you like some wine with your breakfast, Master Buchanan?" she called, pulling his attention.

"I typically stick to ale in the morn," he answered, coming up to them.

Lucy stopped, her glance meeting Greer's gaze briefly. "You called for us?" she said, looking to Walsingham.

"Yes," he said. "You were seen exiting the wine cellar last eve. Were you meeting anyone in there?"

Being the excellent actor she was, Lucy shook her head slowly as if in thought. "No. I needed a break from my assignment as jester and sought some solitude." She glanced at Greer and then looked back to Walsingham. "When I entered the wine cellar, I realized it was completely dark within. I spent perhaps a minute there collecting myself and departed."

The queen shook her shoulders slightly. "No one would stay in a pitch-dark cellar for more than a minute. At least no one sane."

Walsingham held up a golden clasp. "This was found by the wines at the back of the cellar. No one goes into the cellar unless they are there to fetch or turn the wines. Servants only, not someone who would own something so rich."

"Perhaps someone was having a tryst amongst the wine," Cordelia said.

"A tryst?" the queen said. "That never happens at court." Her sarcastic declaration did not make anyone grin.

"Or," Walsingham said, "someone was trying to poison the wine through the corks."

"No syringes have been found," William said, keeping his gaze on Walsingham and the queen.

"We will have the dogs in the royal kennel drink some of each bottle opened," the queen said.

Lucy gasped. "That would be cruel." She looked horrified. "Spirits could kill a dog even without poison. I would rather drink the samples myself then risk a dog's life."

"My father and I will check each cork for holes and a sample of each can be fired to search for poison," William said. He glanced at Lucy and looked away quickly. "There's no reason to have Lady Lucy sample them."

"Nor the dogs," Lucy said.

Elizabeth huffed. "I'd forgotten your notion about animals. I suppose you will not do your duty as Lady of Misrule at the cock fights this midday."

Lucy sunk low into a curtsey, her head bent. "I will but wail and swoon, Your Majesty."

The queen shook her head and rolled her eyes. "The weakness of my sex shames me at times," she said, glancing toward the cellar door. Behind it lay a mass of darkness, which her ladies and closest advisors knew frightened her more than a Spanish fleet.

"To refuse a queen," Greer said, "seems more courageous than most men I know."

Elizabeth turned her back on the dark room, sniffing with disdain. "Now if she would feel the same protectiveness over her queen," Elizabeth said, "she'd be as dogged in her pursuit of assassins as is my spy master." She flapped her hand at Walsingham. Before anyone could agree, Elizabeth continued. "My Robin can call the cock fights. We will be there anyway, and he is naturally good natured."

"Thank you, Your Majesty," Lucy said, rising with her head still tipped down.

"Master Darby," Walsingham said, his voice full of authority, "I will send down fifty bottles for you and your father to inspect before dinner."

William nodded, his face still tight.

Walsingham held up the gold clasp. "And I will try to discover why there was a gold clasp left in the wine cellar." He looked at Cordelia. "I seem to remember you wearing a pearl necklace last eve, Lady Cordelia, and then it was missing from your neck at the end of the evening."

Everyone turned to look at Cordelia. Lucy had mentioned her sister's enquiry about her broken necklace.

Cordelia stared back, her face as if she'd bitten a lemon. "I was having a tryst in the wine cellar." She spit out the words as if they were a bad piece of fish. "'Twas the outcome of too much wine and a flattering lord." She looked at William. "I doubt you will find anything wrong with the bottles."

"He will check them anyway," Walsingham said.

"A disappointment, Lady Cordelia," Elizabeth said. "I'll have to think of a suitable husband for you. Without parents, I must take on the responsibility of finding you properly wed."

"Thank you, Your Majesty," Cordelia murmured, curtseying.

Elizabeth stalked away. "Give her back her necklace clasp,

Lord Walsingham."

Cordelia rose, and Walsingham set the clasp in her palm. He and the guards followed the queen into the Great Hall where Greer heard breakfast being served.

William Darby shook his head. "The Cranfield sisters. Courageous enough to lie to the queen and her watchdog. Perhaps your mother would have been proud of you." His words held poisonous censure. He turned on his heel and stalked away, leaving the sisters and Greer in the corridor where small groups of courtiers walked to the Great Hall, glancing their way.

Cordelia put the clasp in Lucy's hand.

"Thank you, Cordy," Lucy whispered. "You didn't have to—"

"I did." She glanced at Greer and then back to Lucy. "To earn your forgiveness."

"Forgiveness?" Greer asked, looking between the sisters.

Cordelia whipped out her fan and began to brush it in the air even though it wasn't hot. "'Tis between sisters," she said. Several people past to enter the Great Hall.

Cordelia crossed her arms, leaning toward Lucy. "And Walsingham wouldn't have quit looking until he traced the clasp back to you. Your silence would mark you as guilty of much worse, possibly treason."

She looked at Greer. "You might be able to ride off to Scotland, but we have a life here at court, a tenuous one." She narrowed her eyes at Greer. "Do not tear my sister apart. I would never poison the queen, but I certainly know how." She turned and strode toward the Great Hall.

"I have the distinct feeling that your sister does not approve of me," Greer said.

Lucy huffed. "She means well. At least for me. As for you..." She looked at him. "I wouldn't eat or drink anything she gives you."

"SIMMONS?" LUCY CALLED out as she and Greer entered Cranfield House from the back by the kitchen. The roosters seemed cozy in the coop out back, and the house sounded quiet. She looked at Greer. "I'll check on the children and pups."

"I'll see if Simmons is about," Greer said.

Lucy gathered her petticoats and hurried up the steps. "Don't scare him," she called. Which was rather pointless. Greer's build and frown frightened everyone. *Except me.* The whole time they walked together, she couldn't help but remember the power in him as he'd loved her.

She breathed past the flush in her cheeks. "Alyce," she called at the top of the grand staircase. "Catherine? Nick?" Barking came from her bedroom, but no one came running out. She went inside where everything was neat except for feathers strewn everywhere. The dogs had destroyed a pillow. Probably in retaliation for being left behind.

"The two of you cause such mischief," she said. "Off," she commanded, pushing them down. "We need some manner lessons before you grow too big to control."

They ran past her and out the door. She'd ask the children to clean up the feathers. At least they seemed to have let the dogs out to relieve themselves.

"I swear, I'm not planning to poison the queen or anyone." Simmons's voice trembled slightly, but he stood tall before Greer. The dogs rushed forward, jumping around him, barking at Greer. It looked like they were trying to protect the elderly man.

Simmons's hand went out to brush one of the dog's heads while he stared, wide-eyed at Greer.

"Of course you're not," Lucy called above the barking and cast a frown toward Greer. "Come!" she called, slapping her leg to get the dogs' attention. She led them out back to get some of their playfulness out.

She strode back into the front room where the impasse continued. "We overheard you talking with Mistress Wakefield last eve at Whitehall," Greer said. "You mentioned catching the queen when she's vulnerable at Twelfth Night."

"Not to harm her," Simmons said. He worked his hands before him, and sweat marked his brow even though the house was cold without a fire in the main room. "We but want to petition her."

"Which is what I've already explained to Master Buchanan," Lucy said.

"I but need to hear it from him."

"Mistress Wakefield, and another, along with Richard and myself..." Simmons rubbed his mouth. "We have plans to pool our resources to buy the old Channing Abbey. Then we can become landowners instead of simple merchants and servants. 'Tis reaching above our breeding, at least for me, but 'tis possible. And certainly not criminal."

Simmons looked to Lucy. "I have given your mother and Cranfield House thirty years of service. If I want to have a place of my own before I die, I must do so now."

"Who is the fourth man?" Greer asked.

"Jasper Lintel," Simmons said. "Come from Ireland."

"What does he do now?" Greer asked.

"A server at a tavern, I believe." Simmons clasped his hands nervously. "I'm afraid I haven't asked much about him, only about his money. He spends time on London Bridge, so he may work there."

"Mistress Wakefield said he works at the Bear's Inn or Tavern," Lucy said.

"Oh," Simmons said, tugging on one ear. "That's right, Jasper did say that."

Greer's stare was intense as he judged the man's answers. "You had no dealings with Agatha Cranfield's associates?" Greer asked.

"Not at all," Simmons said, standing straight. "I am a loyal Englishman, faithful to the crown and my queen."

After a long moment, Greer nodded. "Thank ye, Goodman Simmons."

They walked outside to the back where the dogs ran around the chicken coop, and the roosters squawked inside.

Simmons held his fingers to his thin lips and blew a sharp whistle. The dogs ran right toward him.

"If you can train them to mind people, I'll pay you extra for your efforts," Lucy said.

"I will endeavor to make them behave, Lady Lucy," Simmons said, pushing the dogs inside the house. "Come along, mongrels."

She and Greer walked down St. Martin's Street. "I need to fetch something at the apothecary on the bridge while we are there," she said. "It'll be open despite Christmastide."

"Why do ye not go to one of the shops we passed on Bucklerbury Lane? It seems all the apothecaries are there."

"I don't approve of how they display the poor animals, dead and stuffed above their doors. Jars of piglets and unborn goats. Master Wendel doesn't deal in exotics. My mother always brought Cordelia and me to his shop for our soaps." Agatha Cranfield had also tried every cure Master Wendel could think of to treat Lucy's stubborn marks.

Lucy walked on, stopping to purchase several small mincemeat pies, sweet buns, and treats for the children. She had some gifts for them hidden away at Cranfield House for New Year's the next day.

"Do you give gifts at the New Year in Scotland?" she asked and handed him a small mincemeat pie.

"Aye, but the big celebration is on the eve before. Hogmanay is celebrated with parades and fireballs being flung about in the dark night."

"Fireballs?"

"A hollow ball filled with dry peat that we light on fire. If ye swing it around on the end of a rope, it blazes through the night. With many twirling, 'tis wonderous to see."

"And dangerous. Here you would hit people and light them on fire," she said, indicating the masses.

He chuckled. "A place is cleared before Edinburgh Castle, but we also celebrate with fire out on the moor before my home. At least when I was a lad."

"What else do you do on Hogmanay?"

"Mother sprinkles holy water throughout the house, seals it up, and lights juniper. When we start to cough and insist we are all going to die, she throws open the door, and we open all the windows to let the smoke out and the cold air of the new year inside, washing away the evils of last year." He shrugged. "'Tis only her now, so I don't know if she still does it."

"How long ago did your father and sisters die?" she asked, her words soft, although she tried to keep pity out of it.

"Nearly five years now."

"And you don't go home to stay with her through Hogmanay?"

"She wishes for me to be up at the castle, garnering Lord Moray's favor and then the king's. I bring gifts the next day and a steak pie for our feast."

Lucy hooked her arm through his. "Maybe we can find some fire for you to throw around tonight. The queen would love the spectacle."

They turned down New Fish Street, which led to London Bridge. Despite the mandate of no work, the narrow walk between the shops lining the bridge on both sides was crowded with people hawking food. Many of the shops had removed their signs to show they were closed, but their doors were cracked, allowing for illegal commerce. The apothecary was open, and Lucy stepped inside the exceedingly small shop that smelled of herbs and the tang of chemicals. There was barely enough room for Greer and her to shut the door behind them without climbing over the counter.

"Master Wendel," Lucy said, giving the middle-aged man a warm smile. With her quest for cures and coverings, she'd known the ornery man for years.

He nodded to her but frowned at Greer. "Good Christmastide, Lady Cranfield," he said, pulling his gaze back to her.

"I have need of some sweet-smelling soaps for my sister and three friends, one being a lad," she said.

"He ain't no lad," the apothecary said, glaring at Greer.

She laughed lightly. "The soap 'tis for a boy of ten years, and I agree, Master Buchanan is not a lad."

"Buchanan," Wendel said. "A Scot." He nodded to Greer's wrapped plaid. "I don't sell to foreigners. Not Irish, Scots, Walloons, French, Spanish, none of them." He waved his hands.

"He's visiting the queen from Edinburgh," Lucy said, trying to keep cheerful in the face of such prejudice. The two men had taken on defensive stances. Well, Greer always stood in a battle stance, but Master Wendel looked ready to pull a sword.

"My father was killed by a Scot on a battlefield," the apothecary said, accusation heavy in his words.

Greer crossed his arms over his chest. "Likely a Scottish battlefield where he'd come uninvited."

"He fought for good King Henry."

"Then he probably slayed a good number of Scots before losing his life," Greer said.

"That he did," Wendel nodded. "And anyone who the good king thought was a threat."

Lucy held her gloved hands out. "Then the two of you are even with the… killing of family and countrymen."

Wendel grunted. "I sell only to English, like Lady Cranfield here." He turned to a shelf that had various chunks of cut soap. "Strawberry soap for you, jasmine for Lady Cordelia Cranfield?"

"You have a sharp memory, Master Wendel," Lucy said in her most complimentary voice.

"Do ye sell poisons, Master Wendel?" Greer asked.

Lucy raised her hand to her forehead and gave Greer a silent, wide-eyed reprimand.

The apothecary continued to select bricks of soap without turning around. "Anything could be a poison if used incorrectly. If Lady Cranfield ate this cake of lye soap, it could make her sick enough to die."

"How about arsenic, ratsbane, henbane, and nightshade?" Greer asked, ignoring Lucy's silently waving hands.

Wendel turned around, and she dropped her hands. "All things that have another purpose other than poisoning. Aye, I have them. Arsenic is part of a remedy for syphilis when the typical mercury elixir and ointment don't work. 'Tis in ratsbane as well."

"Have you by chance sold any recently," Lucy asked. She set a penny on the counter. "Arsenic or ratsbane?"

Wendel scooped it up, pocketing it. "There was a man a week ago. Came in dressed like a servant but with a hood hiding most of his face. Said he must treat the disease."

"Did he purchase other ingredients of the cure or the arsenic alone?" Greer asked.

"Said he had the other ingredients, although he hadn't gotten them from me." The old man wrinkled his nose. "I detected an Irish accent but couldn't be sure."

Lucy set another penny down. "Do you remember what he looked like besides the hood and clothes and possible accent?"

Wendel pocketed the coin and shrugged. "Had brown hair from what hung out of the hood. He was much taller than you, Lady Lucy. More like the Scot. Thin chap though. Shaved chin."

Lucy looked to Greer, who wore his baby-bird-eating frown. "And he gave no name?" Greer asked.

"Nay."

Lucy clinked a third penny down on the man's counter. "If he comes again, please send a runner around to Whitehall. It may be a matter of treason, and Lord Walsingham would reward you for certain."

He bobbed his head. "I will, milady." He slid his hand over five chunks of soap. "Be there anything else for you this festive day? Some ceruse to hide the skin perhaps?"

Lucy had bought the white makeup to hide her marks whenever she'd gone home to visit her mother. Never again would her mother inspect her, so she didn't need it. "No, but some of the queen's favorite rose and musk scent," she answered. "A gift for the New Year."

"Certainly," he said, fetching a glass vial, and she laid out the proper payment for the gifts.

"Thank you and a very happy New Year to you," Lucy said.

"And to you, milady." Wendel frowned at Greer. "Not to you, though."

Lucy tugged Greer's arm to get him to follow her back outside. "You don't know how to question people very well," she said.

"I'm certain the prejudiced bastard knows more," Greer said.

"And I'm certain he wasn't going to tell you more even if I poured all my coin onto his counter."

His gaze followed a cloaked man walking down the bridge. "He described Jasper Lintel."

"Possibly," she said.

Greer grabbed her hand and began to pull her after him. "Did ye see that man?"

"In the cloak?"

"Aye."

"No."

Greer had to slow or trample an old woman whose width took up the entire center of the narrow path. "He stopped in the flow of people as if to come to the apothecary," Greer said without looking back. "He was tall and thin and had red hair."

"Can you still see him?"

"Nay." The heaviness of the word made her shake off his tether.

"Then go get him."

Greer pushed two steps into the crowd when gasps filled the air.

"Watch out!" someone called. Lucy ducked. Greer spun back to her as a ball of fire flew over the crouched people.

CHAPTER THIRTEEN

"Fireballs purify the world by consuming evil and warding off witches and evil spirits."
Pre-Christian theory from Clan.com

A SMALL FIREBALL flew toward them, and people scattered screaming. On London Bridge, with all the houses made of wood, a fireball was bloody dangerous.

"'Tis Hogmanay!" a man yelled as he staggered forward.

"Wait there," Greer yelled over the noise and raced after the flaming ball. He stomped on it, his heavy boots breaking through the ball of peat. He kicked dirty snow onto the flames and several men stomped along the singe mark that the ball had left as a trail.

A tin whistle chirped out a warning as two men dressed in official livery ran toward the scene. "You, there!" one called at Greer. They both charged toward him as if he were the guilty party.

Greer left his sword sheathed. If he sliced one of the queen's guards open, it would be difficult to continue his investigation. So he crossed his arms over his chest, his legs parted in a battle stance. People scurried to get out of the way, and faces appeared in all the windows lining the narrow path along the bridge.

"You could burn the whole bridge down with your filthy fireball, Scot."

"It wasn't his," Lucy yelled, coming forward. Her usual smile was replaced by stern rebuke. "Master Buchanan was escorting me to purchase a gift for the queen. I am Lady Lucy Cranfield. The fool you should be apprehending is passed out next to the apothecary. And he is *not* a Scot." Her stern words condemned the two men, calling them out as fools before the onlookers.

"Pardon, milady," one of the guards said, his face taking on a reddish hue. "'Tis a Scottish tradition."

"Which that inebriated Londoner apparently heard about," she said, pointing back the way they'd come. Several other people mimicked her action, pointing toward the man slouched against the waddle and daub wall.

"'Tis a dangerous custom," the second guard said, still glaring at Greer as he had created it.

"When done on a crowded bridge made of wood, aye," Greer said. "Done in a gravel clearing at night, 'tis quite festive."

The guards moved on to the man against the wall, and Lucy wove her arm through Greer's. People resumed their business, gathering food and gifts for New Years. It was a slow-moving river of humanity. The tang of human bodies mixed with the smell of food and human waste, making Greer long for the open moors of Scotland.

"Have ye visited the countryside?" he asked Lucy.

"When the queen goes on progress, we travel with her. 'Tis much better smelling in the country."

When they stepped off the bridge, Lucy tugged him toward a narrow, uncrowded street where the noise and press of people lessened to a tolerable level. "To the Bear's Inn?" Lucy asked, tugging his arm before he could even answer.

"Maybe Jasper Lintel or the man on the bridge will be there," he said, and they hurried along the narrow avenue, stepping around the filth that was dumped onto streets. *Daingead*. He preferred the cow shite in the fields to the open sewers in the cities. Lucy held her skirts aloft and they dodged puddles, snow, and shit. He couldn't imagine the stink in the heat of the summer season.

The Bear's Inn was quiet that early in the day, with one barkeep inside wiping the tables.

"Excuse me, Goodman," Lucy said, walking forward with her sweet smile. The man stopped immediately to smile back, although it faded when he spotted Greer.

"We are looking for an employee of yours," she said. "An Irishman named Jasper Lintel."

The man's face pinched in, and he rubbed his long beard. "Don't know a man by that name."

"He has a wife, both of them recently from Ireland," Greer said, coming forward. "Said he served here."

The barkeeper's brow rose. "Then he lies. The only servers I hire are English, and there is no one by that name."

Jasper Lintel, or whoever he was, had lied to Simmons and Mistress Wakefield. "Thank ye," Greer said.

Lucy held a coin out for the man. "If you happen to hear of a Jasper Lintel, please send word to Lucy Cranfield up at White-hall."

They brushed by two rough men on their way out, both of them turning to inspect Lucy. Too closely. Greer sent them a fierce frown and slid his arm around Lucy's shoulders.

"I hope ye don't venture often into the London streets alone," he said. The thought of Lucy being attacked sent a wave of fury through him.

She slipped her hand in her pocket, pulling out a sheathed dagger. With it fell a parchment. "I am armed," she said.

He stopped to pick up the unfolded letter. "Do ye know how to use the dagger?" he asked, but his gaze fastened on his name on the letter. His gaze scanned the script that was a combination of fine swirls and boxy letters as if to hide the identity of the author.

"What's to know?" she said, unaware he'd stopped. "You poke the point into someone if they get close." She turned around. "Oh," she said, hurrying back. "That's nothing." She pulled the letter from his hand, shoving it back in her pocket with the dagger.

"Someone sent ye a forged letter, signing my name," he said. "That is *not* nothing."

Lucy continued walking along the lane. "Cordelia slid it beneath my door last night. I found it this morning and confronted her."

Greer ran through the letter in his mind, each word making the stone in his stomach grow heavier.

As beautiful as you are, it will never work. Lucy Cranfield was beyond beautiful.

I must return to Scotland, and you must remain at the queen's service. Both true.

I do not wish to harm you further.

Whatever was to be between us cannot be.

"Lucy," he said, catching her arm to stall her. "Everything she wrote is true. Except the 'Never Yours.'"

Hurt tightened her eyes, but she kept her familiar smile. As if pain no longer registered on her exterior.

"I would not have written that I was never yours," he said. "I was completely yours last night."

"You want me to ignore you?" she asked. "'Twould be difficult with you following me into London."

"Nay. I *should* want ye to ignore me, but I don't," he said.

The tightness in her face relaxed. "Then I am happy you're not so noble." She smiled broadly.

He glanced at her pocket and back to her face, his chest tight. "If ye had not been with me last night, would ye have ignored me this morning? Thought that I'd be coward enough to leave a note under your door without a spoken word?"

"Cordy would have given herself away somehow. She's a terrible liar." Lucy turned away and continued to walk, both of them silent for several dirty cobblestone streets.

When Twelfth Night was over, he would leave, and she would stay. *I could stay.* No, he couldn't. He rubbed a hand down the short beard covering his jaw.

"What would you have done if I'd ignored you?" Lucy asked,

her voice breaking the silence between them. "Would you have assumed I wanted nothing further of you?"

They walked around a large puddle of melted snow where a cat drank, sitting back on its haunches. It ran as Lucy tried to pet it.

When he didn't answer, she continued. "'Tis a good thing we were together last eve, then."

He caught her arm before she could turn back onto the busy thoroughfare along the Thames. "I would have asked for an explanation, thinking I had incurred more of your anger."

"And I would have agreed that you had," she said.

"And I would have demanded to know what I had done."

She smiled at the back and forth. "And then the game would be over with Cordy's letter revealed." Her arched brows rose. "See, the letter is not important. It would have delayed us by half a day."

She stepped into the throng of people like a golden fish caught in a stream. He followed, walking beside her in a game of dodge the puddles, people, and filth.

Greer frowned, the ache in his stomach turning completely to stone. Because even if the letter was easily seen as a forgery, that didn't make it any less true.

'Twas the eve of the New Year, and the night was bright and clear. Many of the courtiers had ventured into the open bailey before Whitehall to chat and stare up at the stars, which were bright enough to be seen even with the torches set about.

Lucy had donned her bright gown and taken up her scepter as Lady of Misrule once again. To make up for her lack of jumping around, which her skirts hindered, she used her arms and voice to add a merry spectacle. Elizabeth loved to dance and could easily laugh when given a reason. So Lucy made certain the minstrels played all her favorite songs, and she encouraged the courtiers to imbibe in wine and recite some poetry or a song.

"In the north," she said, raising her scepter to draw the attention of the clusters of people in the bailey, "they celebrate Hogmanay on the eve of the New Year. They swing balls of fire on rope and chain to make paths of light in the darkness." She swept her scepter about as if it were aflame. "Perhaps our Highlander can demonstrate," she called and signaled to the two guards she'd asked to make balls of dry peat.

Greer stood near her, looking out at the people. But with her declaration, he turned to her and gave a shake of his head.

"Come now," Lucy said, her voice loud and her smile broad. "You know the way of it, and we are in a pebbled courtyard where people will stand back."

"Yes," Queen Elizabeth called from her spot with Walsingham and Leicester. "Let us see this spectacle. I have heard about it but never seen it."

The guards came forward, handing the ends of two ropes to Greer. "What are these made of?" he asked.

"Peat covered with pitch," one guard said and held up a torch. "Same as what we use to keep the torches burning."

Lucy looked closer at the balls. "I should have told you, but I knew you'd have refused."

"But now 'tis a request from a queen," he grumbled.

She patted his arm. "Exactly."

Lucy hurried over to the minstrels. "Please play a fast and festive jig for Master Buchanan's fiery balls."

"Fiery balls?" the man asked and laughed.

"Look, they are on fire," the lute player said with a snort. He pointed to where Greer stood, the guard backing away with a torch. The two balls flared, the fire spreading around the globes so that Greer held them out from himself, measuring how much slack he needed on the lengths of rope.

The flute player started a festive rhythm, and the crowd drew closer to Greer.

"Everyone must stay back," Greer's voice easily overrode the rumble of conversations, and the people retreated several steps, leaving him and Lucy in the center of a dark bailey. The guards moved the lit torches set at intervals along the wall toward the back of the bailey which made the space darker.

"Ye too," Greer said to Lucy.

"Thank you," she said. He answered with a grunt, and she ran back to the edge of light.

"Perhaps we need to hire a Scottish piper," Lord Leister called out and laughter wove out to accompany the flute.

Greer stood in the center, wearing his plaid wrapping over a bright white tunic, the sash flung over one shoulder and across his short jacket. His boots were laced and lined with fur. They braced apart as his arms swung outward, and he started the balls turning. The golden orbs of fire flew up into the air, crossing before swinging down, the trails of their light bright in the darkness like comets.

Ladies gasped as Greer swung the fireballs out along the perimeter as if they'd fly off to burn them. He lifted them, spinning with the rhythm, displaying the control and strength in his well-muscled form. She could imagine him swinging his blades.

"Is there no end to his talent?"

Lucy looked next to her where William had come up. Her stomach tightened. "William, I am sorry about…" What was she sorry about exactly? "That I hurt you." She touched his arm. He was tall, strong, and handsome. "If you thought…"

"I don't want you to get hurt, Lucy," he said. "And everything about that man screams danger."

"Danger to me?" she asked. "Or danger to your idea of how things could be between us?" Her words were slow and soft, but his stiff stance showed that they slashed. She squeezed his arm. "I would not hurt you, William. You are like family to me."

"And that's the problem," he said, turning to walk off into the darkness.

Around her, everyone cheered as if on cue to William's exit in a play. But there was nothing to cheer about hurting a friend.

Lucy looked to the center where Greer threw one of the balls high into the air, catching the rope on the way down to send the flash of light into an arc around the circle of spectators. Greer's strength kept the heavy balls moving exactly where he intended, and his footwork danced with the grace of an experienced warrior on a battlefield. He was glorious, and Lucy's skin tingled in the dark. She ran her hands over her arms, remembering the feel of his touch. She'd mistakenly thought one night would be enough with him. Could she entice him into a second?

Greer spun. The power in his arms, chest, and back were so obvious. The brightness of the flying globes imprinted on her vision, and she blinked to clear them so she could see him better.

The crowd gasped, and Lucy's gaze followed one of the fiery balls. The ball had broken away from the end of the rope and hurtled straight toward the queen. Ladies around her screamed and ran away from the miniature sun as it raced toward their sovereign, ready to strike her dead.

CHAPTER FOURTEEN

*"In the Dark Ages, a shooting star appeared above what is now
Stonehaven. As a result of this appearance, those living nearby
had bumper crops. The seers of the tribe then attributed this
prosperity to the coming of the shooting star. The fireball is a
mimic of this star and the prosperity it brings those who are
around it."*

Dark Ages theory from Clan.com

*B*LOODY HELL! GREER dropped the second orb at his feet and
surged toward the queen. Leister leaped before Elizabeth as
the heavy fireball arced downward to bounce and roll at her feet.
Its greedy flames caught ahold of her skirts as Leister stomped at
them, kicking the pitch-covered ball away and catching his own
boot on fire as some of the pitch stuck to it.

"Out, damn it," Elizabeth cursed, stomping and spinning,
which only fed the flames. It feasted like a hungry pestilence up
the silk and lace, catching her velvet cloak too, which she threw
off onto the ground.

Rushing past Walsingham who yelled for water, Greer
reached the queen, grabbing her burning skirt. Yanking out his
sgian dubh, he sliced through the silk, the fire biting at his bare
hands.

"God's teeth," Elizabeth yelled as Greer yanked the petticoat
so hard, she stumbled into him. For all her strength in character,
she was as frail as any other pampered woman who lifted nothing

for herself. Greer steadied her and quickly slapped the flames trying to creep up her heavy petticoats.

"Hold her," he yelled to Walsingham, who ran after him to defend his queen against the dagger-wielding Highlander.

Walsingham, bright enough to realize what was going on, grabbed hold of the queen's torso, and Greer yanked again. The sound of ripping marked success, and he pulled the flaming skirts from Elizabeth's legs. She was left in her ornate bodice with ruff about her neck, but her bottom half was free of the farthingale and petticoats. Only her hose, smock, and bum roll hid her lower body.

Leister, having put out his boot, ran to take the queen from Walsingham's hold.

Lucy stood near, her face distraught with surprise. "Your Majesty," she said, her tone full of remorse as she laid her own cape around the queen's shoulders. Elizabeth's ornate costumes were another layer of her queenliness, and stripping her skirts away showed the world her mortality.

"If there was any a doubt as to the danger of the Scots," Elizabeth said, looking first at Greer and then at the fiery ball a guard was dousing with water, "let this be a lesson to us all."

"The rope gave way," Greer said. Would he end up in the Tower? That did not fit his plans to convince Lucy to consider another night with him. "'Tis why we use chains at Hogmanay in Edinburgh," he said, taking the extinguished orb from one of the frowning guards. At least six of them had run up with torches to light the area.

Greer spun the blackened ball, catching it in his hands to show where the rope had been burned, releasing the ball to drop amongst the ruined petticoats.

"Who fashioned the balls?" Walsingham asked.

"Let me get you inside, Bess," Leister said.

"First I would know who decided to use rope instead of chain," Elizabeth said, her eyes narrowing at Lucy.

She curtseyed low. "I would never have asked for the fireball entertainment if I'd known it would endanger you or anyone in the area."

"Did you choose to use rope?" Elizabeth asked.

"No, Your Majesty," Lucy said. "I asked for flammable balls to be made on the end of rope or chain. I should have asked Master Buchanan for instructions. I surprised him with the request at the last moment."

Daingead. She'd get herself locked in the Tower.

Greer stepped before Lucy as if protecting her. "A properly soaked rope would work without burning through. I should have checked for dampness. I am—"

"Enough," the queen said. She took a full breath and leveled her gaze at Greer. "Did you know that the rope would break at the exact moment you swung in my direction?" Before either could answer, the queen turned away. "This was obviously an accident. Robert, see me to my room so my ladies can find me an ensemble that is not charred, shredded, and thrown into a muddy puddle."

Walsingham came before the guards. "Giles and Henry, we will discuss your choice of dangerously dry rope."

"Aye, milord," one of the men said.

"You're burned," Lucy said, picking up Greer's blistered palms in her cupped hands. Her hands were gloved as usual. He yearned to pull them off to feel the coolness of her touch. "We need to tend these before they fester," she said.

Reginald Darby walked over to look at the damage to his hands. "I have ointment that calms burns. William and I get quite a few working with the flame and compounds in our laboratory."

"Thank you, Master Darby," Lucy said.

The balding man smiled. "We are always prepared to help those who keep the queen and her court safe."

He'd said "we," but Greer was fairly certain that William Darby would allow him to die of festering burns.

They strode into the castle through the front double doors, the crowd of courtiers expounding loudly for those who hadn't seen.

"We could have all been set aflame."

"Barbaric custom that tests courage."

"Complete foolishness."

When Lucy had handed him the fireballs, he'd hoped to teach them about one of Scotland's unique customs. *Mo chreach*. They would only remember the danger to their queen.

"You were so brave."

Greer looked down to see one of Elizabeth's ladies pouting up at him. As he met her gaze, she smiled. "I can tend your burns, Highlander."

"Thank you, Lady Bixby," Lucy said. "Master Buchanan is being tended by Master Darby."

The woman's gaze did not shift away from Greer's, and her smile turned into an open invitation to her bed. "I am sure I could tend to his pains better than Master Darby."

Lucy snorted softly. "Licking them will do nothing but make them fester."

"Perhaps," Anne Bixby said. "But he will fester while feeling no pain."

"To my laboratory," Reginald said, beckoning him to follow.

"Thank ye, lass, but pain lets a man know he's still alive." He nodded to her, and Anne Bixby smiled.

"Pish," Lucy said, walking beside him.

Behind him, Anne whispered. "He called me 'lass' like I was his lover. We would do well together."

"If you ever made it out of bed," another woman said.

Lucy snorted again, apparently having heard. They walked side by side toward the glow of Reginald's candle up ahead. Was she jealous? The idea drew his attention from his burns. He leaned toward the shadow of Lucy's ear, pausing slightly. "Doing well together is nothing compared to being magnificent together."

He watched her profile as she stared straight ahead. A mischievous smile blossomed. "Perhaps two nights would be best," she whispered. She turned her face to him. Shadows and the golden glow of a lit sconce cut along her lovely features. "In order to make sure you suffer no pain."

"TRUST ME," LUCY whispered, pulling Greer's arm to get him to follow her toward the kitchens. It was late, after everyone had finished their guarded meals, sweetmeats, and wine. Dancing and games, with just the courtiers this night, had dragged on until Lucy thought she would scream.

"Jam, ye say? How do ye know 'tis free of poison?" he asked.

"I made the jam myself, four months ago. The crocks are sealed and in the storeroom beside the hearths. I will know if they've been tampered with." She glanced back at him, her heart beating faster. "'Tis delicious jam, strawberry." She said the words with heat like Anne Bixby's suggestive comment.

"I do love strawberry," Greer murmured, sending lightning through Lucy. Her heart pattered, and the ache below intensified.

She took his hand, which was bandaged around the palm, leaving his fingers thankfully free of burns. She'd left her gloves off, and his skin was warm. They moved on silent feet across the dark kitchen, the glowing coals in the three large hearths making the room warm. No food sat out, all of it being accounted for and locked away for safe keeping against poisoners.

They wove between the broad tables set about as work-stations to the storeroom door. Lucy brandished her taper before her and pushed into the windowless room that smelled of fall apples. Crates of the hardy fruit sat in the coolness, and shelves ran the length of each wall. Lucy let go of Greer's hand and bent to the lowest shelf in the back corner where her labeled clay pots sat. The wax seal on the one she pulled was perfectly intact. Not that anyone would try to poison her anyway. She wasn't important enough to be a target.

She turned to see Greer's broad back as he lit a sconce near the door. Her stomach squeezed in a giddy pinch. A second amazing tryst with him would surely help when he left her to return to his mother and young king in Scotland. The thought of him leaving pressed against her heart.

As if feeling her gaze, he stretched his arms over his head to rest on the low timbers holding up the ceiling. The press of his muscles against the white linen tunic made her mouth go dry, and she wet her lips. He turned around, and she walked forward, the undone jam in her hand. Did Greer throb as much as she?

"Ye found your jam, lass," he said, his voice like a sweep of velvet against her skin.

"Yes," she said, holding the cool clay pot in one hand. She sunk her finger into it, feeling the cold, sweet jam. Pulling it out slowly, she held it to his lips. "Taste."

Without hesitation, Greer's warm mouth came down on her finger, his gaze never leaving her. Everything inside Lucy clenched as he sucked along her digit, his clever tongue pulling the sweet from her. A smile softened the serious lines of his face. "Lucy Cranfield, your jam is as delicious as ye."

He took the clay pot from her and dipped the tip of his finger in it. Her breath caught as he painted a spot on her neck with it. His mouth followed, and her lips dropped open as he kissed the jam off her neck, continuing over to her ear.

"I will never be able to sample strawberry again without growing hard and ready," he whispered.

Her hands went up to capture his head, bringing his lips to hers. She tasted the jam on his tongue and slanted against him, her hands seeking out the muscles of his chest. She yanked up his tunic, her fingers sliding up his smooth skin, through the light curls of hair, over the chiseled contours. His heat drew her completely.

He pulled his tunic off, a white ghost going over his head to drop on the stone floor. His mouth dropped to the skin between her neck and shoulder, trailing along it. Lucy felt the heavy table at her back and leaned backwards onto her hands, tipping her head back to give Greer as much access as he wanted to her skin. With a grasp around her waist, he lifted her to sit on the table, her skirts around her.

Lucy kissed him with abandon, her one hand rucking up her skirts. She spread her legs, raising them to encircle his hips. She wiggled her shoulders, tugging on her body, to slip her bodice far enough down that her breasts rolled out of the top. Greer looked down at them, sitting pale in the dim light.

He growled and descended, his mouth encircling her nipple as he palmed the other. Lucy moaned softly, her foot stroking his arse. Gently he leaned her back. She heard the scrape of the strawberry jar and then his finger touching the inside of her thighs.

He inhaled. "I love the smell of strawberry." His head ducked down where her skirts were bunched.

Lucy gasped as he licked her inner thigh, kissing the tender flesh there and working higher. She'd heard whispers of women being loved so. "Oh Greer," she said, breathless as he touched her very core, loving her so thoroughly that her hands clenched in her skirts. Her eyes were closed but she could imagine him below. The images and sounds made her coil tighter until she shattered, groaning.

As the waves carried her, he pulled her forward, her legs spread still around his waist. He slowly impaled her. Her whole body shook as he filled her, and she clung to him, half on and half off the table. They rocked together, moving faster, the table creaking. His mouth moved between her breasts, her neck, and her lips without breaking contact. Lucy kissed him wildly, frantically. Over and over, they rocked together, climbing higher for long, exquisite minutes, the table taking the force of Greer's thrusts. Lucy clutched hold of him as her pleasure swelled once again, and when he reached between them, rubbing her, she burst.

He followed swiftly, his groan muffled against her mouth.

"Yes, Greer, yes."

"I AM STICKY all over," Lucy said, laughing lightly.

Greer watched her tug up her bodice, once again hiding her

breasts. "Jam is now my favorite food."

She smiled brightly. "I knew you would like my jam."

He almost threw her skirts back over her head. His grin felt natural and genuine. No woman had ever robbed him of his focus like Lucy Cranfield, but no woman had ever made him smile.

Bloody hell. He was on a mission from Lord Moray, and yet here he was in a kitchen larder licking and loving jam off a woman. And he didn't feel guilty. His mission had become less about saving the queen of England and more about seeing Lucy Cranfield's scars and proving to her that she was indeed beautiful.

"I would like to make ye moan in the light," he said, pulling her to him and kissing her softly. "Where I can kiss every inch of ye."

Her smile wavered. "We have proven that we can have great pleasure with our clothes still on."

He kissed her neck under her ear and whispered. "Oh, but ye have not experienced inch by inch kisses and nibbles."

A sound in the kitchen made their heads turn in unison toward the storeroom door. "No one should be about this late. And 'tis too early for the morning cooks," Lucy whispered and pulled away from him. He felt the absence immediately.

Lucy tugged the door open an inch. Greer stood behind her, watching through the crack. A woman stood at the counter, her back to them. Was this the assassin? A woman sent to poison something that only the queen would eat? Or would she kill more in her attempt?

They let her work for a few minutes. He would catch her in the act so she could not deny her evil intentions.

The woman turned toward their hiding space as if she'd heard them, and he found himself holding his breath. It was the Irish kitchen maid; O'Brien was her last name. Her brows were furrowed as she stepped directly toward them.

With a yank, she pulled the door open. "I've got you," she said.

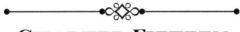

CHAPTER FIFTEEN

*"On the daie of the Epiphanie at night, the kyng with a. xi.
other were disguised, after the maner of Italie, called a maske, a
thyng not seen afore in Englande, thei were appareled in
garmentes long and brode, wrought all with gold, with visers
and cappes of gold & after the banket doen, these Maskers came
in, with sixe gentlemen disguised in silke bearyng staffe torches,
and desired the ladies to daunce... [sic]"*

Chronicler Edward Hall, Epiphany in 1512, Henry VIII's
reign

MARY O'BRIEN LOOKED first at Lucy and then Greer.
"Actually, Goodwife O'Brien," Lucy said, "we've caught
you."

Her surprise at seeing them, with Lucy looking quite ravished, turned to confusion. "Caught me? What do you mean? And
what are you doing hiding in the larder?"

"We... we weren't hiding," Lucy said, and stepped back to
pick up the clay pot. "I was but showing Master Buchanan all that
I've jarred this past summer." She held the pot out and pulled it
back to her bodice, which she hoped was up and straight.

The woman looked at the pot and then back at Greer. Holy
Mother Mary, was he dressed? A quick glance brought relief.
Lucy had not stripped him totally bare in the larder, and he'd
thrown his tunic back on.

"What are ye doing here at this late hour, Goodwife

O'Brien?" Greer asked. He took the jar from Lucy's hand and dipped the tip of his finger in it, tasting it ever so casually. But the action made Lucy's insides clench with longing. Lord, she was incorrigibly wanton.

Mary O'Brien turned, walking quickly back to her workstation. "I freeze the jam into balls to put inside the cakes when I bake them later. I forgot to put them outside in the snow." She pointed to the dallops of jam she'd been dropping onto a flat stone.

"Why freeze the jam?" Lucy asked.

Mary smiled. "'Tis a secret from my mum. That way the jam stays in place in the cake instead of spreading out in the batter. So there's a concentrated surprise in the middle of each slice."

"Clever," Lucy said, and pulled Greer's hand to get him moving. "I hope you find your bed soon, Goodwife."

Mary smiled at her. "I hope you do, too, milady."

Lucy felt her face heat as she led Greer, still holding her strawberry pot, out of the kitchen. They walked quietly up the dimly lit corridor. She looked over her shoulder at her handsome lover. "Do you think she believed us?"

"Nay," Greer said, the corner of his mouth tipping upward. He pulled her into him, his arms cradling her back so that the stone wall didn't bite into her as he pressed her against it. "So I think we should get all the ravishing in that we can before the whole court is whispering about us."

She smiled as she closed her eyes against the assault of hot kisses he was plying along her neck. "Agreed."

With a slow groan, he pulled away, tugging her after him. "I want to make ye moan my name without fear of someone walking down here."

Lucy laughed softly as they nearly raced along the hallway. After several turns, she realized that they weren't headed toward her room nor his. "Where are you taking me?"

He glanced back at her, and the look of intense passion in the set of his eyes and sensuous mouth sent chill bumps over her skin. It was as if he were already touching her. She shuddered slightly and didn't care in the least where he took her.

"I found a suite that's not being used," he said. "Far from others." Greer produced a key, holding it before her nose.

She smiled, letting all her yearning out with it. "Well then, Highlander, take me somewhere I can moan your name."

LUCY SMILED UP at the ceiling where the firelight bathed the ornate spiraled design in golden light. They lay before the hearth on blankets and furs from the bed, another warm nest. Snuggled down in the layers, she faced the fire, with Greer at her back. His fingers stroked her slightly rounded belly, sliding up to her breasts and then back down. They'd finally sated themselves, at least for the time being. She sighed softly.

Greer kissed the exposed spot at the base of her skull. Her hair was swept to the side under her. Slowly, he began to rub the bunched muscles of her shoulder.

"Mmmm... that feels good," she said. She smiled up at him. "Every time you touch me it feels good."

"Then I believe I should touch ye all the time."

"Then we will certainly become the talk of the court."

He pushed her slightly forward so he could reach her other shoulder, her head held by pillows. She groaned softly at the languid feel. Her muscles were sore from loving, and the heat from the fire and Greer's rubbing felt heavenly.

No one had ever touched her like Greer Buchanan had. No one made her feel like this. So free, so trusting. When she felt the blanket slide lower, she didn't move. She was on her stomach, the fire warming her exposed skin. Little by little the blanket slipped lower.

He must see them. She waited, holding her breath as his hands stopped.

The silence stretched, and Lucy nearly pulled the blanket back up. She knew how horrible the scars looked. Puckered skin that lay in thick circles where her mother tried to burn off her dark marks.

She stiffened.

"Relax, Lucy," he murmured, his hands beginning the massage again, kneading her muscles down her back, over the smooth skin and the burns. "They do not pain ye?"

"No," she whispered.

He continued to stroke, sweeping down with his knuckles and the heels of his strong hands. Little by little, she relaxed under the pressure. The blanket slid lower, exposing her buttocks, where she knew another scar marred the flesh. But he didn't even pause at it, stroking her. He worked the blanket down her legs, but she didn't feel cold between the fire and the warmth of his hands.

The scars were surely still there. William swore that nothing would make them disappear. But Greer did not avoid them. Instead, he continued to rub her muscles that lay under the puckered, thick skin patches. He got to her feet where he massages the arches, making her moan.

"That feels so good," she murmured against the pillow.

"Turn over," he said in a soft rumble.

It took her several breaths to start to turn, but he didn't rush or push her over. Slowly, she rolled to her side, facing away from him. Then she scooted to lay on her back, her knees bent. She kept her eyes closed.

Lucy startled as he kissed her lips gently, and she blinked to stare into his rugged face. "I see ye, Lucy Cranfield." Pity was absent. Anger was muted. The strength she heard in his voice and saw in his face was something much more powerful. It was truth.

He kissed her forehead, and went down to her feet, rubbing the tops of them until she sighed with pleasure. Strong thumbs worked up her shin and into the muscles of her thighs, right over one of the worst scars above her knee. He avoided the crux of her legs, which clenched with demands and made her shift. But he continued up her abdomen where she knew several marks had been burned, marring the softness of the pale skin there.

Lucy's eyes were closed, following him in her mind. But they opened when she felt his lips on her skin. His bent head was full of dark waves as he gently kissed the scar on her abdomen. He moved up to the next, kissing it. Not in a passionate way, but in a soft accepting way.

Lucy blinked at the pressure of tears in her eyes. He lifted his head to meet her gaze. She felt a tear escape, running in a line across her temple to her ear. He leaned down again and kissed another scar farther up under her breasts. Gentle. Reverent.

Another tear escaped, sliding into her ear, and he continued to kiss each scar along her body. Taking her left hand, he massaged it, each finger and the hollow of her palm. When he took her scarred right hand, she nearly pulled it away, an impulse she curbed.

He rubbed each finger and her palm like the other, but then he turned her palm up. His gaze met hers as he bent, kissing the center where the skin was blotchy and thick. Another tear slid to her ear, and she sniffed slightly.

Greer laid back on his side, raised on his elbow as he stroked her uncovered body gently. They stared at each other, and her heart swelled with emotion. His bent finger caught the next tear as it slid out, and he leaned in to kiss her lips ever so gently.

His eyes were beautiful as he looked into hers, and he brushed her hair back from her damp cheek. "Ye are beautiful, Lucy. Do not doubt that."

"They are hideous," she whispered, and more tears came, making her blink.

"Whoever told ye that, whether it be your mother or yourself, was wrong. What was done to ye was hideous, but ye are beautiful. Ye are strong, a survivor. Ye are compassionate and kind, and your smile lifts the suffering of those ye encounter." He leaned slightly forward, their gazes tethered. "If that is not beauty, then the meaning of the word has been corrupted. So, I will call ye bòidheach."

The word made her heart beat hard, and worry must have shown in her face. He smiled. "'Tis Gaelic for beautiful. If the word is corrupt down here in England, I will use my language of warriors long past, fighting for those they love, and seeing the truth beyond a picture in a polished glass. Bòidheach, Lucy, lass. Ye are that from your sweet little toes to the strands of flaxen gold on your head."

Her throat was closed with emotion, and she cleared it softly. "Thank you," she whispered.

Greer pulled the blanket back up over them both and kissed her lips. "Nay, lass, thank ye."

He pulled her close against him. Lucy hadn't realized how stiff she must have been before, worrying that he would feel the roughness of her scars. Because now she relaxed, truly let go, and cuddled into Greer. This was trust, the first time she'd ever experienced it. Trust and some other fierce emotion. Lucy's heart squeezed with fear. How could she survive when he left London, left her?

GREER STRAIGHTENED HIS sash. He picked up the three gifts wrapped in velvet cloth and tied with colorful spun cording. One was from Lord Moray in the name of King James for Queen Elizabeth and the other two were from him to Lucy.

Lucy. He hadn't been able to get her out of his mind. He'd walked her back to her room at dawn, and then he'd been busy all day finding her a Hogmanay gift. He'd thought of getting her a looking glass but didn't want it to seem contrived to remind her that she was beautiful. After she'd trusted him through the night to see her scars, he didn't want to ruin it with a foolish gift.

He'd meant every word he'd said to her. The only thing he'd

kept in check was the fury he'd felt that she'd had to endure the physical and mental pain of having her body mutilated. Her mother was truly a criminal, not only to the crown. Her father, as well, if he knew what was going on and hadn't stepped in to stop it. And Greer knew enough about scars from his own mother that he knew one night of loving Lucy wasn't going to heal her inside. He would need to remind her for a long time before she truly loved herself.

I don't have a long time.

Daingead. After Twelfth Night, Lord Moray expected him back in Edinburgh with news of the assassin's failed attempt. He'd written him to tell him about the poisoned courtier and the precautions Walsingham was taking to ensure Elizabeth's welfare. If anything happened to Elizabeth before James came into his majority, Catholics would rally to put the imprisoned Mary Stuart on the throne of England, something the Protestants in Scotland feared after their persecution all over Europe and under Elizabeth's older sister, Mary Tudor.

Greer locked his room and walked down the corridor toward the Great Hall where Lucy had said they should meet. Greer had spoken with Mary O'Brien earlier to make certain she wasn't going to talk about them inspecting the larder. She seemed accommodating but asked him not to talk about her mum's secret of freezing jam in cake. He'd assured her that he was not in the habit of discussing baking techniques with anyone.

Greer whistled a light tune as he walked along. When was the last time he'd spontaneously whistled? Had he ever? Surely England hadn't made his heart lighter. It was an Englishwoman.

Laughter came from the Great Hall as he neared, his boots tapping on the stonework. He rounded the corner and stopped before a small crowd that had opened a thoroughfare down the center of the room. Two ladies held large wooden spoons with one egg each balanced on them. One hand on the spoon and one clutching their skirts, they raced with even steps down the center, their faces tense in concentration.

Lucy stood at the finish holding out her scepter. She was *bòidheach*, beautiful. She wore a bright green gown that was dotted with pearls. Her stomacher was embroidered with gold thread into holly leaves. The hood she wore was made of cloth of gold and allowed some of her curls to show about her shoulders and long neck, which she did not cover up with a ruff. Her already lovely face was open with mirth, making her even bonnier.

She glowed of happiness and laughed out loud with the room when one lady dropped her egg. It splattered on the floor in a pile of yellow yolk and clear muck. The second lady continued slower, reaching the end.

"Lady Margaret is the winner," Lucy called above the applause. She held the lady's egg up high.

A set of young lords took up the spoons next as Jane, one of the kitchen maids, ran out onto the floor with rags to wipe up the mess. She looked a bit haggard from the game.

Elizabeth sat talking with Leister on her dais. Walsingham nodded to Greer as he continually surveyed the room. The man must never have a moment of peace. He was always on guard. *As I should be.*

Greer walked along the perimeter, and Lucy caught sight of him. Her smile relaxed as her gaze followed him, making his groin tighten. Her simple look would render him hard. Perhaps tonight he would teach her another position. Neither of them had mentioned a third night together, but their mutual desire seemed a bloody good predictor.

His smile faded. What if she became with child? He should stay in London until it was clear that she was not. Aye, he'd write about his findings to Lord Moray and send word to his mother that he must delay. 'Twas the honorable thing to do.

Honorable would mean he should also stop tupping her. *Mo chreach.*

"Why such a frown, Highlander?" Queen Elizabeth called. "'Tis a day of gifts and laughter." She raised her arms in the air as if declaring everyone to be merry.

He bowed his head to her. "I fear I am always serious, Your Majesty."

She blew her exhale out from between her dark red lips. "You and my spy master are cut from the same lot." She nodded to where Walsingham frowned at the table set up with sweet meats. He gestured to several that the servers had to sample.

"If it were up to Walsingham," Leister said, "he would have the servers eat all our food first. Then if they didn't die, he'd order them cut open to retrieve your safe fare."

"Don't be grotesque, Robin," she chided.

"I have a gift to present to ye from Lord Moray on behalf of King James," Greer said and bowed, holding out the one gift for the queen.

She took it with her long, uncovered fingers. "Interesting ribbon," she said.

"'Tis a strand of spun Highland wool, colored by the heather flower that grows on the moors."

"How appropriate," she murmured and unwrapped the woolen cloth to reveal a chain of gold with a ruby hanging from the center. She smiled at the rich gift, lifting it out to dangle from her beringed fingers. "Lovely," she said and looked to Greer. "I will send a letter of appreciation, but please also relay how pleased I am. I believe that Lord Moray and I are on the page of peace, and I am glad for both of our peoples."

"Aye, Your Majesty," Greer said.

"How lovely." Lucy's voice pulled Greer around to see her standing behind him. Even though she spoke of the necklace, her gaze rested on him.

He nodded to her. "Happy New Year, Lady Lucy," Greer said.

Behind him Elizabeth snorted, and Greer saw Leister whispering something in her ear. The queen nodded and looked between Lucy and Greer. "Well, Lady of Misrule, perhaps you will receive something as lovely from Master Buchanan. There are whispers that you two have been seen in each other's company muchly."

"I am but helping Master Buchanan stop the assassin he was sent to London to find," Lucy answered without hesitation, reminding Greer what a talent she had for lying. "Since my predecessor was killed by chance, 'tis in my best interest, as well as yours, to help him succeed in his mission."

Elizabeth tilted her head while studying Lucy. "Well said, Lady Lucy." Her smirk said that she wasn't convinced. Elizabeth looked past them where the minstrels had begun a jig. "Take me to dance, dear Robin."

Leister stood, offering his arm, and the two walked away, Lucy curtseying as she passed. Greer stopped beside her. "I have a gift for ye, too, but I don't know where or when I can give it to ye."

"I have a gift for you as well," she said, her gaze shifting outward on the room as if they simply happened to be standing next to one another. "Count to one hundred and meet me in the chapel."

Perhaps the reminder of a condemning God would keep him honorable.

She walked away, speaking with several guests. Her scepter swept over a group playing Snapdragon in the corner and ladies shrieked and laughed as men kissed them soundly. Slowly she made her way to the door and slipped out into the corridor.

Greer walked along the sweetmeats table. Most of them were untouched. Would they be given to the poor if not eaten? Lord, he hoped none were tainted.

Ninety-eight, ninety-nine, one hundred.

Greer strode out of the room and walked directly into the chapel. He would use restraint and then tell her he would stay in London until they knew she was not burdened with his child. The grand chapel, pews lining the center aisle, seemed empty. His boots clicked on the marble floor as he walked toward the front where a movement in the shadowed alcove caught his eye.

Lucy stood in a small, boxed room partially behind a curtain. It must have been a confessional back when Queen Mary renovated the chapel. He walked over and took a deep breath. "Lucy, lass—" he started but her hand curled into his tunic, pulling him into the tight space. She pressed her body against his, and his blood jumped to life once more.

There was no holding back, even if his soul was at stake. His arms wrapped around her, and his mouth descended on hers as she stroked down his back, squeezing his arse through his plaid. They kissed and touched there, tucked away from spying eyes.

His hands raised to cup her face. "Lucy," he murmured. "I want to take ye right here."

"Then do," she whispered.

"'Tis a house of God...and I need...to talk with ye...about my plans." Her kisses kept interrupting him until his head swam with the heady strawberry essence that permeated her skin.

She took a deep breath and rested her forehead on his chest. "'Tis so hard to be modest when you appear in all your rugged glory. You are much more in control of yourself."

He smiled at her poetic words and held her against him. "If ye could feel through all your layers, ye would see how out of control I am."

He held his breath as her hand snaked down the front of him to feel his hard jack through his plaid. "Oh," she said, but there was a happy satisfaction in the word. When she began to rub, he snatched her hand away and pulled her out of the unused confessional. Although, it was a place for the revealing of sin. And what he wanted to do with Lucy inside was truly sinful.

He took a deep breath and adjusted himself. "I came to give ye your gift."

She smiled and looked down where his plaid tented out. "Then please give it to me." Her words were so suggestive that he nearly pushed her back into the box.

"Och, but lass, I have no wish to burden ye with my bairn."

Her smile faded. "That would be difficult."

"As it is, I will stay in London until we know for sure ye are not."

Her smile returned. "So if I am, you will stay?"

"I…I have a duty, lass."

She sniffed, nodding quickly. "Of course." She dug her hand into the pocket underneath her petticoat and pulled out a small box. "Happy New Year." A less joyful, less lustful smile returned to her lips.

He took the box, unfolding the top lid to reveal a circular gold charm, a locket. He pressed the small lever open to see a miniature portrait of Lucy on one side and a lock of her golden hair tied in a braided knot secured into the other side. "For when you have to return to Edinburgh." Her words were soft.

"'Tis rich indeed, and I will cherish it," he said. *Daingead.* He should have gotten her the mirror. It was priced closer to her gift.

He exhaled long. "I fear I am not as rich with gifts." He pulled his package out. "There are several things to it."

Her gloved fingers untied the knot and opened the cloth. Two collars lay there. "They are for Pip and Percy," he said, picking one up. "Their names are burned into the leather. Pip Cranfield," he said, pointing out the name that had scrollwork etched into each, making them decorative. "So no one can say they aren't yours if they get away."

She smiled at him as she lifted Percy's. "They are perfect," she said. "Thank you."

He pulled forth a slender gift. "I also have this."

CHAPTER SIXTEEN

"Now poisons do not onely kill being taken into the bodie, but
som being put or applied outwardly."
Ambroise Paré, 6th-century French royal physician

LUCY PULLED THE woven ribbon on the second package. "You
didn't have to get me a second gift," she said. The collars for
her pets meant more than Greer had probably intended. They
were a tangible way of showing his support in her quest to save
the two dogs from the abusive bear-baiting sport. Pip and Percy
were hers to keep. Perhaps she'd leave court and live at Cranfield
House so she could love them and the three children every day.
Certainly all five of them needed more attention than Simmons
could give, especially if he moved away.

"I wanted to also give ye something to wear," he said.

She laughed lightly. "Do I get a collar too?"

She let the flaps of soft wool fall off and stared at two silver
sticks about a quarter inch thick and seven inches long. They each
had a pearl at one end opposite a vicious looking point at the
other.

"They're to hold your hair, but..." he lifted one up like a
miniature sword, "ye can use them as weapons if needed." He
thrust the ornamental hair stick at an invisible foe. "Very effective
and easily concealed."

The pair was beautiful, practical, and evidence that he wanted
her to be safe. But her heart squeezed slightly. "For when you're

no longer here," she said. "For me to protect myself."

He didn't answer, and she forced a sweet smile. "They are lovely, Greer. Thank you."

He studied her closely as if not convinced. "Ye like them?"

She relaxed her smile into a genuine one. He'd said up front that he would leave when his mission was done. His mother needed him as well as his king. Lucy stuffed the disappointment down inside with all her other dark emotions. "Yes, I truly do." She rose on her toes to kiss his cheek. "And the collars for the dogs mean so much. Too," she added. His frown showed that he doubted her. "And you like the locket?" she asked.

"Aye. Your likeness is finely made." The pinch between his brows deepened.

They stood there before the altar with their gifts, and Lucy felt the press of the silence. It was as if the gifts had sucked the passion out of the room.

"I should get back to the Great Hall," Lucy said, wrapping the collars and lethal hair sticks back in the cloth to carry. "The queen will be formally opening her own gifts. I should be there to poke jests about them."

They walked up the marble aisle, their footsteps echoing in the silence. She shivered slightly at the feel of judgement and remorse.

Greer opened the heavy chapel door, and an angry voice came from the open Great Hall.

"Are you trying to kill me, Lady Cranfield?"

"That's the queen," Lucy said, hurrying across the corridor, Greer right by her side.

The minstrels had silenced, and the full room stood still, watching the drama unfold before the queen's dais. Elizabeth stood tall, looming over Cordelia. Even without the white makeup, Cordelia looked as pale as the queen. Elizabeth's white face was pinched, and her red lips sealed tight. William and his father were crouched around something lying on the floor.

"'Tis definitely a powder of some composition," the older

Darby said. "I will have to test it in my laboratory to know for certain, but it looks like ratsbane."

Lucy rushed forward, shouldering her way through the press. People let her through, and she saw the grand ostrich-feather fan lying on the floor.

"I swear to you, Your Majesty," Cordelia said, "there was no powder when I wrapped it yesterday. I would never taint a gift with poison to give to you."

"The snake doesn't stray far from its sire in beliefs. Even with your mother dead, you carry on her treasonous work. Arrest her!" Elizabeth called, and several guards came forward.

"Please, Your Majesty," Lucy called, grabbing onto her sister. Tears ran down Cordelia's face, but she held her head high. "Certainly, a traitor has sabotaged my sister's gift."

"It would be foolish for her to taint her own gift to ye, knowing ye might see the poison or be accused if ye became ill," Greer said.

But Elizabeth's face was tight with anger, and worse, fear. And people and animals were much more dangerous when fear ruled them, even more so than anger.

"Take Lady Cranfield to the Tower," Elizabeth said.

"Just to be certain," Walsingham said, his gaze drifting to Lucy, "which Lady Cranfield are you imprisoning?"

Lucy held her breath, frozen for a moment. Who would take care of the children and dogs if she were locked away? Her house and money taken by the crown?

"Cordelia Cranfield," Elizabeth said, her small, sharp eyes darting to Lucy. "For now."

Before Lucy could say anything, Greer took her arm, pulling her back step by step until the crowd enveloped them. It was as if he coaxed her away from the ledge of a deadly precipice.

"I must stay with her," she said.

His lips came near her ear. "Ye must not. Not when Walsingham could easily convince Elizabeth to lock ye up too. Come." He took her hand, his fingers intertwining with her gloved one, locking her to him as he hurried them down the dim corridor.

"Where are we going?" she asked.

"Gather things. We will go to Cranfield House first and decide if 'tis safe to stay."

Her fist tightened in the folds of her petticoat. "I can't leave Cordy."

"Ye must right now. Before the Darbys confirm 'tis poison and Walsingham writes up your arrest warrant."

"But I had nothing—"

"Fear multiplies suspicion until it either fades or ends with a beheading," he said as they raced along the corridor.

"Won't I look guilty running?"

"Ye look guilty now because your name is Cranfield."

"God's teeth." He was right.

As they rounded the corner, a sliver of light shone out in the hall across from Lucy's room. The door was open. Greer pulled her flat against the wall, and they returned around the corner.

"Who's in my room?" she whispered. "We raced right here."

"Who has a key?" he said softly.

"Any servant."

"Damn. Stay here," he said.

She let him take several steps around the corner and then followed. He frowned back at her, and she shooed him to continue.

Before the door, Greer surged forward. The door banged against the wall as he held his sword before him. She ran up behind, but the room looked vacant. Greer strode about, opening the clothes press and pushing back the drapes. "Search the room."

She bent to look under the bed. "For a person?"

"For something that would send ye to the Tower with your sister. Something that may have been placed—"

"Under here," she said. She had sunk all the way to the floor to lay upon her stomach, her petticoats swelling outward to settle around her. "There's a pot like my jam." Her words were strained as she tried to reach it, stretching her muscles in her shoulders and back. "But I didn't put it under here. I can't even reach it."

Greer's face appeared on the other side, and his long reach was able to grab the pot. They both pushed up, leaning on the bed across from one another, Lucy's breath coming fast. He pulled the knotted leather string to remove the thin hide that capped it. "'Tis not jam," he said and met her gaze.

"What is it?"

He looked back at Lucy. "Poison."

"How do you know?" she asked, pushing to her feet to run around. She looked in the clay jar, but it was the label on the outside that proclaimed it ratsbane. The white powder looked identical to what was infused into the feathers on the fan Cordelia had given to the queen.

Several sets of footsteps sounded far down the hallway. Panic ripped through Lucy, making stars appear in her periphery. Before she could even think, Greer strode to the window that sat two stories off the ground, pushing it open.

Lucy watched his shoulder and arm rotate with such power, and he sent the clay jar hurling out into the night to fall somewhere in the manicured gardens. He quickly pulled the window closed and straightened the drapes just before Walsingham and several guards filled the doorway.

"Lucy Cranfield," he said, "I am under orders to search your room for dangerous substances."

She plopped down on the edge of her bed, her breaths shallow. Was the pot the only damning evidence placed in her room? *Holy Mother Mary.* She swallowed. "Of course, Lord Walsingham." Should she say her door was open when they returned? Would that look like she was casting blame?

The guards filed in, pulling back her blankets and squeezing all her pillows with their thick hands. Greer came up to stand next to where she sat, and she stood, nearly throwing herself into his arms. But that would show a definite attachment and might implicate him too.

Walsingham didn't question his appearance there. Which was

fortunate since Lucy's mind was clenched in anxiety and unable to formulate any stories, believable ones or not. She was like a bird caught in the gaze of a stalking cat, waiting for the teeth to bite into her.

One of the guards ran her wrapped gift over to Walsingham, who quickly pulled the ribbon exposing the soap she'd purchased as a gift for the queen. "What is this?" Walsingham asked.

"My New Year's gift for the queen. Her favorite scent in soap from…Which I purchased for her." If she told him she'd gone to the apothecary, he might question the man who could reveal they were asking about poisons. Lord, where else could she have gotten it. All the names of the vendor carts and little shops had vanished from her mind like smoke caught on a breeze.

He studied it as it balanced on the wrapping. Could the assassin have poisoned her soap as well as Cordelia's fan? Walsingham held it out to her. "I would see you smell and touch the soap, Lady Cranfield."

"Someone could have added poison to it like they did to Lady Cordelia's fan," Greer said, coming closer.

Would dying of poison be better than being imprisoned and executed? "I don't see anything," Lucy said and gingerly touched the sides of the blocky cake.

"Without your gloves, milady," Walsingham said.

None of Elizabeth's ministers had seen the scars across her right hand. She took a settling breath and pulled off the left glove.

"Both gloves, milady," Walsingham said.

She swallowed and pulled the fingers, one by one, of her right glove until she slid it completely off. If Walsingham was disgusted by her red, blotchy scars, he didn't say anything. Lucy picked up the cake of soap and brought it to her nose, inhaling. She looked at Walsingham. "Rose and musk. 'Tis the queen's favorite." She rubbed one finger over the top and held it up for Walsingham to see. "No residue."

Walsingham studied it, too, and her finger. "You may rewrap it."

"Nothing but the gift was found that does not normally belong to a lady's room," one of the guards said. "Except the gold clasp next to a broken pearl necklace." He pointed to the dressing table where Lucy had laid it out.

"Does that not belong to Lady Cordelia?" Walsingham said. His voice was conversational, but Lucy knew he was probing for anything that hinted at the sisters lying.

"I was going to take it to a goldsmith to fix it for her. She doesn't go outside the walls of Whitehall as much as I."

Walsingham stared at her. "You do go often into town, dressed covertly."

"To help the poor, Lord Walsingham. As I have said before." She kept his stare without blinking. He would see no lies in her eyes.

Walsingham sniffed, the one side of his mouth twitching upward as if the strain of staring had made his face pinch. He looked to his guards. "Lady Cordelia's room is next door. Search it now," he said, producing a ring with keys on it, probably one to each bed chamber along the hall.

"Someone could have put something incriminating in my sister's room," Lucy said, trying to follow him, but Greer caught her arm, anchoring her close.

"Noted, Lady Lucy," Walsingham said and continued out into the corridor to Cordelia's door.

Lucy turned to Greer. "He needs someone to blame," she whispered. "He will see her executed, and the assassin will either flee safely or finish his mission."

"And ye getting imprisoned will not swing either scenario into our favor."

"What do I do?" she said, her words snapping with ire even though she felt the pressure of tears gathering in her eyes.

"Nothing," he said, and her mouth opened to argue. But he continued. "*Ye* will do nothing. *We* will come up with a plan." He looked at the doorway. "But not here. Walsingham is looking for a reason to send ye to the Tower." He glanced at the window.

"And things will be found, and ye will be blamed."

"If we go to Cranfield House, he will find me there," she whispered. Her mind flipped through other possible hiding places. She looked back at him. "I think I know where we can go."

⤜⟫⟫⟫⟪⟪⟪⤛

THE NARROW HOUSE looked abandoned, like a hollow skull with its windows vacant and dark. "Who owns it?" Greer asked as he followed Lucy behind it where it sat on the Strand.

"The crown now," Lucy said as she tried the back door, which was locked. "It used to belong to Thomas Howard, fourth Duke of Norfolk."

"One of those involved in the Ridolfi Plot?" Greer asked.

She nodded and frowned at the building. "'Tis been empty since he was executed." The sound of horses coming down the Strand made them press against the back where timbers criss-crossed the daub. The carriage passed, and Greer moved his jaw back and forth to release the tension. He had to keep Lucy out of the bloody Tower.

"I need a rock," he said, and Lucy pulled her skirts back to kick at shadows in the yard. He withdrew his *sgian dubh* and worked the six-inch blade into the crack of the back door.

"Here's one that might fit your hand."

He reset the point of the blade along the locking mechanism. *Clang.* He delivered one heavy strike, and the blade broke through the old iron. "Inside before someone investigates the sound," he said, and they hurried through the door, shutting it.

Greer blinked to help his eyes adjust to the near black. The fleeting moonlight through two glassed windows showed they were in a kitchen with a hearth that looked as lifeless as the rest of the house.

"There's a lamp," Lucy said, her voice soft in the tomblike

manse.

Greer met her at the raised workstation and used his flint and bit of wool to light the wick. There was enough oil in it to feed the flame, casting a glow about the room.

"I have no tie to this place," Lucy said. "Walsingham shouldn't search here if he wants to arrest me." She looked at him. "You may want to go somewhere else, distance yourself from me."

He stepped up to her. "I'm not leaving ye in this mess, lass."

She exhaled as if she'd worried over it. In the candlelight, her lashes looked longer and darker. "You are honorable, Greer, but I don't want to see you locked away because of it. Your mother—"

"Is strong and safe up in Edinburgh. I will stay to see ye out of this." And to make certain she wasn't with his child. If she was, he'd steal her away to Scotland. No child of his would be birthed in the Tower of London.

"Thank you," she said, her voice soft, "but I don't know how we can find my way out of this tangled mess."

"We need to find the true assassin before they go into hiding or fulfill their quest to kill the queen."

"But how? Especially now when we are in hiding from Walsingham?"

"A close study of all the facts," he said. "They will lead us in a direction." At least he hoped so.

Lucy led them out of the kitchen into the interior library. Greer set the lamp down and made certain the curtains hid the light from outside while she sat in a leather-backed chair.

"At the apothecary, before the fireball, someone seemed to run from us," Lucy said. "Could he be our culprit?"

"The fact that he ran makes it a possibility." And there'd been something familiar about him.

He sat across from her in an identical chair. It was large enough to accommodate his frame. Lucy looked like a wee lass in hers, having to perch on the edge so her feet touched the floor.

"And Jasper Lintel lied about his working at the Bear's Inn," she said. "But would he have access to Whitehall? The food and keys to Cordelia and my rooms?"

"What would be the motive for making Cordelia and then ye look guilty?" he asked.

"There needs to be a guilty person," Lucy said, her usual smile gone. "Since our mother was revealed as a traitor, everyone has looked upon Cordelia and me as possible plotting traitors, probably waiting for the chance to strike."

Greer rose and lifted his chair, setting it down right before Lucy so he could reach her hands. They were still bare, and he held them, rubbing them with his thumbs. "We're assuming these are English Catholics who want Elizabeth gone so Mary of Scotland can take the throne. Elizabeth has enemies all over Europe, Scotland, and Ireland."

"The French are talented with poison," Lucy said.

"But this wasn't subtle," Greer said. "And Richard Whitby being poisoned was a mistake as well."

"It wasn't even Elizabeth's sweet that was tainted, since he didn't take hers, and William didn't find anything in the queen's food when he tested it. He didn't find poison in anyone's remaining food or wine."

"Yet we know Whitby ate or drank something poisonous. Whose plates did he eat from?"

"Several of the ladies down the table."

"And at the top of the table?" Greer asked.

"I believe he only ate from Lord Burghley's plate," she said.

"Burghley," he murmured. "What are his true religious beliefs?"

"He's as Protestant as the queen," Lucy said.

"He has strong opinions on creating a unified kingdom of England, Scotland, and Ireland," Greer said. He slid even closer until their knees touched.

She nodded. "He's pushing for her to use force towards that end. At least in Ireland. I think Lord Burghley believes Elizabeth will make your King James her heir if she has none herself. That will connect Scotland and England, but Ireland is still apart. King Henry brought Wales under English rule when he was on the throne, and Lord Burghley wants to see more of that. He's an empire builder."

"And Jasper Lintel is Irish."

Lucy's eyes raised from their hands to Greer's eyes. "You think Lord Burghley was the target, not the queen?"

"I think 'twas meant for someone who stands in the assassin's way."

"Well then you certainly shouldn't eat anything at court," Lucy said. "Everyone knows you're there to warn the queen about them."

"Anyone who protects the queen is in danger." Greer watched Lucy fight a yawn. "Ye need to rest." He stood. "We will find a bed."

He pulled her from the chair and wrapped her in his arms.

"And you think I will get rest in the same bed with you?" She snorted softly against his chest.

He felt a smile tug on his frown. "Aye, we both need rest. Although if ye think ye won't be able to keep your hands to yourself, I'll find a second bed far down the hall."

She laughed. A loud bark that she quickly hushed as if remembering that they were intruders and fugitives.

He picked up the lamp, and they walked hand in hand toward the steps that led above. "Although," she said, "perhaps you should get me with child. Pregnant women are not executed until the babe is born."

The thought of Lucy pining away in the Tower, her belly growing with his bairn, Lucy being dragged away to the block after it was born made his hand fist. "Or I will take ye away to Scotland, bairn or no bairn."

He felt her stop and turned to look down to her on the step behind him. "I could... go with you to Scotland?" she asked.

He'd never considered it before when her world was comfortable. That she might want to give all this up. "Aye, Lucy, ye could be safer there even if 'tis not as luxurious."

"Safer with you?"

"You are always safer with me," he said.

Her lips opened and closed twice before she said, "I do believe that."

They kept climbing until they reached a landing. Richly wrought portraits lined the hall where bedrooms opened on either side. He led Lucy into the last one. "'Tis best to be away from the stairs if anyone enters the house."

He handed her the lamp while he picked up and shook the quilt atop the bed to rid it of dust. No creatures stirred on the fine tick. Norfolk's house had been well kept. Probably by a contingent of hired servants.

"Greer?"

"Aye?" He watched her walk over to the side table, setting the lamp there. She pulled her French hood from her head, letting her hair fall about her shoulders.

She set it onto the table and turned to him, taking a full breath to look him in the eyes. "Will you marry me?"

CHAPTER SEVENTEEN

"Ill bread and ill drink / Makes many ill thinke."
Thomas Tusser, *Five Hundred Points of Good Husbandry,*
1573

THE QUESTION HAD been on the tip of her tongue all night, ever since he mentioned she could be with child. She'd known the risks, of course, but the danger seemed so far off compared to the other dangers around them that she hadn't thought things through.

"If I'm with your child?" she said. "I must know so I can start to make plans."

He stood there as if the mythical Medusa had turned him to stone, a mighty warrior made immobile by a woman's simple question. Although, there was nothing simple about wedding him. He was Scots and she was English. She had a house here in London, and of course, there was the fact that she was probably going to be declared a traitor by morning. Even King James's regent might support Elizabeth's declaration of her guilt. And could she leave London if Cordelia was still locked in the Tower?

"I don't mean to put you to the rack," she said.

"I will not abandon ye, lass, or my child," he said.

She frowned slightly. "That's not an answer to my question."

Greer ran a hand through his thick hair. "I have so little to offer ye as a husband, Lucy."

"You're right," she said and waved her hand as if brushing off the ludicrous notion. "You have strength, cleverness, and courage. You helped me save Pip and Percy without complaint and encouraged Alyce to look past her scars." She looked down at her gloved hands. "And me perhaps."

She walked to the opposite side of the bed. She'd sleep in her clothes in case they must rise quickly to flee. "I can see how deficit you are as a potential husband."

"Lucy," he said, coming around the bed to capture her shoulders. He turned her toward him, and she blinked, hoping he couldn't see the shine to her eyes. "I could not keep ye in what ye are accustomed. Silks and velvet and jewels. I am but a soldier for my king. I come from a humble home."

"And I come from a traitor's home," she said. "A torturous home." She looked past him. "Silk and velvet stings against burns."

She turned away, pulling out of his hands. *I am pathetic. A fool.* Lucy turned to him, a smile back on her mouth, even if she couldn't make it authentic. "I will do well wherever I am, Master Buchanan. Let it not concern you."

"Lucy," he said again, and she looked into his eyes then. They stared at one another without a word between them.

She saw worry, determination, and something like remorse there. "Don't you dare pity me," she whispered. "I will not stand for it."

She pulled out of his grip to sit on the bed. No wonder women didn't ask men to wed. It was too painful when they didn't say yes. Let them be the ones to flay open their hearts.

She untied her boots, kicking them off and climbed into the bed, pins, stays, and stockings all in place. She laid on her side, back to the center, listening to him walk around. The tick sloped as he sat on his edge, and she clung to her side so as not to roll into him. In the dark, she let a hot tear roll out. *Fool.* When had she let herself fall in love with Greer Buchanan?

"THESE FIT WELL enough."

Greer turned to see Lucy standing at the bottom of the stairs dressed in what was probably Lord Norfolk's servant's liveried clothes in green and blue. Hose ran up her slender legs and under breeches that fell to her knees. A tunic, tucked under a green wool jacket, hid her curves. Her hands worked to coil her long hair up to pin so that a cap could cover its golden glory.

"Aye." He pulled at his crotch where the English trews fit too snuggly. "Norfolk was a bit smaller than me. But these will stand out less than my plaid."

After a long night of half-sleep, dreaming of losing everything from his sword to his mother, Greer had risen before dawn to investigate the house for anything useful. He'd left Lucy sleeping, her face too beautiful to look at for long.

Will you marry me?

Why hadn't he just said yes? *Mo chreach.* Because she lived at the English court and had a house in London richer than any in which he'd ever lived. How could she be content living in a cottage on the moors?

"There were some old apples in the cold storage with jars of jam, vegetables, and ale. I mixed some milled flour with a few things to make a few pancakes," Greer said. "I cooked them over the kitchen fire before dawn so passersby wouldn't see the smoke."

"Clever," she said, tying off her plaited hair.

"They're good with...the jam." It was strawberry jam. Just the smell of it made him want to carry Lucy upstairs and stroke her until she forgot about his foolish non-response last night.

"Thank you," she said cheerily as if nothing painful had happened between them. "I plan to go back to the apothecary and ask about ratsbane purchases. Maybe Jasper Lintel will show up there."

"He's not the only apothecary in London," Greer said, watching her sniff the jar of jam. A slight blush came to her neck, creeping into her cheeks. She didn't look at him as she spread some on the pancakes.

"'Tis a place to start," she said. "And then I must get word to the children that I will be hidden for a while." She chewed for a moment and swallowed. "The children can find information from Whitehall for us."

"People know they are tied to ye," he said. "It could be dangerous."

Her lips pinched in thought. "They could speak with the barn lads, stay hidden, but I'll warn them of the danger and leave it to them."

"They'll help ye anyway."

She nodded, her brow furrowed. "But without Cordelia, I have no other contact. Well, except William."

William Darby. Just the thought of the swain made Greer's stomach tighten. He would have said "yes" as soon as Lucy had asked him to marry. *Bloody hell.* The smitten man would have asked her in the first place. "Has William asked ye to wed him?"

Fok. What had made him ask that aloud?

She blinked. "Actually, I didn't give him the chance."

"Why?" Why the hell was he still talking?

"I told him I only thought of him as a brother or friend." She tugged on her jacket, pulling the sleeve down over most of her right hand, because wearing lady's gloves would look odd. "Let's go."

She walked away before he could say anything or feel anything except a loosening of his chest. *Relief.*

Lucy walked with her face down whenever anyone came their way on the roads. In her livery clothes, she looked like a lad. He probably looked like a man who couldn't afford properly fitted clothing. Well, he *was* a man who couldn't afford a set of English clothing. He had brought only two dress tunics and one extra length of plaid with him. His mother had made him a court costume with breeches, hose, and jacket so he would look appropriate at the Scottish Court in Edinburgh, but he'd left the costume up north.

They dodged around people who were still wishing each other merry. Sometimes he and Lucy would separate to work their way through the tight streets where laundry hung above to dry, and an occasional baker hawked his buns from a cart. But Greer always knew exactly where Lucy was.

The group at the head of London Bridge was thick, and they ended up on opposite sides of the street, making his heart pound when he lost sight of her. But they met before the apothecary shop, which was doing a good business.

Two customers exited the tiny shop, and they walked in. The man frowned at first, but his face opened in surprise when he looked at Lucy. "Milady?" His gaze shifted to Greer, and he frowned. "Still keeping foreign company, I see." He looked back to her. "And in a new disguise."

Lucy leaned into him. "We are hunting an assassin, Master Wendel, one who struck again yesterday with ratsbane."

His eyes opened wide. "The queen?" he whispered.

"Is well," she said. "It was detected before anything could befall her."

"Thank the good Lord," he murmured.

"Did anyone buy ratsbane recently?"

"Aye," he said, and Greer moved closer.

"Did they say what was the purpose?" Greer asked.

The man narrowed his eyes. "Well, no one said, 'Wrap me up some ratsbane so I can poison the queen.'" He looked at Lucy and then up at the ceiling, thinking, and Greer and Lucy were unfortunately afforded a fine view of the wild hairs growing in his nostrils.

"The man asked for a small amount. I thought he might have mice."

"Did he give ye a name?" Greer asked.

"Nay, but I knew him." He nodded to Lucy. "He wore richer

clothes like a gentleman, with a cap and everything, but he was that butler of yours, Lady Lucy."

"Simmons?" she whispered.

"Aye. He's come here off and on for years for your mother. Well… before."

"Thank you, Master Wendel," Lucy said and set a coin on his counter, which the man quickly tucked away.

"He also bought rose-scented soap," Wendell added. "And something with spice that he said he planned to use on furniture to stop dogs from chewing it."

With Pip and Percy working their puppy teeth out, that certainly sounded like Simmons. Greer escorted Lucy out of the shop where she walked around the corner to rest against the rail over the water.

"Simmons was buying poison?" she said, her words numb.

"Are there mice at Cranfield House?"

She shook her head, her face slack. "Never."

He offered her his arm and then dropped it when he realized how it would look for him leading a lad along like a courtly lady. "He could be only wanting to poison Nick's cocks," Greer said. That would be horrible for Lucy, too, but at least it wouldn't make her trusted housekeeper a traitor.

"We need to ask him," she said, striding forward. The gentle sway of her hips was obvious even in her trousers.

No words passed between them as they made their way across the city to St. Martin's Lane. They circled behind Cranfield House, stopping when they heard a voice.

Greer leaned up against Lucy to look over her head around the corner. The warmth of her against him made his chest squeeze. *Bloody hell.* Why couldn't he focus? All he wanted to do was take Lucy back to Norfolk's house and hold her close until everything between them was good and easy again.

"Sit and stay," Simmons said where he stood with Pip and Percy in the snow.

"They are doing wonderfully," Catherine said. "We must give

them a sweet."

"Sweets aren't healthy for dogs," Alyce said next to her.

Nick hopped down the plank leading up to the chicken coop with such gusto that the two pups broke rank and ran to play with him. Simmons frowned, his hands on his hips. "This is training time, young man," Simmons called.

Nick ran back where Pip and Percy had stood. "Sit," he ordered.

"Now make the sit signal," Simmons said, his voice even like a tutor instructing his pupil on an arithmetic equation.

Nick tipped his pinched fingers up. "Sit." The two dogs sat in unison. Catherine hopped up and down, clapping, making the dogs rise again.

"Sit," Nick repeated, and they settled back down. This time Catherine held still.

"They are coming along, Goodman Simmons," Alyce said.

Lucy pulled away from the safety of their spot and stepped around the corner. Pip and Percy jumped up, running and barking at her. She yanked her cap from her head, letting her long braid tumble out. "'Tis me," she said as they ran up.

Fierce barking turned to happy yips as they recognized her. The dogs leaped around Lucy, and Catherine threw herself into her arms. "Lady Lucy! Happy New Year and thank you for our warm gifts." She stepped back and spun around to show her bright blue petticoat. "And the hose keep me so warm." She lifted the hem to show woolen hose underneath. "I can be outdoors all day without freezing."

"Thank you," Alyce said, and gave Greer a nod. "You have new clothes too."

Simmons shook his head. "As does Lady Lucy." He frowned at her masculine costume.

"See what a good job we're doing with the dogs," Nick said, hugging pup. "And the cocks are liking their new home." He looked to Greer. "Cabbages do work."

Greer nodded to him. "Ye've kept your promise to see the

cocks comfortable and are helping care for these growing beasts. Very good." Nick stood even straighter, his smile broad.

"Master Simmons is doing most of the training," Alyce said. "We merely help."

Greer studied the old man. Simmons crossed his arms over his chest, watching the children with a softened expression, the bite out of his frown.

"Master Simmons," Greer said, "Lady Lucy and I would like to have a private word with ye."

His arms slowly dropped, his eyes growing wider. "Certainly. Is there more trouble up at Whitehall?"

"Aye," Greer said and walked toward the back of the house. "Maybe the children could continue to train Pip and Percy while we talk inside."

"Excellent idea," Lucy said, striding after Greer. "Come along, Simmons."

The elderly man followed behind without another option. He was still Lucy's paid servant and obviously loyal to Cranfield House. Was he also loyal to the late Agatha Cranfield, Lucy's traitorous mother?

They walked in a single line into the library off the entry hall. Greer closed the door behind them.

"What is this about?" Simmons asked.

"Did you buy ratsbane at the apothecary on London Bridge?" Lucy asked.

Simmons took a small stagger backwards. "Good Lord." He looked to Greer. "Has ratsbane been used at Whitehall?"

"Cordelia has been accused of trying to poison the queen with ratsbane dusted through the fan she gifted her last night," Lucy said.

Greer watched Simmons closely. His face turned reddish. "And someone tried to make Lucy look guilty by putting some more ratsbane in a clay jar under her bed," Greer said.

Simmons's hands fisted before him as if in prayer. "Is that why you're dressed like a lad?"

"They've sent Cordelia to the Tower," Lucy answered. "I may be next. We felt it prudent to leave Whitehall until this was figured out." She glanced around and then back at the man. "Do we have mice or rats at Cranfield, or were you planning to poison the animals?"

His mouth dropped open and closed twice before he spoke. "No to both, milady."

"But ye bought ratsbane at the apothecary," Greer said.

"Yes, but it was for my associate. He said he needed it for rats at his employers' establishment. A small amount, anyway."

"Why would you buy it for him?" Lucy said, walking closer to the butler. She touched his arm. "Are you continuing my mother's work?"

Simmons sunk onto the edge of a chair by the cold hearth. "Certainly not. I... He asked me to purchase it because Master Wendel wouldn't sell to an Irishman."

"Jasper Lintel," Greer said.

"Why, yes," Simmons said, looking up at him. "How—?"

"The mysterious Jasper Lintel doesn't work at the Bear's Inn," Lucy said. "We think he's been getting poison to use at Whitehall," Lucy said, sitting in the chair opposite him.

"My lord," Simmons whispered.

"Why didn't he buy it himself from another apothecary?" Greer said.

"He said they are all prejudiced against the Irish," Simmons said. "He also asked Catolina to purchase ratsbane from the chemists on Bucklersbury Street."

Lucy glanced at Greer and then back to Simmons. "How did you meet this man?" she asked.

"Mistress Wakefield said he and his wife frequented the shops on Gracechurch Street. They came into her lace shop and spent time talking with her about the poor conditions in Ireland. When Catolina, Richard, and I decided we wanted to better ourselves, she mentioned it to them. They were interested, and Lintel started meeting with us."

Simmons leaned toward Lucy, his face pinched with worry. "What will become of Lady Cordelia? And you?"

"Has anyone come from the court for me and Master Buchanan?" Lucy asked.

"No. Should I...close up the manor?"

Walsingham's hounds would find him soon enough. "Pack a bag," Greer said, and looked to Lucy. "If Walsingham's men question your prejudiced apothecary, he will point them here to Simmons."

"Blessed Mary, protect me," Simmons said, making the sign of the cross before him.

"And don't do that before anyone," Lucy said. "They will immediately think you are Catholic."

Lucy exhaled. "Can you stay with Mistress Wakefield?"

He flushed. "I could, but she's a single woman. 'Twould be unseemly."

"Either her or some other safe place," Lucy said. "The children can remain here."

Simmons grabbed Lucy's hand. "If I helped get Lady Cordelia sent to the Tower...I will never forgive myself."

The man seemed sincere. His eyes were glassy, like he fought tears. He shook his head. "I didn't trust Jasper, but Catolina likes his wife." He clutched his hands together. "If Lady Cranfield was still alive, she would protect all of us."

"She is the reason we were instantly suspected of treason," Lucy said, acid in her voice.

His face flushed redder. "She wouldn't have allowed you or Lady Cordelia to be cast in suspicion at the court, even if she intended evil. She loved you."

Lucy snorted. "She hated me."

He shook his head. "No. She worried about you being judged, milady. I heard her praying nightly for you."

"For me to be different, beautiful," Lucy said.

"Yes."

Greer watched Lucy's face tighten. She wasn't loved for who

she was, and the butler's confirmation stung, even though she knew.

Greer wanted so badly to reach out to her, but their stilted discussion this morning had driven a wedge between them. *Will you marry me?* Would she move away from the English court? Live on the moors in a cottage that he'd built a mile away from his mother. Did she think that Lord Moray would have Greer up at Edinburgh Castle for fetes like Elizabeth?

"You should leave here as soon as possible," Lucy said to her butler, "because it won't take long for Walsingham to question all the apothecaries that may have sold ratsbane."

"YE WALK LIKE a woman," Greer said.

"Pardon?" she asked, looking at him as they hurried toward Gracechurch to warn Mistress Wakefield about Walsingham's investigation.

"Ye sway." He tipped his head toward her lower half. "Even in breeches, ye look...curved, and ye sway when ye walk. Like a lass, not a lad."

"How does a lad walk then?" she said, her gaze scanning the people up ahead.

"Straighter. Less hips."

Greer kept his grin inside as she tried to walk without her hips moving. Even with treasonous poisoners, false accusations, and danger everywhere, Lucy lightened his soul. And she wanted to marry him. What would it be like to have her by his side through the challenges of life? At the Edinburgh court, she'd know how to work around royalty, winning their hearts, while still taking risks to help animals and the less fortunate. But could she be satisfied going home to their cottage outside town?

"Lucy," he said as they turned onto another road.

She stopped, her brow pinched. "Jasper Lintel has got to be

the traitor," she said, her voice low. "He showed up a month ago from Ireland. His wife befriended Mistress Wakefield."

"So they suddenly had a good reason for needing to be up at Whitehall," Greer said. This topic was much easier to discuss than his lack of riches.

"To make the acquaintance of the queen," Lucy said. "The same thing Richard Whitby was doing."

"And Mistress Wakefield," he said. "She obtained access during the festivities when the queen invited simple townsfolk inside."

"We need to find him," Lucy said. "And prove he's the traitor." She huffed. "Because if he's not, I don't know how we can save Cordy."

And Simmons and probably Mistress Wakefield now.

"I'm not even sure I could spot him," she said. "I only saw him briefly that night when we took Pip and Percy to Cranfield House."

"Simmons knows what he looks like."

"He shouldn't go near the court right now," Lucy said.

Greer stopped, and they looked at each other. "The children," they said in unison.

Lucy caught his arm as if it were the most natural thing. The two of them against the darkness in the world. "They saw him those nights he came for their meetings."

"If Jasper Lintel is up at Whitehall, they could identify him."

They rounded the corner onto Gracechurch Street where Wakefield's Laces and Baubles stood. Mistress Wakefield had a sign hanging that had white lace painted on it, with what looked like a vial of perfume.

Before Greer could ask if she would be in since it was still Christmastide, two guards dressed in red and gold tromped out of the store. Greer grabbed Lucy's arm, leading her in a casual walk to the alley where they could see.

"Mistress Wakefield," Lucy whispered, as the woman was marched out of her store, Lord Walsingham following her.

"Hear ye! Hear ye!" a town crier called at the corner, making Lucy jump. Criers went about telling the latest news and gossip, stopping every street or two to repeat it. This lad stood on a barrel under a tall lamp that would be lit at dusk.

"'Tis the second day of January in our Lord's year fifteen seventy-three. Twelfth Night is in three nights hence. Food and shoes for the needy and destitute are being given out at Whitehall gates.

"Harry Hunks, the vicious bear, will be tried at the Bear Garden on the morrow." The boy cupped his hands around his mouth. "No executions today, but Lady Cordelia Cranfield is to be put to death for treason by the end of the week."

Chapter Eighteen

If this were played upon a stage now, I could condemn it as an improbable fiction.
William Shakespeare, *Twelfth Night*, 1600

"**P**UT TO DEATH," Lucy whispered, her knees buckling. Greer's hand came under her arm, and he pulled her farther into the shadow of the building. "My God," she breathed, sucking in large draughts of air as she sunk down, her behind in the trousers sitting on a pile of wet snow.

"Even breaths, Lucy."

"Poor Cordy," she said. "Executed? Why are they acting so fast? Oh, my poor Cordy."

"Even breaths, lass," he said, near her ear and lifted under her arms. "Else ye will swoon."

Lucy's heart squeezed so hard, she rubbed it through the tunic. How would she survive without her sister? Cordy didn't deserve to die. Would it be hanging? Or by the axe?

Greer stood before her, his hands continuing to hold her up.

Lucy swallowed and focused on the tie at his throat. "My friend, Maggie, was able to break her husband out of the Tower. We could get Cordy out and all of us ride to Scotland."

"I'm certain Walsingham learned how to tighten his defenses after that escape."

Lucy pressed her hands, one over the top, to her forehead, making her cap fall off. "I cannot let Cordy be killed." Greer caught her braid, and she leaned numbly against the wall as he coiled it back around into a knot on her head and pushed the cap over it. She looked up into his face.

It was hard, his brows pinched. He knew how dire things were. She didn't have to convince him of that. Even if he wouldn't marry her, he would help her. *Unless I'm with his child. Then he might marry me.* The hope surfaced easily, bobbing as if on the top of the Thames.

But there was no time to think of babes or weddings or happiness. *I will have no one if Cordy dies.* Lucy dropped her face in her hands. "I am a coward," she whispered.

Greer squeezed her shoulders. "Ye are not a coward."

Fear gripped her throat. She swallowed, tipping her face to his. "I am," she said. "The thought of losing Cordy is too much." She shook her head. "I can barely stand."

Greer looked up and down the vacant alley as if making sure no one was nearby. "I believe that Walsingham is setting a trap for ye with Cordelia's sentence. It may not even be true."

Tears filled her eyes. "But what if she thinks it is? She must be terrified." Lucy's heart pounded as if tethered to her sister's wildly flying pulse.

He exhaled and squeezed her hands. "We need to find the real culprit. And fast."

"And it must be Jasper Lintel," she said.

He caught her chin gently in his fingers. "And if the worst happens, I am stealing ye away to Scotland before Walsingham can grab ye too."

Lucy wiped her eyes to clear them of tears. "I cannot even think about the worst." Cordelia dying by the blade or hanging. Even touching the very edge of the thought made a swollen tear break free to run down her cheek. Greer wiped it with his thumb.

"We need to hurry back to Cranfield House," Greer said. "Walsingham is acting quicker than I anticipated. We'll take the children, Simmons, and the dogs to Norfolk's to plan our next step."

Lucy nodded, taking an even breath to push back against the immobilizing fear. "Let's move, then."

They traveled back the way they'd walked, hurrying this time. As they rounded the corner onto St. Martin's Lane, Greer grabbed her arm, pulling her to the side of the road. "No," she said, her voice low. She stopped as she spotted a wagon bearing Elizabeth's coat of arms outside Cranfield House. Neighbors had come forth from their own houses to watch the spectacle.

John Simmons was led outside, his balding head bowed.

Lucy gasped softly, and her heart clenched as Pip and Percy trotted out on the ends of ropes about their necks. She hadn't even had time to put their collars on. Walsingham would no doubt return them to the Bear Garden kennels.

Greer pressed his arm firmly against hers. Thank goodness they had quartered Greer's horse in Norfolk's stables, or Darach might have been seized as well.

Greer and Lucy waited until the wagon, with Simmons sitting bound in the middle, rumbled over the cobblestones east toward the Tower. Once the sound of the wheels had faded and the neighbors had dispersed, Greer tugged her arm to follow him. They stepped back out, walking casually until they reached the side of Cranfield House where they ducked around behind.

The house was silent as they stepped in the back door. "Walsingham may have left a guard or two," Greer whispered in her ear. She nodded and they walked lightly through the ornately furnished home that she'd always known. Now it seemed as cold and hollow as a tomb.

Whispering came from the study, and they crept that way. Peeking around the door, Lucy saw Alyce hugging Catherine as Nick tried to start a fire in the hearth.

"Are you well?" Lucy asked. All three children spun around, their eyes wide with terror and then relief when they saw them.

"The queen's guards took Simmons," Alyce said.

"And Pip and Percy." Catherine ran to Lucy, throwing her arms around her. Lucy hugged the girl tightly.

Nick looked pale. "The head guard said you stole the dogs and that Lord Walsingham was taking them back."

Alyce looked close to tears but was being brave. "They said Simmons bought poison to kill the queen."

"How terrifying for you all," Lucy said, pulling the three in together to hug. The panic that had taken her strength before was no match to the need to protect these three children. They needed her to be strong. Her gaze found Greer's. "We need you three to be brave."

"We must save Pip and Percy," Catherine cried.

"And Simmons," Nick said, nodding. Apparently, the children had grown to care for their biggest critic.

"He's done nothing wrong," Alyce said. "Just like Pip and Percy."

Nick nodded, wiping a hand across his cheek. The movement reminded Lucy how young he was.

Lucy looked at each child. "Did any of you get a good look at all the people who met with Simmons?"

"Mistress Wakefield was the only lady," Alyce said. "And we saw the other two men. You said one of them, Richard Whitby, was killed."

"He had that walking stick," Catherine said.

"But ye saw the other man?" Greer asked. "The one named Jasper Lintel."

All three of them nodded. "He is tall and thin and has really bushy eyebrows," Nick said.

"And he spoke with an Irish accent," Alyce said.

Lucy glanced at Greer and then back to the children. "We need to get back into Whitehall so you can find him."

IT TOOK ANOTHER night and day to work out the costumes that Lucy said would blend in with the troop of actors Richard Whitby had employed for Twelfth Night before he died. Greer and Lucy had considered going to the troop itself to ask to blend in but worried they might give them away to Walsingham for a reward. And women were not permitted to act on stage unless they were part of a masque up at court.

Lucy had already been accused by the crown, and the town crier read out her description in the streets each day asking for the good people of London to turn in the traitor. If Greer and Lucy didn't uncover the real assassin, at least three innocent people would be put to death, and the assassin might still strike the queen.

"Ye look tired," Greer said as they dressed in their costumes at Norfolk's house. Darkness had fallen, and the mystery plays would begin soon up at Whitehall for Twelfth Night. "Are the children keeping ye up?" he asked.

They had spent the last two nights at Norfolk's empty townhouse, Lucy sharing a room with the girls and Greer with Nick.

"I keep expecting Walsingham to charge through the doors," she said softly so the children wouldn't hear. Alyce helped Catherine into a fluffy sheep costume. Nick worked to tie his ancient wrap around himself while balancing his shepherd's crook over one arm.

"Set it down," Alyce told him.

"Oh," he said, and it dropped to the floor. The bang made Catherine jump and gasp. Alyce rolled her eyes.

The fact that the older girl no longer hid her face around him cheered Greer. Thanks to Lucy's unconditional love, she didn't seem too lost to shame. With the right guidance, Alyce might see herself worthy of moving about without hiding half her face all the time.

Greer caught Lucy's hand and pulled her into the hallway. It was lit by the soft glow of a lit sconce. "I would have ye sleep with me tonight," he said. Two nights without her next to him had left him cold and worried.

"If we survive tonight," she said with a dark laugh.

"We will survive." And he would take her and the children away from London if they couldn't find Jasper Lintel and prove him the traitor. "I think we will both sleep easier next to one another."

"First of all," she said, clearing her throat slightly, "I would not set such an inappropriate example for the children."

She inhaled and met his eyes. "And second...I'm not with your child."

The information stopped his inhale. His stomach tightened, like a loss. "Ye know for certain?"

"Yes." She looked down at the floorboards. "So you are free to go."

Free to go? *Daingead.* Nothing could be further from the truth. He caught her arms. "I am not free to go."

"Once your mission is complete," she said, but kept her face down. "I know you must return to Edinburgh."

"Lucy." He waited, but she didn't look up. He gently lifted her chin so that she met his gaze. "I do not live at the castle in Edinburgh. I live in a thatched cottage a mile from my mother. I care for her as best I can. I don't own velvet and silk. I have a cow and a few goats and sheep."

"And chickens," she whispered, without looking away.

"Aye. I plant carrots and turnips to harvest, and I go to war when my king calls me. I am not a nobleman. Ye would not be...satisfied there."

Lucy frowned. "How do you know that? I love animals. I could be happy on a farm."

"How do *ye* know that? Ye've never lived on a farm." He glanced about the hall that had carved molding and polished floors. "Ye've lived at Cranfield House or at the English court. A cottage on a farm is squalor compared to thick rugs and tapestries draping the walls. Gold plates and crystal chandeliers."

"We are dressed," Alyce said from the doorway. Her brows rose as she looked between them. "Pardon," she said and disappeared back into the room.

"Let's get Cordy released," Lucy said, her eyes narrowed in anger, "and then we will talk about what requirements I have for being happy and satisfied."

She pulled a shawl up over her head. It hid her golden braid. Even with her face peeking out, she was beautiful with the gentle strength in the lines of her face.

The five of them kept to the shadows as they walked toward Whitehall in silence. Catherine held Greer's hand, her small fingers clutching his. He bent near her head. "Ye do not need to go inside," he said. "Alyce and Nick have seen the Irishman."

She looked up at him and scrunched her nose in a way that reminded him of Lucy when she was seriously irked. "I'm as brave, and I'm smaller, so I can scurry into places that others cannot reach."

"Quite so," he said, squeezing her hand. "We are fortunate to have ye."

Whitehall was lit for Twelfth Night with torches lining the thoroughfare up to the entrance. The children, Lucy, and Greer moved as a group under the watchful eyes of the gatekeeper. To them, they looked like another group of actors hurrying inside to entertain.

Lucy led them to the right under another arched gateway so they could enter near the chapel and wine cellar. The door opened as one of the actors from another troop stepped out into the night. Lucy caught the door before it could close.

"Stick the rock in there," the man called, pointing. "I've gotta piss."

Greer set a rock in the door so it wouldn't close, and they hurried inside. About twenty men stood in various types of dress outside the Great Hall, bantering and holding scripts, some of them making wide gestures as if practicing.

"Oh, my heart," Catherine whispered. She smiled and raised excitedly onto her toes. "I want to be an actor."

"Girls aren't actors," Nick said, straightening his cloak.

"Tonight I am," Catherine shot back.

Lucy knelt before her, checking the straps that held the sheep skin over her back. "Tonight you are also an assassin hunter." The wee lass nodded, her face serious.

"Who are you?" asked a man as he walked up, his nose tipped high so that he looked down on the children. He wore a deep red velvet jacket with gold thread along the seams.

"The Scottish Thistle group," Greer said.

"You have children and a woman working for you?"

Lucy walked up. "Aye. 'Tis allowed in Scotland," she said in something similar to a northern accent. "We Scots are more modern and practical."

The man snorted. "I wonder what the queen has to say about that."

"A queen?" Lucy continued. "A woman who has had to defend her position against outdated ideas about women? I think she would tell ye to hold your wagging tongue before she orders it cut out."

The leader of the acting troop gave her an evil look. "Just stay out of our way."

Lucy followed him with a steely gaze as he walked off. "Are all actors so horrible?"

"Ye are the first I've met, so I would say nay," Greer said.

She grinned at him. "I am a fine actor, am I not?"

"Especially when ye are on a mission to save animals or a sister."

She inhaled deeply, her smile flattening into determination, and she gave a quick nod.

A couple came out down the hall, a liveried man and a kitchen maid. Behind them walked William Darby. *Daingead.* He would recognize them right off.

"That's him," Nick said, his whisper frantic. "That's the man who came to Cranfield House to meet with Simmons."

CHAPTER NINETEEN

*"The Twelfth Night Cake has a bean and a pea baked into it.
The man who finds the bean in his slice of cake becomes King
for the night while the lady who finds a pea in her slice of cake
becomes Queen for the night."*

Smithsonian Libraries and Archives

L UCY LOOKED AT William, who luckily did not seem to notice her. "He's not Irish," she said.

"Which man?" Greer asked Nick.

"The one talking with the woman," Alyce said. "That is Jasper Lintel, the man who met with Simmons at Cranfield House."

Lucy released her breath. Thank God it wasn't William. He was a good man, and in his position as poison detector, Elizabeth would have been dead months ago if he wanted her gone.

"Are ye sure?" Greer asked.

Catherine, Alyce, and Nick all nodded.

Greer moved Catherine before him and crouched down as if fixing the ties of her sheep skin. "Have ye seen the woman before, Catherine?"

Lucy had and so had Greer. Mary O'Brien had been the cook who had caught them in the larder when she and Greer had been spreading strawberry jam on each other. Her cheeks warmed at the memory.

Catherine shook her head and looked to Alyce. "Not the woman, right?"

Alyce shook her head. "Only the man." She turned away from the couple as if talking to Lucy. "But he was dressed differently. Not in red and gold. Yeoman clothes."

Greer lowered to the ground as if tying his boot, and William walked past. The man and woman nodded to one another and turned in opposite ways. The woman toward the kitchens and the man toward the Great Hall.

Lucy tugged Greer over to the wall, and the children clustered around them. "Mary O'Brien is said to have a husband," she said, "who must be Jasper Lintel."

"A false name." Greer crossed his arms over his muscular chest. Even in the English garments he looked powerful. "He wanted to get into Whitehall and used Simmons and his cause to do so."

"But it looks like they were already in Whitehall. He as a guard and she as a baker," Lucy said.

"He needed someone to buy the poison, and happened upon Simmons, Richard Whitby, and Mistress Wakefield." Greer suggested. "So it wouldn't be traced to them."

"I didn't see him the night Richard was poisoned," Lucy said. "But his wife was questioned about the sweetmeats."

"They are Irish," Greer murmured, his lips tight. "I would gamble a bag of shillings on the target being William Cecil, Lord Burghley."

"The Irish dislike his policies," Lucy said. The old man was very determined and opinionated but worked in the background while Elizabeth took center stage and therefore was considered at risk from Catholics.

"Many Irish citizens have raised arms against English occupation and governing," Greer said. "Burghley is the target, not Elizabeth."

"It could be both," Lucy said. "Take out the one who is pushing so hard for unification *and* throw the country into chaos by then killing off the queen," she whispered. "There would be no unification then."

Lucy's heart thumped hard as she looked toward the Great Hall. "'Tis Twelfth Night. There must be poison in their food."

"You said that guards were watching closely, though," Alyce said, "making them eat what they are serving."

"They can't eat every part of what they are making, or they will fall to their own poison," Greer said.

"Perhaps they are putting a little bit in a specific piece or slice," Catherine said. She pinched her little fingers together.

"Keeping it contained, like a piece of ice inside a snowball," Nick said. "The rest of the snowball is just snow, but 'tis the ice that makes it hit so hard. But then it melts away."

Lucy's breath stuttered to a stop, and she looked at Greer. "Ice. A ball of ice." Her face snapped back to the doorway where the other actors filed inside with a great flourish. "Mary O'Brien, the night we were in… when I was fetching some of my strawberry jam in the larder," she said. "Mary O'Brien was up very late, and she was dabbing small balls of jam on a sheet to place outside to freeze overnight."

"Her grandmother's secret technique," Greer said. "Ballocks." His hand went to clasp the back of his head before dropping.

"The ice pieces could be stuck into very specific areas of a cake before baking," Alyce said.

Lucy began speaking quickly. "So the poison wouldn't seep into the rest of the cake but stay there, melting as the cake bakes."

"Then after the assassination," Greer said, "the poison part would have been ingested and therefore undetectable in the rest of the cake."

Lucy grabbed Greer's arm. "We need to stop them from eating their cake." She dropped her hold and ran forward.

"Lucy, wait," he said, but she continued.

"There's poison in the cake!" she called out at the same time the Great Hall erupted in laughter over the play that was being enacted. The two guards at the doors grabbed her, stopping her from running inside. "Let me go! The queen and Lord Burghley."

"We've got you, traitor," the guard, Giles, said, yanking the shawl off her head.

Slam. Greer's fist hit Giles square in the jaw, making him reel backwards. Lucy wobbled, but Giles released her as the other guard attacked Greer. Lucy surged forward into the room, leaving Greer to deal with three other guards who rushed past her.

The Great Hall was full of courtiers dressed in splendor and masks made of velvet and jewels. The actors performed off to the left in a cleared area where she and Greer had danced the La Volta days before. It seemed so long ago now.

Elizabeth sat on her throne with Lord Leister to one side and Lord Burghley on the other. Mary O'Brien hovered near them, slicing pieces of her Twelfth Night cake.

"Stop!" Lucy yelled as another guard caught her arm.

"Lucy?" William said, blocking her.

She shoved against him, trying to break away from the guard. "I must get to the queen and Lord Burghley," she yelled. "There is poison in the Twelfth Night cake."

People around her gasped, but the rest of the room continued to watch the play, laughing at the antics of a lad dressed as a woman who shrieked at her father for making her wed.

"Let go!" Lucy yelled.

"I don't want to kill ye," she heard Greer say behind her. She couldn't move forward. Between William, the guards, and the crowd, it was as if she were caught in thick mud.

"Don't eat the cake," she yelled, but Elizabeth was looking to Walsingham, who had stood up, his gaze falling on her from across the hall. The queen couldn't hear her.

Mary O'Brien was setting sliced cake on plates at the head of the table, nodding to something one of the ladies nearby said. Mary's smile was calm and her gaze sharp on the cake as she carefully pulled a slice to place on the queen's plate.

Walsingham began to push toward Lucy through the crowd. Lord Burghley, as fond of sweets as Elizabeth, picked up his fork. Holy God! They wouldn't make it.

By Lucy's legs, a sheep hurried past, scurrying on hands and knees. *Catherine.* Behind her came Alyce, draped as the Virgin Mary, and Nick, dressed as a shepherd. While the guards held Lucy back and kept Greer fighting outside the room, the children raced toward the dais. Alyce's cloak caught on a chair back, and she threw it off, pushing forward. Catherine continued to crawl under the table like a mouse.

"Stop," Alyce yelled, her voice finally reaching Elizabeth.

Elizabeth stood. "What is this?"

Mary O'Brien backed away.

"Get her, Nick," Lucy yelled. Nick hopped onto the well-dressed table, running along it, kicking off holly and overturning goblets of wine, most of which had been untouched by the wary courtiers. The white tablecloth was fast becoming a bath of crimson.

Leister jumped in front of the queen, but Nick leaped to the side to race around, grabbing Mary O'Brien.

"The cake is poisoned," Lucy called to Walsingham as he got close enough to hear.

The actors on stage paused, and everyone turned to watch the spectacle, several people saying, "Poison?"

Lettice and Margaret gasped, and murmuring rose in volume as everyone glanced between the ruined table, cakes, Lucy, and the queen.

"Let me go save your bloody queen," Greer yelled as he forced his way forward even with two guards clinging to his arms, their heels trying to find purchase on the polished floors. He dragged them along using brute strength.

Catherine climbed up from underneath the trestle table. She jumped onto the table where Nick had already run and threw off her sheep skin to race forward. "Don't eat it, Your Majesty." She kicked it away from her and then made a little curtsey in her breeches before turning to Lord Burghley. "You neither," she pointed, and he immediately dropped his fork. It clanged against the gold plate.

"The baker woman," Lucy said, yanking her arm from a guard to point at Mary where she struggled against Nick's hold. He was strong, but he was only ten years old. "For God's sake, grab her."

Walsingham pointed at her, and three guards surrounded Mary and Nick, two catching her, while one held onto Nick. "We'll get to the bottom of this now," Walsingham called out and waved the guards to bring Lucy forward. Greer was already headed that way, so his guards finally let go, following him while tugging to right their red doublets.

The glittering crowd parted, letting Walsingham, Lucy, and Greer stride forward. She heard whispers as ladies pointed at her hose, doublet, and ungloved hand. Lucy's heart beat hard in her chest. What if they were wrong? They would all be in the Tower, and Lucy would never live a simple life on a farm with Greer.

Elizabeth waited at the head of the table. "What do you mean?" She threw a hand toward the cake on the plate that Catherine had kicked farther across the table. "The baker ate a piece off my own slice." She made a show of looking over at Mary. "And she seems fairly robust and unaffected by poison."

Lucy's tight stomach uncoiled a bit when she saw the markings on the cake. Mary had decorated the top with swirls and stars made from sugar. The twelve slices were outlined by a design, indicating where she should cut. Lucy nodded toward the cake. "She knew which slice to give you with the designs painted on top."

"The queen and William Cecil, Lord Burghley," Greer said.

Elizabeth snorted. "It seems you are as dangerous as a queen, Spirit."

Lord Burghley stared at his delicious looking cake that he'd almost eaten. "I am hardly."

"Ye are pushing hard for uniting Ireland with England, milord, a joining that some Irish Catholics will not tolerate without bloodshed."

Through all this, Mary stood silent, her face hard like stone.

"What say you, Goodwife O'Brien?" Walsingham asked and motioned to the guards at her elbows to bring her closer. "Why are there slices marked on top of the cake?"

"I saw her turn the cake around until one slice faced you, Bess," Lord Leister said.

"I marked where the Twelfth Night pea would sit in one piece," Mary said. One pea was placed in a Twelfth Night cake so it could be found, marking the finder as the queen for the rest of the night. "I wanted to make certain the queen found it in hers. So she could be the merry queen for the rest of Christmastide." Mary glanced at Lucy. "Since her chosen one is a traitor."

"Lies," Alyce said, frowning fiercely.

Mary nodded toward the plate. "Like Her Majesty said, I ate some of her piece and feel well indeed."

"She froze the poison in small ice balls so it would not spread within the cake or even the slice during baking," Lucy said. "Perhaps she froze the bean in with it, but either way, I am certain Master Darby and Master William will find ratsbane or arsenic inside the queen's piece and Lord Burghley's piece."

"The apothecary on London Bridge said Simmons bought ratsbane," Walsingham said.

"Because Mary's husband, who has been masquerading as Jasper Lintel, asked him to, as well as Mistress Wakefield."

"I've never heard of a Jasper Lintel," Mary said, narrowing her eyes. "You saw some innocent baking that night after I caught you and the lady tupping in the pantry."

Another round of gasps followed a wave through the hall.

"The man is in Whitehall now," Greer said. "He pretended to be part of a business deal with Simmons, Mistress Wakefield, and Richard Whitby," Greer said.

"All they planned was to find favor with the queen so they could petition to own a small, abandoned abbey in the west," Alyce said. "We eavesdropped."

"Simmons would never poison the queen," Catherine added with a serious head nod. "He is too proper to do anything as such."

Walsingham took Lord Burghley's fork and cut through his cake until he came to the center where the cake batter was still raw. Leister did the same to Elizabeth's piece, finding the bean in the center surrounded by raw batter.

Lucy chest expanded with relief. They were right! "The ice kept the batter cold in that spot, so it did not bake properly," Lucy said, speaking quickly. "'Tis still raw there."

Walsingham nodded to the guards who started going down the table to check the cake slices and uncut cakes. Reginal Darby came up with William to the queen, who studied the wet part of her cake. "May I, Your Majesty?" Reginald asked.

"By all means, master chemist," she said, and let him take it.

He poked around the area. "There is a bean," he said, "and the batter around it is uncooked as if the bean had been frozen in liquid."

Reginald Darby moved the knife around in the wet batter, holding it up with some white substance on the tip. "And white powder." The elderly chemist looked to Walsingham.

"Just some uncooked flour," Mary said, her eyes wide.

Reginald ignored her, looking up at Walsingham and then Elizabeth. "If 'tis ratsbane, there's more here than the size of a pea. 'Twould be a fatal dose."

"There's some of the powder in mine as well," Lord Burghley proclaimed. "In the uncooked spot."

Greer cut into one farther down. "The cake is fully cooked in this piece."

"Here as well," another guard called as he cut through some other cake centers, mushing the sponge with the back of his dagger.

"With so much required tasting, she would have been very careful where she put the lethal substance," Lucy said.

A murmur rose near the door as two guards lifted the baker's husband under his arms to bring him inside the Great Hall. "Ye have the wrong man," he called out in a thick accent.

Catherine stood on the table, her thin legs braced wide as she pointed. "And that is Jasper Lintel."

"Also known as Jacob O'Brien," Walsingham said.

"The two of you killed Richard Whitby by accident when he took the tart meant for Lord Burghley," Lucy said. "You likely added ratsbane to Cordelia's gift for the queen. Three innocent people, Cordelia Cranfield, John Simmons, and Catolina Wakefield, are imprisoned in the Tower because of you." She looked between Mary and her husband. "And now you try to kill the queen."

"And me," Lord Burghley said. "Imagine, the queen and me dead." His eyes opened wider. "The whole of England would be in chaos."

"And ye'd be too busy fighting your own people to worry about our isle," Mary said, her voice full of scorn.

"Hold your tongue, woman," Jacob O'Brien said.

"Ye incompetent fool," she yelled at him. "We could have been done with this whole mess if ye'd let me do it my way with the tarts on Christmas."

"Foolish woman," Jacob muttered, glancing around, but Mary O'Brien didn't seem to care that everyone around was witnessing her confession.

She looked at Elizabeth with disdain. "Ye royal bastard." Gasps sounded through the hall. "Ye and your council of overly fed Protestants deciding to doom us to Hell, taking over our beautiful isle and imposing your religion on us." She turned her glare on Lord Burghley. "We will never be a part of your Protestant England."

"'Tis for the safety of the realm," Lord Burghley said. "France and Spain cannot have a foothold in Ireland, or they will invade it, Wales, and England."

"Safety of the realm?" Mary said. "And yet ye do not care if we starve or die of plague. 'Tis the safety of England ye care about."

"You know nothing of the politics that keep this land—and

your land—safe," Lord Burghley said. But to Lucy, it sounded like Mary O'Brien had a pretty good grasp of the world she endured. Enough that she was willing to kill and die for it.

"Arrest this woman and her husband," Elizabeth said.

Lucy's gaze snapped back to Elizabeth. She curtseyed, her head bowed. "And release my sister, Your Majesty?"

"'Tis obvious the poison was placed in the fan by someone other than Cordelia Cranfield," Greer said, reminding them of what he'd said before. "It makes no sense for her to poison her own gift to ye."

Elizabeth stared at the cake with the uncooked center and then at Mary O'Brien. "It grieves my heart so," she murmured.

"But your loyal subjects will do anything to keep you safe," Lucy said, her hand going out to the children and Greer. "Like my sister."

"Hm..." Elizabeth stood straighter, her gaze going to Walsingham. "If you have no proof to implicate the young Lady Cranfield, she may be allowed her freedom."

Lucy leaned against the table, her relief so intense that she had to blink back the moisture in her eyes.

Walsingham bowed his head. "There is no evidence of her wrongdoing, except for the powder on the fan and a jar of it shoved under her bed. Her door was also left unlocked when we came to search it."

"Very well," Elizabeth said, waving her hand. "Let Lady Cranfield come back to Whitehall."

"Thank you, Your Majesty." Before the queen could turn away, Lucy murmured, "and Simmons and Mistress Wakefield?"

Elizabeth exhaled in a huff. "John Simmons and Catolina Wakefield may also go free, and if they have a business proposal, they must present it, not sneak around."

"Huzzah!" Catherine yelled from the tabletop.

"Huzzah!" Nick repeated, pumping his fist in the air.

Alyce wrapped her arms around Catherine, lifting her off the ruined table and onto the floor.

Mary and Jacob O'Brien were led out of the room by several guards, and other kitchen maids scurried around with trays collecting all the cake. Even though it seemed only two slices were tainted with poison, no one was taking any chances.

"So, Master Buchanan," Lord Walsingham said as he drew close to Lucy and Greer, "it seems Lord Moray muddled the source of the danger." He frowned. "'Twas not Mary Stuart from Scotland who sent an assassin but Mary and Jacob O'Brien acting on behalf of Ireland."

"Unless there's another assassin," Elizabeth said.

"Heaven help us," Lord Burghley said. He looked to one of the maids. "Is there any untainted cake tucked away in the kitchens?" He followed her in that direction.

Elizabeth stood regally next to Walsingham. Her gaze fell between Lucy and Greer. "And what will you do now, Lady Lucy? Remain here at Whitehall dodging assassins and..." her eyes lowered to Lucy's exposed arm, "hiding your infirmaries? Or will you follow your friend Maggie Darby to Scotland?"

Lucy's mouth opened and closed. "I do not know, Your Majesty."

"Well, you better make up your mind soon," she said with a glance at Greer. "Twelfth Night is over." She turned and glided out of the hall.

CHAPTER TWENTY

"As a Protestant Queen, Elizabeth was forced to live with the threat of assassination from Catholics throughout her reign. But there was an army of men working in secret to protect the Queen. These were her spies, her secret service, and they were overseen by the most ruthless spy master of them all: Francis Walsingham."

BBC

"AND I REMEMBERED how Nick used to take bits of ice and put them in the center of a snowball," Lucy said. "It hit as hard as a rock, but nothing could be seen of it once it melted."

Cordelia shook her head. "You really are brilliant, Lucy," she said as she folded another smock to lay upon the others in her traveling trunk.

Lucy didn't feel brilliant. In fact, she felt rather like a fool. After the theatrics of Twelfth Night, Greer had walked her back to her bedchamber at Whitehall. There had been time to ask him what he thought she should do, but the words would not come. Because she didn't want to hear him tell her to stay.

Instead of being able to sleep, Lucy had paced her room far into the night. She'd only settled down after she'd written a letter to Maggie Darby asking if the invitation to join her in Scotland was still open. She was living with the Gordons way up north at Auchindoun Castle in Banffshire. It was several days' ride north of Edinburgh. Perhaps they could stay in Edinburgh before continuing on to the Gordons.

What was left for her in England? Despite their innocence, Cordelia and Lucy would be treated with cold indignation. The Cranfield name was already associated with treason, and now the shadow of guilt would follow them. If the whole assassination attempt weren't enough, William had told her that people were coming to ask him if the deformity on Lucy's arm was contagious. And slanderous comments were being made about Lucy's lack of virtue.

"Are the children packing?" Cordelia asked her.

Lucy left her gloves off and rubbed her injured hand absently. "They will, but they haven't much to take."

"Of course. And we have time." Cordelia motioned to her trunk. "I really could wait, but I confess I want to leave now." She turned away from the trunk to look at Lucy. "You've sent off the letter to Maggie?"

Lucy nodded. "This morn. It went out with the same carrier taking Lord Walsingham's letter of what has occurred to Lord Moray and King James. He will pass it to another courier in Edinburgh to take it up to Banffshire. So it may take a fortnight to hear back."

Cordelia's brows rose. "Why didn't Lord Walsingham send his missive with Master Buchanan?"

Lucy turned away from her sister's questioning gaze. "I believe Greer wishes to stay a few days more to…wrap up stray details for his full account."

Cordelia walked over, the heels of her slippers tapping the floor. She squeezed Lucy's arm, making her turn. "What is he to you?" Cordelia asked.

Caught in her sister's piercing stare, Lucy's pleasant mask of confidence fell. Her eyes closed as tears gathered behind them and her brows felt heavy, bending low like her lips.

"God's teeth," Cordelia swore softly. "You're in love with him."

The words didn't shock Lucy. She'd guessed the ailment

already. She blinked her eyes open, sniffing helplessly at the two tears that had swelled over her lashes to slide down her cheeks.

"Are you with child?" Cordelia asked.

Lucy shook her head. "My courses came, and we haven't been together since."

Cordelia released an exhale that could have been relief. "You must tell him."

"I did. He knows I'm not with child."

"No, sister," Cordelia said. "You need to tell him you're in love."

LUCY WALKED ALONG the Strand, lost in thought. She hadn't seen Greer since he left her alone in her bedchamber at Whitehall two nights ago. When she'd gone to the stables, his horse wasn't there. At first panic had slammed into her chest, but then she'd remembered that he'd stabled the horse at Lord Norfolk's house. Everything had been moving so quickly this past week, but now it felt like she was walking through thick tar. Its weight seemed to drag her down.

What would she say to Greer when she saw him next?

I love you. So, marry me and take me up to Scotland with you. Lucy shook her head. Even she wasn't so bold.

We seem well suited for each other. Perhaps I should travel with you north toward Maggie's home. Too vague. But he might fall in love with her on the journey.

Lucy clasped her hands. She'd donned her gloves, but only because it was cold. Let others judge her because of her scars. She did not care. Hopefully Alyce would see her as a good example and not hide away all her life.

Lucy stopped before the big old Cranfield House and looked up at it. Lord Burghley said that Elizabeth was letting the sisters keep it, but there were too many bad memories there. She and Cordelia would sell it and use the money to make a new home up near Maggie.

"Good. You're here."

Lucy spun to see Greer walking out from beside the house. "Greer? I thought you were with your horse."

"Darach is being heartily patted and brushed by the children out back, but we have somewhere to go."

"Go? Where?"

He took her hand, tugging her to follow him. "Another mission."

"Another assassin?" she asked. Her heart leaped. Would Greer stay in London longer?

"Nay, but something that needs our attention."

She hurried along with him into the streets. It was the day after Epiphany and shops were once again open. Shopkeepers were tidying their front stoops, brushing them free of snow and cracking off the ice that had gathered while they'd been away making merry with their families.

Twice, Lucy slipped, but Greer had her arm, keeping her upright. "We best get ye some boots with grip," he said.

Greer stopped to purchase two buns. He handed one to her. "Are people eating at the castle again?"

"I don't know. I haven't eaten much, and Cordy has brought me things."

He frowned and handed her a bun. "Then eat." He wouldn't proceed until she took a bite. Then he nodded and nearly dragged her along.

"Why are you in such a hurry?" she asked, but the loud call of another town crier describing the cold weather covered her words.

When Greer turned onto London Bridge, she thought he'd stop at the apothecary, but he continued to dodge people, bringing her behind him.

At the end, he turned them down Southwark along the Thames, her heart squeezed. She picked up her pace, bringing herself alongside him. "We are going to the kennels?"

He looked at her and gave a small nod. "We have two innocent pups to break out. 'Tis a worthy mission."

Pip and Percy. He hadn't forgotten them in all the chaos. Lucy's eyes filled with tears, and she blinked them away, nodding.

Her breath puffed out white as they jogged along, her holding her skirts higher to keep from catching the hem with her toes. "A worthy mission indeed."

They stopped beside the kennel, flat against the wall. Greer glanced around the corner and then held his finger to his lips as he turned back to her. They waited, his hand clasping hers. Lucy's heart swelled. He was helping her steal back her dogs. He understood her and her love for animals.

She tugged on his hand, and he looked down at her. Her heart was already pounding so hard that exposing her heart might kill her if Greer stomped on it. But then her suffering would be over. "I love you," she whispered. "Will you marry me?"

Greer's brows rose, giving him a playful look. "Right now?"

"After we complete our mission?" She held her breath, her heart pounding in her tight chest. "I know I asked once, but you never answered."

His gray eyes looked down into hers. "Ye will be happy living in a thatched cottage on a moor, Lucy?"

"As long as you're living with me."

He leaned in, his face bending down to hers. "Then aye, Lucy, lass, I will marry ye."

Lucy's heart about burst inside her as his lips touched down for a kiss. He broke away slowly, looking into her eyes. His had a way of smiling even when his mouth was in a straight line. "I love ye too," he said. "Now let's fetch Pip and Percy."

"And free the other dogs too?" she asked.

He snorted softly. "Of course."

"THEY FOUND THEIR way back to Cranfield House," Lucy said, and Greer nearly snorted over how genuine her lies sounded.

Walsingham did snort. "And you had these dogs before?"

"Yes," Lucy said. "Look at their collars, milord. They proclaim them as Cranfield dogs."

"And they happened to find their way home?"

"I heard that another villain released all the dogs again from the Bear Garden kennels," Cordelia said beside Lucy.

"They escaped the scoundrels and ran home, then," Lucy added, and they both nodded in unison. Greer was certain that the two sisters were capable of espionage at the highest level.

Walsingham tugged his triangular beard. "Sisters in conspiracy. 'Tis good you are going up to Scotland, Lady Lucy."

"After we are wed," Greer said, taking Lucy's arm.

Walsingham's brows rose high on his forehead. "Have you asked the queen, Lady Lucy?"

Lucy smiled. "I believe her exact reply was 'Good, then you won't harry me any further.'"

"Yes," Elizabeth said as she whisked into the room. "Let that Highlander tame you."

Greer bowed and the ladies curtsied as the queen stopped before them. She smiled. "Although you and your sister don't seem the type to ever be tamed." She glanced at Greer and then back at Lucy. "And for saving me and my beloved Lord Burghley, I will forgive you the chaos you have caused and grant you my blessing. You may wed in the chapel before you depart."

"Thank you, Your Majesty," Lucy said and smiled at Greer.

"I will be happy to correspond with you, Your Majesty," Cordelia said. "If there is news from Edinburgh."

Elizabeth waved her hand. "Your sister can do that."

"But…" Cordelia's brows pinched. "I'm going with my sister."

"Along with the children, Simmons, the pups, and two roosters," Lucy said.

"Spy master," Elizabeth intoned, and Walsingham looked at

Cordelia.

"We have a mission for you, Lady Cordelia, before you go north."

"A mission?" Cordelia asked.

"To completely clear the Cranfield name and retire to Scotland with your sister, you must first go on progress for the queen," Walsingham said.

"You mean *with* the queen," Lucy said.

"No," Elizabeth said, and touched a reddish curl falling upon Cordelia's shoulder. "You will be going for me, Cordelia Cranfield, as the Virgin Queen Elizabeth."

THE GOWN WAS exquisite, a gift from the queen herself. Lucy walked slowly down the aisle between the rows of people in the chapel at Whitehall, the train of blue and lace following. The blue silk was shot through with white silk thread sewn into patterns of roses and leafy vines along the petticoat, and pearls were knotted into the centers of the flowers. Lucy's French hood matched with a blue velvet drape in back, and pearls and silk adorned the front. The one item that she decided to forgo was the pair of white gloves that had come with the ensemble. Instead, she clutched the small bouquet of holy and mistletoe with her bare hands.

Catherine, Alyce, and Nick stood near the front, smiles across all their faces. They wore new clothes of soft wool for warmth. Simmons also stood up front, along with the queen and councilors. Cordelia and William stood by as official witnesses.

Lucy inhaled a jagged breath, her nervousness at so much attention making her knees feel weak. But then Greer took a step out from the side, turning to face her as she walked slowly forward while a flute played a sweet melody.

Greer Buchanan was tall and broad and beautiful in a rugged way. His hair was clipped to just below his ears, and his short beard was trimmed. But it was his eyes, their intensity as he watched her, that pulled Lucy's breath from her chest. She glided slowly, step by step. He wore his plaid and pristine white tunic, looking very much the handsome, honorable, talented man who had loved every inch of her.

Just the sight of him made her heart beat hard with courage at the same time she felt dizzy with joy, and she had to check herself so she wouldn't run down the aisle to him. Drawing closer, she could see the slight rise at the corners of his mouth. 'Twas his way of smiling, and she met it with her own.

"Och, but lass, ye are bòidheach," he murmured in his thick accent. "I love ye, Lucy Cranfield."

"I haven't started yet," the pastor said.

"Pardon, milord," Lucy said. "We tend to break the rules." She smiled back at Greer. "I love you, too, Greer Buchanan, my Highlander." She took his hand, and the two of them turned to recite their vows, vows that etched a new belief across her heart. A belief that would snub out the scars that Lucy had always carried inside. A belief that she too could be loved for who she was.

Return to the Queen's Highlanders to journey with Cordelia Cranfield on her dangerous mission. To protect Queen Elizabeth and find her own freedom, Cordelia must partner with the most lethal man she's ever met.

Acknowledgments

Thank you so much for following Greer and Lucy's adventure! I've been having so much fun exploring Elizabethan England, and I'm honored to be able to write the great Queen Elizabeth I.

Thank you to Kathryn Le Veque for inviting me to the Dragonblade Clan and to Amelia Hester, my wonderful editor. What a fabulous opportunity you've given me to dream of life in Tudor London!

And of course, my heart goes to my very own Highlander, Braden, who more than once found this manuscript when my computer decided to hide it in a dusty, dark corner.

Also…

At the end of each of my books, I ask that you, my awesome readers, please remind yourselves of the whispered symptoms of ovarian cancer. I am now a ten-year survivor, one of the lucky ones. Please don't rely on luck. If you experience any of these symptoms consistently for three weeks or more, go see your GYN.

- Bloating
- Eating less and feeling full faster
- Abdominal pain
- Trouble with your bladder

Other symptoms may include: indigestion, back pain, pain with intercourse, constipation, fatigue, and menstrual irregularities.

About the Author

Heather McCollum is an award-winning, Scottish historical romance writer. With over twenty books published, she is an Amazon Best Selling author in Highlander Romance. Her favorite heroes are brawny and broody with golden hearts, and the feistier the heroine the better!

When she is not dreaming up adventures and conflict for rugged Highlanders and clever heroines, she spends her time educating women about the symptoms of Ovarian Cancer. She is a survivor and lists the subtle symptoms in the backs of all her books. She loves dragonflies, chai lattes, and baking things she sees on the Great British Baking Show. Heather resides with her very own Highland hero and three spirited children in the wilds of suburbia on the mid-Atlantic coast.

Twitter: @HMcCollumAuthor
FB: HeatherMcCollumAuthor
Pinterest: hmccollumauthor
Instagram: heathermccollumauthor
Goodreads:
goodreads.com/author/show/4185696.Heather_McCollum
BookBub: bookbub.com/authors/heather-mccollum
Amazon: amazon.com/Heather-McCollum/e/B004FREFHI

CPSIA information can be obtained
at www.ICGtesting.com
Printed in the USA
BVHW031712180922
647223BV00036B/1069